ABOUT THE AUTHOR

Icelandic crime-writer Lilja Sigurðardóttir was born in the town of Akranes in 1972 and raised in Mexico, Sweden, Spain and Iceland. An award-winning playwright, Lilja has written ten crime novels, including *Snare*, *Trap* and *Cage*, making up the Reykjavík Noir trilogy, and her standalone thriller *Betrayal*, all of which have hit bestseller lists worldwide. *Snare* was longlisted for the CWA International Dagger, *Cage* won Best Icelandic Crime Novel of the Year and was a *Guardian* Book of the Year, and *Betrayal* was shortlisted for the prestigious Glass Key Award and won Icelandic Crime Novel of the Year. The film rights for the Reykjavík Noir trilogy have been bought by Palomar Pictures in California. *Cold as Hell*, the first book in the An Áróra Investigation series, was published in the UK in 2021.

She lives in Reykjavík with her partner. You'll find Lilja on Twitter @lilja1972 and on her website liljawriter.com.

ABOUT THE TRANSLATOR

A series of unlikely coincidences allowed Quentin Bates to escape English suburbia as a teenager with the chance of a gap year working in Iceland. For a variety of reasons, the year stretched to become a gap decade, during which time he went native in the north of Iceland, acquiring a new language, a new profession and a family.

He is the author of a series of crime novels set in present-day Iceland. His translations include works by Guðlaugur Arason, Ragnar Jónasson, Einar Kárason and Sólveig Pálsdóttir, as well as Lilja Sigurðardóttir's Reykjavík Noir trilogy, standalone novel *Betrayal* and the Áróra series. Follow Quentin on Twitter @graskeggur.

RED AS BLOOD

Lilja Sigurðardóttir

Translated by Quentin Bates

ORENDA BOOKS

Orenda Books
16 Carson Road
West Dulwich
London SE21 8HU
www.orendabooks.co.uk

First published in Icelandic as *Blóðrauður sjór* by Forlagið in 2020
First published in English by Orenda Books in 2022
Copyright © Lilja Sigurðardóttir, 2020
English translation copyright © Quentin Bates, 2022

A catalogue record for this book is available from the British Library.
B-format paperback ISBN 978-1-914585-32-6
eISBN 978-1-914585-33-3

The publication of this translation has been made possible through the financial
support of

[] ICELANDIC LITERATURE CENTER

Printed and bound by CPI Group (UK) Ltd, Croydon CR0 4YY

For sales and distribution, please contact info@orendabooks.co.uk or visit
www.orendabooks.co.uk.

PRONUNCIATION GUIDE

Icelandic has a couple of letters that don't exist in other European languages and which are not always easy to replicate. The letter ð is generally replaced with a d in English, but we have decided to use the Icelandic letter to remain closer to the original names. Its sound is closest to the hard th in English, as found in *thus* and *bathe*.

The letter r is generally rolled hard with the tongue against the roof of the mouth.

In pronouncing Icelandic personal and place names, the emphasis is placed on the first syllable.

Guðrún – Guth-ruen
Flosi – Flow-si
Áróra – Ow-roe-ra
Sara Sól – Sara Soul
Hraunbrún – Hroyn-bruun
Garðvís – Garth-vies
Kristján – Krist-yown
Gúgúlú – Goo-Goo-Loo
Ísafold – Eesa-fold
Sigurlaug – Sigur-loyg
Bergrós – Berg-rose
Oddsteinn – Odd-stay-in
Tækjakistan – Tie-kya-kistan
Garðlager – Garth-lager
Miklatún – Mikla-toon
Laxaslóð – Laxa-slowth
Thorlákshöfn – Thor-lowks-hoepn
Rannveig – Rann-vayg

We have your wife, Guðrún Aronsdóttir.

The price for her freedom is two million euros, to be delivered in two-hundred-euro notes before the end of this week.

You will be told where to deliver the cash.

We do not wish Guðrún to come to harm, but we will kill her if you contact the police.

We will kill her if you don't pay.

Her life is in your hands.

MONDAY

1

The letter lay on the kitchen table, a single A4 sheet of paper, inkjet printed. These few lines in the middle of a mostly blank page failed to explain what had happened, but at the same time their meaning was so terrifying that Flosi was left weak at the knees, certain he was about to collapse. He sank onto a chair and read the message again, a tense knot forming in his gut as he fought for breath and surveyed the chaos in the kitchen.

That evening's dinner lay uncooked on the island unit. The export-grade Hornafjörður langoustines had clearly been on the worktop for a long time as the shells were starting to blacken. Guðrún had obviously been in the middle of preparing dinner: there were herbs on the chopping block, and in the pan on the stove was a knob of butter, over which Guðrún had squeezed a lemon, as she always did. Her langoustines were always fantastic, and to his astonishment, Flosi felt his mouth watering at the thought of langoustine á la Guðrún. He could almost taste them, flash-fried in the pan with lemon garlic butter, fresh herbs and freshly ground black pepper.

As if it was some new discovery, the thought came to his mind that he was fortunate to be married to a wizard of a cook. Some husbands had to put up with food cooked as a duty rather than as an art. Others had to cook for themselves. He should have been aware after twelve years that she was a fine cook, but it was suddenly obvious that he was lucky in so many ways to be Guðrún's husband. But now a catastrophe had befallen them.

Sometimes he had wondered when misfortune would come crashing into their lives. He was fifty-five and had seen his contemporaries having to deal with cancer, bankruptcy or car crashes. One had even lost a child. Everyone seemed to get their share of trouble and sorrow. Except for him. He had sailed on a tide of good luck, hoping to escape the storms that life, almost at random, seemed to make everyone else endure.

Of course, he had been through a divorce and all the drama that went with that, and it went without saying that Sara Sól's behaviour had been challenging when she had been a teenager, plus he had often had to put in the hours to keep the company afloat. It had also been a disappointment he had been forced to swallow when he and Guðrún couldn't have children of their own. But nothing genuinely bad had ever befallen him. Until now.

As he sat, fighting to draw breath, it occurred to him that this was what he deserved. Recently he hadn't appreciated Guðrún properly. He had even begun to find her tiresome, and she also seemed to have lost interest in him. She kept the house spick and span, and still put her heart and soul into cooking, and they chatted about this and that over dinner, until, when everything had been put away, routine took over – the sofa awaited them. It was as if nothing could dislodge her from lying there, in front of the TV, until she fell asleep, while he sat in his chair and hopped between channels as she snored softly, her mouth open and her face lolling against the cushion.

She wouldn't be dozing in front of the television tonight. There was no doubt about that. She had clearly resisted those who had taken her away. There was a broken glass on the floor and puddles of white wine around it. She must have poured herself a glass while she was preparing dinner, as she so often did. A red pepper and a fork also lay on the floor, and one of the stools was on its side, as if it had been kicked out of the way as she was dragged from the room. The fridge stood wide open. Guðrún would never have left the fridge open.

As he looked over the scene, his sense of smell seemed to come to life. He could smell burning. He stood up and sniffed. The oven was switched on, and it hummed, telling him that the fan was running. Guðrún had persuaded him to buy this ruinously expensive oven precisely because of the fantastic fan that she had to have.

Flosi opened the oven and saw a long baking tin inside. Without thinking, he reached in and grabbed it, and it took his brain more than a second to process the pain. He yelped, snatched his hand back and hurried to pick up an oven glove so that he could take the bread out. The top was black, and while the tin's contents resembled burnt embers, he recognised it all the same. This had been Guðrún's mountain-herb bread, which was always so delicious with langoustines. He switched off the oven, and then his legs finally gave way as he sank to the kitchen floor, his eyes brimmed with tears and he could feel the pain flood through him at the same time as he felt the sting of the burn on his hand.

TUESDAY

2

Áróra had to keep a firm grip on the wheel of the jeep as it bounced down the gravel road that led away from the Hafnir road. It was an exaggeration to call it a gravel road, as this was one of these pitted tracks that had neither a number nor a name. Shortly, this little detour through the lava fields would undoubtedly rejoin Highway 44, the Hafnir road. When she had started investigating, back in the summer, she could hardly believe how many of these tracks there were leading off into the wilderness from every numbered road in the south-west corner of Iceland. Highway 44 alone had more than a dozen of these trails leading this way and that. A few of those that meandered off to the north led to the service road for the airport runway or towards the Svartsengi geothermal plant. But most of them didn't end up anywhere. They just faded away out there in the lava, becoming dead-ends. Just like her efforts to find her sister.

Áróra glanced over her shoulder and up through the jeep's open top. The drone followed obediently, keeping an altitude of twelve metres, just as she had programmed it to do. This was high enough to capture images a few metres either side of the road, but low enough for the pictures to be clear – and to get anything worthwhile out of this, she would need clear images.

She was surprised when the track came to a sudden end, as she had been certain that this was one of those that lay in a half-loop away from the Hafnir road and back to it, but when she compared the drone footage against the map, she found that she wasn't where she had thought she was. Not that it mattered. She could take that particular half-loop next time. This was the first calm day for a week, and she was determined to use the few days she had to fly the drone. She'd heard that the weather would worsen before long, bringing with it high winds, and she recalled from her childhood in Iceland that apart from a few breaks, these could last all winter long, and on top of that there would be falls of snow that would cover the ground and hide anything that might be there.

She got out of the car, landed the drone, folded it away and placed it carefully in the front seat. Standing by the car, she scanned the drone's footage on her phone. She could see that the lava fields had taken on their autumn colours, which you couldn't make out from close by; the drone's point of view, however, showed patches of rust red and mixed shades of brown where plants had established themselves among the grey-green moss that looked to be the black lava's only covering.

Her heart lurched as she saw something blue on the screen. It looked to be about two metres from the track, not far from where it ended. She zoomed in but couldn't make out anything other than a sky-blue surface, half buried under a lava outcrop. Further back, not far from where she had turned off the Hafnir road, there was something white. Considering how large and pale it was, she was surprised that she hadn't noticed it earlier.

She got back in the jeep, turned it around and went back the way she had come, now irritated at not being able to go faster. But putting her foot down wasn't an option, as that could lead to shredding a tyre on the razor-sharp lava, and changing the wheel would take effort and time. Time better spent continuing the search.

Without bothering to shut the car door, she jumped out and strode over a bulging lava dome towards the outcrop that hid whatever she had seen on the drone footage. The regular warning pings from the car to tell her she had left a door open accompanied her heart beat, which grew faster the closer she got. The blue shape was plastic, and she felt disappointment blending with the relief that always came when something the drone had picked up turned out to be garbage. This time it was the broken lid of a bin.

Áróra sighed and tugged at the plastic. It had clearly been there a long time as it was as good as fused to the lava and she had to pull hard a few times to free it, so that she could drag it to the car and dump it with the rest of that morning's junk. The white object the drone had seen turned out to be the remains of a tarpaulin, and Áróra folded it away in the boot. At any rate, collecting rubbish was a worthwhile thing to do, she thought, as usual preventing her thoughts from wandering too far in the direction of what she would do if she were to stumble across what she was searching for – if she were to find her sister's remains.

She had made herself comfortable back in the car when her phone rang. Usually when she was on these trips, she made a point of not answering the phone. It seemed wrong to pollute the time spent searching for Ísafold with anything else, but as it was her friend and colleague Michael calling from Scotland, she allowed herself an exception to her rule.

'Hi, Michael,' she said cheerfully, but he seemed so preoccupied that he wasn't able to reply in kind.

'I have an extremely strange favour to ask,' he said, and it was clear to Áróra from his tone that this wasn't a request that she would be able to refuse.

3

Anyone who has experienced such a shock knows the moment of mercy between the end of sleep, when your mind is just beginning to come alive but it's still so quiet, and the instant reality comes flooding back, ice cold and harsh, like a deep plunge. Flosi lay for a while and stared upwards, wondering why he was in the living room. And then it came to him. The previous day. Guðrún.

More than likely he had passed out on the sofa sometime after his conversation with the accountant in Britain who he'd called to ask him to make cash available to pay the ransom. He had told him the whole story. He had to. He'd had to tell someone. Michael had told him to keep calm, pour himself a double and try to relax; he would send someone to him, to support him. Flosi had just gone along with it. He needed some kind of support. He felt that he was on the brink of a well of despair, and if there wasn't someone or something to hold on to him, he'd be sucked deep into it in a flash.

He snatched up his phone and sent a message to Sara Sól: *Come now, my darling. I need you.*

She'd be there in less than an hour if he knew her right. They had always been close, and she would do anything for him. It had been Guðrún who complicated things, a typical step-parent situation. Maybe that was why Sara Sól had been so keen to be at his side in everything to do with the company. When it came to the business, Guðrún was nowhere to be seen.

The thought of Guðrún brought him out in a cold sweat. Under what conditions was she being held? How was she feeling? Was she frightened? Had she been hurt? Mental images flashed through his mind. He had no idea where they came from – maybe from crime movies or news items about kidnappings. He visualised Guðrún in manacles on a filthy, cold floor, and then on an unmade bed with a cord of some kind around her neck. But the worst was the thought of her shut in a tiny, windowless room. In his mind the room wasn't dirty and everything necessary was there – even a television; but this was the worst thing he could imagine for Guðrún. She suffered from claustrophobia, to the extent that getting in a lift was a challenge.

He still had his phone in his hand and for some reason he selected Guðrún's number from the memory. Flosi heard her phone ring out in the hall, where it had been when he had come home. He tried to stand up, but it felt as if the sofa dragged him back down. It was a cruel irony that he now sat and longed for her in precisely the spot that had irritated him so much because she preferred it to him in the evenings. He missed her so much that it was painful – he missed her so desperately much. What wouldn't he give to have Guðrún snoring on the sofa this evening, and every evening, while he fought his usual battle with the remote as he searched for something worth watching.

He had shed all the tears he had when he finally heard the front door open and Sara Sól's voice from the hall.

'Dad!'

He tried to call out to her that he was in the living room, but the sound he made was more like the howl of a wounded beast. Sara Sól came into the room and stared at him.

'Dad, what's the matter?'

4

The house was one of the smartest on Hraunbrún. It wasn't immediately visible from the street, hidden away along a drive leading off from a cul-de-sac that three detached houses shared. The appearance of the house itself was magnificent, as if it had been designed with wonderful events in mind, the best dinner parties, dances, visits from illustrious guests. There was nothing whatever about the place that was everyday. There were no garden tools by the garage, no broom left handy by the door, to sweep away the leaves that were piling up along the street and the pavements in shades of russet, and there was no shelter for bins anywhere to be seen.

The drive was paved, as was the pathway that curved to the front door. On each side of the path were outdoor lights, spaced a metre or so apart, and a thick birch hedge, clipped into neat domes that showed off their red-brown autumn foliage.

Áróra rang the bell, and it occurred to her that she should have gone home first to get changed, but the thought was forgotten as soon as the man opened the door. His face was so wracked with desperation that she doubted he would notice minor details, such as her faded jeans and windcheater.

'You're Flosi?' she asked, extending a hand. His palm was sweaty and she could feel the faint trembling as he took her hand and squeezed it. 'My name's Áróra. I've been sent by Michael, your accountant in Edinburgh.'

She followed Flosi inside, through the entrance lobby and a spacious hallway where stairs led to the upper floor and a whole row of mirror-fronted cupboards stretched all the way to the ceiling. In the kitchen Flosi pointed at the floor where a broken glass and some vegetables lay, and then snatched up a printed sheet of paper from the kitchen worktop and handed it to her.

'It was like this when I came home yesterday. And this letter was here on the table. So I called Michael to ask him to make the money available and ... and ... well.'

His words petered out and he looked helplessly at Áróra.

'If that's what it comes to, then I'll be the one to travel to the UK and fetch your money,' she said.

Flosi nodded, and for a moment Áróra thought he was going to crumple, but he coughed and rolled his shoulders as if holding himself back.

'Michael also asked me to give you what support I can, considering you don't want to go to the police. He felt that you shouldn't be dealing with kidnappers alone,' she said.

'Good. Yes. Thank you, thanks,' Flosi muttered. 'To be honest, I don't know where to turn. But I need to have the money ready when they get in touch. I can't wait for days on end for a bank transfer and all the bother that goes with it. I'll have to have the right amount ready. So they'll release Guðrún.'

Saying his wife's name out loud seemed to upset the delicate equilibrium he had fought so hard to maintain since Áróra had been here, and tears trickled from both eyes and down his cheeks. He sniffed hard, reached for a kitchen roll, pulled off a sheet and wiped his face.

'It's unbearable, not knowing how she is, whether they are treating her well, if she's frightened.'

Áróra reached out and placed an encouraging hand on his arm.

'Considering there's a ransom demand, I think you can be confident that they value Guðrún highly.' She glanced again at the letter. 'They seem to think she's worth two million euros. So that means they must be looking after her well.'

'You're right,' Flosi said, as if snatching in desperation at the hope this thought offered. 'Of course you're right.'

Áróra scanned the note again, and then realised what it was about the ransom demand that had been troubling her.

'It's strange that they ask for euros, and not krónur,' she said. 'Who would know that you have money in an overseas account?'

Flosi stretched to take the note, looking at it as if he was seeing it properly for the first time, although he must have read it a hundred times since finding it on the kitchen table.

'I suppose it's one of those foreign crime gangs we keep seeing on the news? They must demand money that doesn't need to be changed.'

He shrugged as he spoke, handing the note back to her. She placed it on the kitchen table where he said he had found it, and took a picture of it with her phone. It bugged her that Flosi hadn't answered her question about who could have knowledge of his overseas accounts, and she wondered if he was simply too upset to think straight, or if he had purposefully dodged the question.

Whichever it was, it confirmed her feeling that this man needed more help than she could provide.

5

This was a tall, muscular woman Michael had sent him. Flosi felt she exuded a calming influence that he wasn't able to define. Maybe it was simply the relief at being able to discuss things with someone who might be able to help him – at sharing the burden of all this with someone.

Once the woman had been through the living room and the kitchen, checking behind paintings and pictures, climbing on chairs, examining the light fittings to check for surveillance equipment, she sat down and looked intently into his eyes.

'I know a cop who I'm sure would be prepared to meet and give us advice,' she said. 'You wouldn't have to tell him who you are, you'd just have to say you know me and tell him about the situation.'

'But the letter said that they would kill Guðrún if I go to the police,' Flosi said. 'I can't take the risk. I can't take any chances with Guðrún's safety.'

Despite his clouded thinking, this one thing remained clear in his mind. He would do nothing that could risk Guðrún's life. He would do everything he could to bring her back safe and well.

He smiled bitterly as he recalled how for months he had felt that Guðrún had him caught in a rut, a day-to-day routine that he had longed to change – break up, re-evaluate, maybe even reject outright. But now circumstances had quite literally swept his feet from under him and he would give anything to be looking forward to one of those mundane evenings: Guðrún dozing off on the sofa after dinner, two glasses of white wine, him sitting on his own, trying to fix his attention on the television screen. Now he could see that loneliness wasn't the most awful thing that could happen. The terror that had him in its grasp right now was worse – much, much worse.

'Let's try and put aside the anxiety you must be experiencing now,' Áróra said. 'It's logical to think that they wouldn't rush to kill a woman they reckon is worth two million euros.'

'But that risk isn't worth taking,' Flosi replied. 'If they find out that I've been in touch with the police, then I've broken one of the conditions. And I couldn't live with myself if...'

He was unable to finish his sentence as the misery that had been with him since he woke up again forced its way to the surface and stifled his words before they could be spoken.

'If I ask the cop I know to wear plain clothes and meet us at a coffee shop, would you be prepared to come? We'd have a chance to get his advice, and there'd be no obligation and nothing to say that you've approached the police.'

'How does that work?' Flosi said when he finally managed to force out a few words. 'Wouldn't the police force their way in and take over? Then the kidnappers would see all the police cars outside, and Guðrún's days would be numbered.' And he realised that this was what he feared more than anything: the complete loss of control, being rendered powerless. That was exactly what he had never been. He had managed his life with determination; some might even say he'd been ruthless in his approach. And he had never curled up and waited to see what would happen next. He was too strong for that, too determined.

'It could be worth finding out if this is something the police are familiar with. Maybe you're just one of a bunch of people in the same situation.'

This hadn't occurred to him. Perhaps he was just one of many who had been attacked like this. He had seen on the news that criminal gangs came and went in waves, were a plague for a short while, and then disappeared until another one came along. There had been the contractor swindle, in which skilled workers were offered at a cheap rate, and as soon as an advance payment had been made, they vanished. Or there were the computer hackers who conned people into downloading software that gave the thieves access to their bank accounts. But there hadn't been a word about kidnappings in the news. Maybe this was just the latest development. He could be just one victim of some ruthless group that the police were about to nab.

Sara Sól brought a cup of steaming tea into the living room to him. She placed a coaster beneath the cup as she put it on the oak table and laid a comforting hand on her father's shoulder.

'Dad and I don't want to take any risks,' she said to Áróra. 'Probably the best thing would be for you to go right away to the accountant to fetch the money so that it's ready when the kidnappers make contact.'

Flosi nodded and patted the back of his daughter's hand. She was his greatest joy and support. She was twenty-two and next year would graduate with a degree in business studies, and then he would appoint her to manage part of the company. She deserved it. She was a hard worker and had always been good to her father, although that behaviour hadn't extended to Guðrún. To be blunt, she had often been downright unpleasant to Guðrún. But that was the way relationships with a step parent often panned out – marred by suspicion and jealousy. But she seemed to have the same outlook on all this as he did. Something as shocking as this often served to clarify things, decluttering emotions. Sara Sól appeared to be as devastated as he was.

6

Áróra's name appearing on the screen was such a surprise that Daníel almost dropped his phone. It had been a long time since she had last called. If he recalled correctly, he hadn't heard from her since sometime in the middle of the summer. Maybe that was because he had been on the sharp side when he'd told her that he'd call if the investigation into her sister's disappearance made any progress. There had been no need to take that tone, and the moment he had hung up, he bitterly regretted his abruptness. All the same, he had been no less frustrated than she was that the investigation had ground to a halt. But she had been pushy, asking the same questions over and over again, and hinting that the police – which included him – were failing to do their job. He understood – knew that these reactions were normal for relatives of victims of violent crime when a case didn't come to a neat conclusion, so he should have been more patient through all the phone calls, paying no heed to her implied criticisms. But there was something about Áróra that upset his usual balance. Her presence had such an effect on him that he wasn't in complete control. He was as nervous as a teenager around her.

'My dear Áróra, there have been no developments,' he said as he picked up, using his gentlest, warmest tone.

'I know,' she replied after a moment's hesitation. 'You said you'd call if there was anything new.'

'Yes, that's right. Unfortunately, nothing new has come to light. Which is why I haven't called.'

'I'm calling about something else,' she said, and his heart tripped an extra beat. 'I need some advice, and it's urgent.'

Daníel stood up and went along the police station's corridor and down a flight of stairs to where he could stand on the landing and look out of the window. Having a view helped him concentrate. Activity around the gate below the window had the same effect as a fish tank, with patrol cars coming and going as smoothly as goldfish, giving the impression that life continued as usual although not much was actually happening.

'Tell me about it,' he said.

'It's not something I can really talk about over the phone,' Áróra said. 'An acquaintance of mine needs some guidance on a very serious matter, so I was wondering if you could meet us? Maybe at a café?'

'Yes, of course,' Daníel said, wanting to ask more but holding himself in check. 'When?'

'Now?' Áróra said, and there was a note of hopeful expectation in her voice.

He felt he owed it to her to respond quickly, and doing so would assuage his own bad feelings too, but he also felt a tingle of excitement running through him at the thought of meeting her.

'OK. I'll come right away,' he said, and thought he could hear her sigh.

'Thank you,' she said, and he could hear it again, a sigh of relief. There was clearly something troubling her deeply. 'And Daníel?' she added. 'Could you come completely incognito, no police car and no uniform?'

Daníel hurried to the changing room and opened his locker. Áróra had suggested meeting in forty minutes at a café down in the Grandi district, so he had an opportunity to smarten himself up. Not that he looked scruffy. He had taken a shower that morning, but hadn't bothered to shave, and he wasn't about to meet Áróra with grey stubble on his face. He pulled off his shirt, stood at a basin and mopped his armpits with the damp corner of a towel. Then he soaped his face, shaved, splashed on a generous amount of aftershave and an equally liberal helping of deodorant. Then he put on a clean T-shirt from his locker, wound the scarf his son had given him around his neck. He picked up a dark grey blazer and set off down the station stairs, his heart full of expectation.

7

It had been with reluctance that Flosi had gone to the café, determined not to give his name. An hour later, however, he had handed over to this detective his name, address, phone number and his national ID number. With that, a formal investigation into Guðrún's abduction was in progress. That was what the policeman had called it: abduction. He had explained to Flosi that he and his colleagues could investigate and monitor developments without any indication that the police were anywhere nearby. He had mentioned plain-clothes officers in an unmarked car.

Flosi had finally agreed to all this when the detective had asked what he would do if Guðrún was not freed on payment of the ransom.

'What are your options then?' the policeman had said. 'Suppose you pay up and they demand more money?'

That had been the breaking point for Flosi. He crumbled and wept in front of the policeman and Áróra as he realised exactly the position he was in. He was not in control of anything. He was in the grip of ruthless criminals; following their instructions and not going to the police would force him into a completely hopeless position. By working with the police he would at least have a few cards to play with.

The policeman put the ransom note in an envelope and said that the forensics division would check it for fingerprints and for any clues in the ink, and would examine the wording carefully. Once Flosi had dried his tears with the serviette Áróra handed him, glanced around to see if anyone had noticed him crying and then taken a deep breath, he sat up straight in his chair as if he was back in the managing director's seat at Garðvís ehf and looked the policeman in the eye.

'What do you suggest?' he asked, and the policeman calmly went through the list, as if he was just an obedient staff member at the wholesaler, outlining the initial steps and sketching a rough plan. It all made it sound like he knew what he was doing.

'Now I'll go back to the station and file the case, set up an undercover team with discreet facilities and Áróra will accompany you home,' he said. 'Later today I'll come to your house, in plain clothes and carrying a cake in a box, as if I'm an old friend stopping by for coffee.'

A moment later they were all on the pavement outside, and Flosi set off towards Áróra's car, turning just in time to see her and the policeman smile at each other. Going by the warmth of the smile and the look that passed between them, it seemed they were having difficulty taking their eyes off each other, and it was obvious that they either knew each other well or wanted to know each other better. Flosi felt the anger swell inside him. Flirting like this was totally inappropriate considering his wife was in mortal danger somewhere. He had no desire to be reminded of other people's love lives.

'That'll do!' he called out to them, startling Áróra, who jogged towards the car, while the policeman didn't seem remotely perturbed by his impatience and took the opportunity to follow Áróra with his eyes, a look on his face that Flosi wouldn't have tolerated if she had been his daughter.

8

Áróra stood speechless in the kitchen doorway. Every sign of the abduction had vanished. The broken glass had been swept up and the floor had been mopped, and Flosi's daughter, Sara Sól, was on her knees scrubbing the kitchen units. A smell of bleach lay heavy in the air.

'What the hell are you doing?' Áróra snarled at the young woman, who quickly got to her feet, pushed a lock of fair hair from her forehead and tugged the pink washing-up gloves from her hands.

'Just cleaning up. So it's nicer for Dad to come home to,' she said, a perplexed expression on her face.

Áróra regretted the harshness of her tone.

'The police are on their way and will be expecting to look for evidence, and you've scrubbed it all away.'

Crestfallen, Sara Sól looked around, and Áróra noticed how alike she and Flosi were. She had the same high forehead and their eyes were the same shade of grey-green, but she had a narrower nose that ended in a slightly upturned tip, which gave her the look of being arrogant when she was simply confused – as she was right now.

'But we weren't going to involve the police,' she said, and looked in dismay at Áróra, who sighed.

'Put all that cleaning stuff away,' she said. 'Your father changed his mind. He wants the police to help.'

Sara Sól followed her into the living room, where Flosi sat on the sofa, outwardly calm, apart from the rapid tapping of his right foot, his heel beating out a rhythm on the floor as if it provided some kind of release for the tension inside him. Sara Sól sat next to him and as he extended an arm, curled into his side. The two were clearly close.

'So you both work in your family company?' Áróra asked, and they both nodded at the same time.

'I just work a few hours, alongside college, this winter, but I've always worked there, every holiday and any break from school,' said Sara Sól. 'In the warehouse or in the office.'

'She'll finish her business studies degree in the spring,' Flosi said. 'And some work experience helps. She'll go straight into full-time work, with responsibilities.'

Flosi gazed proudly at his daughter, who smiled shyly back at him.

'I'm not sure about doing a masters later on. I'm not certain I'll need it. The only plan I've ever had is to go into the business with Dad.'

'Ever since she was tiny,' Flosi smiled. He clearly welcomed this opportunity to focus his mind on something other than Guðrún's disappearance. 'I think she was five when she announced that she'd be taking over one day.'

They were startled by the sound of the doorbell, and father and daughter stared at Áróra with eyes that were wide with fright.

'That's Daníel,' she said and got up to answer the door. He stood outside, holding with both hands a large cake box marked with the logo of a well-known bakery.

'The daughter scrubbed the whole kitchen while we were out,' Áróra whispered to him as he came in.

'What?'

He stopped in the hallway and stared at her.

'Yes,' Áróra said. 'She scrubbed the whole place from top to bottom. Floor, worktop, cupboards.'

'Hell...' Daníel began, falling silent as Flosi appeared. Daníel handed him the cake and strode into the living room, where he drew the blinds shut and pulled the floor-length curtains across. 'From now on,' he said. 'Curtains covering every window as we don't know who is watching the house.' He paused, turned to Sara Sól and extended a hand. 'Inspector Daníel Hansson.'

'Sara Sól Flosadóttir,' she replied.

Daníel continued to issue instructions as if he were a strict teacher facing a class of ill-behaved youngsters:

'In a few minutes there will be two police officers here. Helena is my colleague from CID and Jean-Christophe is a young man from the forensics division. Flosi, you're to go out on the steps in front and hug them both, making it clear in a loud voice that you're delighted to see them and how wonderful it is to have old friends here to support you. There was nothing in that ransom note to say that you shouldn't tell your friends about the abduction, so we can make full use of that.'

Daníel strode to the dining room and drew all the curtains across the windows. They followed him like obedient children. Sara Sól trailed behind her father, and Áróra noticed that her hand was in Flosi's, and that he put a protective arm around her, as if she was a small child.

'There's an unmarked patrol car parked along the street in an unobtrusive spot. It would be ideal, Flosi, if the police could have the use of one of your company's vans – one that's clearly marked as belonging to the business – so that we can come and go without it looking suspicious.'

There was no doubting that Daníel had taken charge, and Áróra sighed with relief.

9

There was a tense atmosphere in the house and Daníel quickly identified Flosi as the key source of it. He paced the floor with slow steps, but his body language showed that he was struggling to control himself. His fists were clenched and he breathed in gasps, as if he had trouble filling his lungs. He stared in confusion at his daughter, who had apparently relieved her own tension by carefully cleaning the crime scene before the police arrived.

'I just didn't want Dad to come home and see all that,' she repeated once again, while Daníel smiled encouragingly and nodded. She had apologised to everyone from the investigative team, Helena, the French forensics guy, and to Daníel, as well as to Áróra, who had been the only one who had taken her to task for what she had done. And despite her apologies, the girl didn't seem to realise that her painstaking cleaning, with bleach and window polish, made her a suspect.

'Now, close your eyes and try to recall exactly what you saw when you came in this morning. We'll help you lay everything out as it was so we can take pictures,' Daníel said. 'This could help. And remember that even minor details can make a difference.' The girl nodded eagerly, and Daníel turned to Flosi. 'I want you to help her. Every detail you can bring to mind.'

Flosi stopped pacing and stared at Daníel. The look in his eyes was of confusion; they looked like those of a rabbit caught in a car's headlights.

Daníel caught Helena's eye and a quick tilt of his head told her that she should supervise recreating the crime scene; she quickly nodded back to let him know that she was thinking along the same lines. This was the way much of their communication took place. Each read the other's body language and sometimes no words were even needed. Helena was an outstanding police officer, but she allowed nobody to become close to her, so many of the lads in CID seemed to be half frightened of her. Daníel liked to work with her, though. Her limitless determination and work rate made life easy for him, so he always chose her as his closest colleague over more experienced officers.

He could hear Helena as she began to instruct Flosi and Sara Sól to re-arrange the kitchen to resemble the scene as they had found it. He went into the living room. Áróra was sitting there on the sofa, and his sense of everything else around them was suddenly cut off. All he could see and hear was Áróra; he felt that he could almost smell her through the cloud of aftershave that enveloped him. She gave him a quick, weak smile. He thought that she wanted to smile more broadly but that she didn't feel it appropriate under the circumstances.

'Jeez,' she said, and he sighed, shaking his head as he sat in an armchair facing her.

'This is a strange situation,' he said. 'I think kidnapping is probably one of the rarest crimes we encounter in Iceland. I'm going to have to get some advice from colleagues in Norway and Denmark. I've never had to deal with anything like this before.'

He knew he would have to take a statement from Áróra, to formally take down the details of her involvement in the situation. But he didn't feel like doing it right away. He was going to enjoy this moment, when he could sit opposite and watch her.

10

Flosi felt his head throb as he sat by Sara Sól's side at the dining table, facing the people from the police as they asked question after question. What got on his nerves most was that the questions seemed to be so random, somehow coming from every direction, as if they were casting their lines here and there in the hope that sooner or later an unwary salmon would bite.

'It didn't occur to you when you went into the kitchen that this was some kind of practical joke? A prank in poor taste, maybe?' Daníel asked, and Flosi shook his head.

'Why would I think that?' he said. 'I don't know anyone who would do something like that to me.'

'I asked simply because the initial reaction of people who are victims of this kind of thing is disbelief. They go into denial about what has actually happened. You didn't have any thoughts along those lines?'

Flosi again shook his head, feeling it swell, waiting for it to explode with a bang. Was this policeman indicating that there were correct and incorrect reactions to this sort of thing? Had his reactions been the wrong ones? Was that suspicious in any way?

'Explain to me again why you decided to clean the kitchen,' the female officer, Helena, said, her words directed at Sara Sól.

'I just don't know,' she said miserably. 'Maybe I needed to have something to do while Dad went with this ... this woman from the accountant in Scotland...'

'Áróra,' Helena said.

'Yes. While Dad went with Áróra to talk to the policeman. You,' she said, pointing at Daníel. 'And I thought he'd come home and he'd be in a terrible state, and it would be awful for him to see all that mess left by the abduction. You know, the broken glass on the floor and half-cooked food going bad on the worktop.' She shrugged her shoulders, and spread her hands, palms up, and for a moment she reminded Flosi of an angel. 'Like I told you before, I didn't know that Dad was going to bring the police in, and it didn't even cross my mind that anyone would want to search the kitchen for evidence. And I like to do the cleaning. Here, I mean, at Dad's place. Not at home.'

Helena smiled and made a note on the pad in front of her, holding it in such a way that what she wrote couldn't be seen. She seemed amiable, but was one of those people it's not easy to get the measure of. She was petite, with short, dark hair and dark-grey eyes that looked warm but which could become so sharp, it was almost painful to be subjected to her gaze. At first Flosi, when he saw her outside the house, had thought she was a teenager, but close up, when he went onto the steps to hug her and give them a loud, clear welcome, as Daníel had instructed, he saw that fine lines had begun to form around her eyes, so she had to be in her thirties.

'Why do you think they asked for the ransom to be paid in euros?' Daníel asked, his gaze now fixed on Flosi, who glanced over at Helena, only to find the same hard stare from her. He sighed. Áróra had told him he'd have to be straight with them, that he would have to be open. This could make all the difference.

'As Áróra has maybe told you relating to her connection to all this, I have money in overseas accounts. Mostly in euros. Michael, the accountant with whom Áróra works, has for many years managed these accounts for me. I'd like to make it clear that the intention has always been to declare these funds and pay tax on them – I've always intended to do it at such time as I bring it all to Iceland.'

This was a lie, and Flosi could see that Daníel was aware of that.

'We're not investigating tax evasion,' Daníel said. 'So we'll keep any discussion about tax until later, as we have more urgent things to deal with. I'm curious to know who knew about this money you have squirrelled away overseas. I need names.'

Flosi felt the sweat break out on his back.

'Are you saying that someone near to me, someone among my closest friends, could be behind this? Could be the person who abducted Guðrún?'

'That's what we need to establish,' Daníel said. 'We need to know if the person concerned has demanded euros because they know you have cash overseas, or if it's just a coincidence.'

Coincidence. Flosi felt himself snatching at the idea. It could be a complete coincidence. That was a thought that was more easily borne than the notion that someone he knew, someone he trusted, might have done this to him, and done this to Guðrún. But his relief was short-lived, as Helena turned her relentless gaze on Sara Sól.

'Let's go through your day yesterday. You went to the pool and then to college...' she began, before two short rings on the door-bell interrupted them. This was the signal the police officers had agreed between them to use.

'Come to the door with me, Flosi,' Helena said, getting to her feet, and he followed her through the living room to the lobby. He felt discomforted by leaving Sara Sól alone with Daníel. He wanted to be there, to know what was said. He wanted to know what questions they asked her. He felt that their last questions had been significant, as if they suspected her of some involvement with this. But it was ridiculous that his wonderful, fair-haired girl would do such a thing to him.

'You're to open the door and let the pizza guy in,' Helena said, and stepped to one side so that she was out of sight when Flosi opened the door.

'Come right in,' he said, which was unnecessary, as this wasn't a pizza delivery man, but a police officer in a Dominos baseball cap. The French forensics guy appeared and took the large insulated bag that the pizza cop handed him, placed it on the sideboard and took out all kinds of stuff in little bags and boxes. Then he took the plastic bag he had brought from the kitchen and stuffed it into the insulated bag. Flosi thought he saw a tin can through the thin plastic, and realised that this was the contents of the kitchen bin. Jean-Christophe handed the pizza cop the bag, and Helena nodded to Flosi as a signal to open the door and let the pizza guy out, taking their rubbish with him. No doubt this would be on the way to some laboratory where it would be inspected and examined under a microscope, just like every other aspect of their lives would be, Flosi thought, and the sweat again began to trickle down his back.

11

Once the items for the forensic team had been whisked away by their colleague Kristján in his pizza-delivery disguise and Flosi had resumed his seat at the table, Helena noticed that he was even more agitated. She also saw that this hadn't escaped Daníel's notice, and so they began to dig deeper to find out what had upset him. While they had gone through the previous day's events with Sara Sól, Flosi had seemed to be on tenterhooks, but now, while they were asking him to detail his own day, he seemed more relaxed.

Helena would have preferred to pile the pressure on Sara Sól, in the hope they'd push Flosi's patience to its limits, but Daníel steered the conversation towards Guðrún, and Helena knew that he was right. They had seen what they needed to and now knew that Flosi was sensitive about anything that concerned his daughter. This could be either because there was something he preferred to keep to himself, or simply a parent's protective instincts at work.

Now they needed to gather all the information they could about Guðrún. There was nothing coincidental about her disappearance. This had been planned. That indicated that Guðrún had been selected, maybe because of who she was, or because of the man she was married to. So that meant that she and her life had to be central to solving the mystery.

'Guðrún isn't on Facebook or any other social media,' Flosi said, and Helena immediately felt a wave of disappointment, which she knew Daníel would share. Social media had become an increasingly important part of their work in recent years. The things that people wrote or confessed in messages was almost beyond belief; it was as if people failed to understand that what happened online was as indelible as if it had been carved in stone.

'Her phone – the one that was left here – is an iPhone, isn't it?' Daníel asked.

'Yes, it's a new smartphone that Dad bought for her, but she doesn't use the smart stuff much,' Sara Sól said.

'That's unusual for someone who isn't exactly old,' Helena observed.

'Yes, I know,' Flosi said awkwardly, as if in Guðrún's defence. 'She didn't have much interest in the internet.'

'Didn't?' Daníel said.

'What?' Flosi seemed unaware of his own words.

'You said "she didn't", and not "she doesn't",' Helena said, her tone deliberately sharp.

Flosi turned pale and instead of correcting himself, or explaining, or going on the defensive, it was clear that he wanted most of all to burst into tears.

'I really said that?' he gasped. 'God help me.'

Sara Sól placed an arm around his shoulders and pulled him comfortingly close. Daníel waited for a moment before resuming his gentle, good-cop role.

'How about text messages? Does she use those?' he asked.

Sara Sól nodded.

'You can send her a text, but you can never tell if she reads them as she rarely replies. And she hardly ever uses email either. She says that computers are a thief of time. If she ever has to give someone an email address, she gives them Dad's.'

'She always wanted...' Flosi began, before stopping short. 'God, I've done it again. Speaking about her in the past tense. Just like she's dead.'

He buried his face in his hands and Sara Sól patted his back with a steady rhythm as if she were comforting a restless child.

When Flosi raised his head, his eyes brimmed with tears and desperation.

'What do you think?' he demanded. 'Do you think she's dead?'

12

'There's a small grey case at the bottom of the cupboard in the hall. Shaving stuff, toothpaste, underwear and a few other essentials,' Daníel said. 'I need that, and the phone charger that's plugged into a socket in the kitchen.'

Áróra nodded, and Daníel stifled an urge to tell her to write this down. There were only two things, so it wasn't as if she was going to forget one of them. He knew he would have to keep in check his tendency to micromanage things that weren't directly connected to work, such as those concerning Áróra.

'Put it in a supermarket bag. You should be able to find one in the kitchen. So it looks like you've just been shopping.'

Áróra nodded and took the key he handed her. For a second he touched her palm and it felt as if the tips of his fingers were on fire. He jerked his hand back.

'What's up?' Áróra asked, noticing how fast he had snatched back his hand.

'Nothing,' he said. 'Take some indirect route both to my place and back here.'

Áróra caught his eye, and he thought he could see a little levity in her expression. A smile seemed to be about to appear around her eyes, and he didn't know if this was directed at him or elsewhere. Maybe she even wanted to laugh at him and the depth of feeling that enveloped him in her presence.

He stood in the hall for a moment, waiting for the door to close behind her, took a deep breath and told himself to concentrate on his thought processes, which had become dull and needed sharpening. By the time he returned to the living room, he was his usual calm, collected self. The thoughts that Áróra triggered in him had settled.

He could hear a murmur of conversation from Helena and Sara Sól in the kitchen. He had asked Helena to compile a family tree and a network of the family's friends, with the girl's help, and to put together a detailed picture of the last forty-eight hours leading up to Guðrún's disappearance. Flosi slumped on the sofa, staring at the blank television screen, as if there was something there that called for his concentration. Daníel sat in an armchair opposite him and cleared his throat.

'We have set up both the landline and your mobile to intercept calls. It'll be either me or another officer listening in here, and all calls are also recorded. I know it's not pleasant, but in a case like this it's vital.'

'Of course,' Flosi muttered. He had looked terrified earlier in the day when Daníel had asked him to sign a consent form allowing them to listen in, but now he seemed to have accepted that as long as his wife remained unaccounted for, the police would be tracking his every movement. Flosi picked up a sheet of paper and handed it to Daníel. On it was a series of hand-written numbers.

'That's the password for Guðrún's online banking. She was...' He coughed awkwardly. 'She is careful with money, and smart too.'

Daníel took the paper. He would check the account later.

'Did she work with you at your company?' Daníel asked.

'No,' Flosi replied. 'Garðvís is my world and Sara Sól's. I tried to keep her and Guðrún as far apart as I could. They didn't get on. Typical step-relationship.'

'My experience is that relationships of that nature can be very varied,' Daníel said, recalling how he would have preferred to hold on to at least two of his step-fathers, unlike his mother, who always seemed to tire of the latest boyfriend shortly after they moved in. 'What's the nature of this difficult relationship between Guðrún and Sara Sól?'

Flosi sighed and waved a hand, as if he preferred to make out that it was of no importance. He clearly regretted having mentioned it.

'Well, there's the florist's shop idea. Guðrún had wanted to open a shop, and I was looking at supporting her, but Sara Sól didn't think it was a good investment, so I pulled back on it.'

'And I imagine Guðrún wasn't impressed?'

'Not at all. It certainly fuelled the hostility between them.' Flosi gasped as if he had emerged from deep water, and Daníel realised that he was struggling to keep himself from bursting into tears again. 'I have huge regrets about not supporting Guðrún on it. I've no doubt she could have made a little flower shop pay its way.'

13

Helena was so elated as she left the house, she was almost floating. She had never heard of a case of kidnapping in Iceland before. There had certainly been instances of people being held against their will – when coked-up guys from gangs had plucked people off the street, held them prisoner and tormented them as payback for some underworld debt – and there were the domestic-abuse cases where men held their wives or exes hostage. That happened now and again. But a planned and executed kidnapping with a ransom demand was such a rarity that the chance to work on and learn from such a case would hardly come her way again.

If ever there was a time to make use of *the system*, this was it.

To be on top form for work in the morning she really needed to get some decent rest and respite this evening. It felt as if her feet didn't even touch the ground as she glided to the car and started the engine, and before setting off, she had fished her phone from a pocket and tapped in a short message to the first one in the group she thought of as *the system*. It wasn't so complicated a setup that it deserved a name, but she liked to call it that in her own mind, as it created a certain distance and reminded her that each of them was part of a greater whole. *The system* was a group of three women in the same circumstances as herself – unwilling or unable to be in a relationship, but who occasionally felt the need for an evening or a night with another woman. None of them knew about the others, but as far as Helena was concerned, they were a single network.

She drove along the gloomy Hraunbrún at a leisurely rate, and it happened that Beta, who wouldn't necessarily be her first choice but was top in alphabetical order, replied before she reached the Hjallabraut junction.

At work, Evening shift.

Helena wrote a reply at the give-way sign, wishing her a good shift and sending a little heart and an *xx*. A heart and an *xx* came right back. All this was so straightforward and free from any drama that it was wonderful. Once she was past the two round-abouts and the junction leading onto Reykjavíkurvegur, she had decided who would be her next choice. Sirra was a night owl, always up for a long evening's fun and never too worried about having to be up early the next morning. Helena's thoughts lingered on Sirra. She had to be at least ten years older than her but kept herself in great form, and like many who discovered their inner self later in life, she needed a couple of glasses of wine before she'd take the brakes off, and then she'd be insatiable in bed; passionate, wild.

There was a red light at the crossing by the filling station on Reykjavíkurvegur, although no pedestrian was anywhere to be seen. Helena took the opportunity to send Sirra a text.

Wanna hook up?

Sirra had made fun of her the first time she had sent such a message, finding it weird that she chose to send it in English. But Helena found it less clunky to use an English expression. Icelandic didn't have the vocabulary that fitted her relationships with these women. 'Hook up' was perfect. To connect, link together. Somehow these foreign expressions reflected the casual nature of all this, that it was somehow arbitrary, free of any obligation.

Helena had tried different routes to this before. For a while she had been constantly on Tinder, always trying out new relation-ships. But that wasn't going to work for long. It was too stressful and there was too much uncertainty about the quality of the sex, on top of which she simply didn't have time for all these coffee dates, take-it-slowly dinners and long-winded I-don't-know-what-I-want conversations. But these three she had tracked down were perfect, all ready for a short-notice shag, and it was rare that they all had other commitments at the same time. Helena got what she wanted without having to go through explanations of why she worked such long days, didn't take a summer holiday and had no interests outside her job. As well as that, she escaped deadly dull evenings in front of the TV, pretending to enjoy romantic comedies.

Happy to hook up but it'll have to be at your place, the message from Sirra read.

Helena felt a wave of contented warmth flow through her. Sirra. This would be a Sirra evening. She could almost feel the aroma of her scent, see that beautiful smile. Normally they met at Sirra's home in Laugardalur, but of course it wasn't fair to have it that way every time. It was time to meet at Helena's place. She mentally checked her flat. The bedclothes were clean, although she hadn't bothered to make the bed that morning. There was white wine in the cooler, and if she was quick she'd be home in time to light candles and pick out some sweet music before Sirra arrived.

She sent an *OK*, and a GPS tag for her address on Mánatún. No chatter or yakking between them. They knew each other well enough that there was no need. Although in reality they hardly knew each other at all. The perfect *system*.

14

Áróra drew a deep breath as she stepped inside Daníel's apartment. It had that distinctive Icelandic smell that she couldn't define but which had something to do with the Icelandic habit of always having open windows with radiators invariably directly beneath them so that they would heat up the air as it flowed in. The air inside the place was dry, and far, far too hot. She could make out a faint trace of Daníel's aftershave in the air, and in the hall she couldn't withstand the temptation to take his motorcycle jacket from its hook and breath in deep the aroma from the collar. The jacket smelled of masculinity and leather, and for a moment Áróra wanted to put it on and envelop herself in Daníel's presence.

She opened the hall cupboard and found the little grey overnight case he had asked her to collect. He seemed to have this ready if he were to be called away for a couple of nights. More than likely, detectives were called out to any part of the country at short notice when something came up.

She took her shoes off in the hall before venturing onto the parquet, tiptoeing on stockinged feet into the kitchen. The charger was where Daníel had said it would be, and she coiled away the cable and put it in the case.

She opened the bottom drawer and smiled to herself at the sight of the rolled-up carrier bags. This was one thing her parents had squabbled over. It irritated her father that British people, her mother included, organised their kitchens as they saw fit, while most Icelanders regarded it as an inviolable rule that plastic bags should be in the bottom drawer, the bin should be under the sink and the eggs in the fridge. Áróra took one of the Króna supermarket bags and dropped the overnight case into it.

This brought her errand to Daníel's home to an end, but before she knew it she was looking around in his bedroom. This was the only room in the place that she hadn't been in before, and it was more stripped back than she had expected. The walls were bare, there was no cover over the imposing American-style bed, just a simple white duvet cover, and a bedside table on only one side. All in all, it was less welcoming than the average hotel room.

Áróra was startled by a sharp bang on the floor-length window and let out a yelp of surprise. Outside in the darkness stood a broad-shouldered woman, pointing angrily at the handle, indicating that Áróra should open it.

'What are you doing in Daníel's place?' the woman asked in a deep voice, and Áróra realised that there was some male physiognomy beneath the imposing wig and false eyelashes.

'I'm fetching some things for Daníel as he's spending some time away due to work.'

'And you are?'

The glare that accompanied the question was arrogant and suspicious in roughly equal measure.

'My name's Áróra and I'm—' she began, but was interrupted by a loud whoop.

'Oh, my God. You're Áróra? Finally, darling!' Áróra was stunned at this outpouring of joy that came with kisses on both cheeks and a hug. 'At last. I've heard so much about you, darling, and you're nothing like I imagined. Gorgeous. Absolutely gorgeous! I'm so sorry, I'm smudging make-up on you. I've just come from an appearance. So pleased to meet you. I'm Lady Gúgúlú, the sexiest and also the most daring queen to be found north of the Alps. My mental state is all right, but it comes and goes.'

Áróra grasped the offered hand and laughed at the theatricality of it all.

'I'm the absolute best, bestest friend Daníel has. I live over there in the garden and he tells me everything. And that includes everything about you.'

Áróra lifted a questioning eyebrow but Lady Gúgúlú didn't seem inclined to share anything more of the discussions she and Daníel had had about her. She couldn't imagine that their short acquaintance could have provided material for any detailed conversations, though. He had been kind to her at the outset of the investigation into her sister's disappearance, and they had spent an evening together when something had almost happened between them, but she had halted, backed off. She had made it plain that she wasn't the type for romance, that she preferred being single. Everything had gone wrong after that when she had been with another guy down town and had run into Daníel, and hadn't been able to explain to him that it had been just a quick fling; nothing serious, no affection there. Over the summer her vexation over her desire to explain herself to Daníel had grown – as had her disappointment at the police's lack of progress in solving the mystery of her sister's disappearance. Her and Daníel's calls had become shorter and colder as the summer passed.

Having happily waved goodbye to Lady Gúgúlú, Áróra went to the hall to put on her shoes, and noticed that there was a lamp switched on in the living room. This was an Icelandic habit that annoyed her. They wasted energy like irresponsible children. They left lights burning for days on end, and allowed water to gush from the taps while they brushed their teeth or washed up. This had been another bone of contention between her parents.

Áróra went into the living room, and as she reached for the lamp on the desk to switch it off, the warm feeling inside, which had begun when she heard that Daníel had talked about her to this odd friend of his, came close to boiling point as she saw what was on the desk. A folder marked *Ísafold Jónsdóttir* lay there, surrounded by papers – evidence files and scrawled notes.

He hadn't forgotten her sister. He was still investigating her disappearance.

15

'Lovely flat,' Sirra said as she walked in. There was a note of surprise in her voice that made Helena laugh.

'What did you expect?' she asked as she poured white wine into
a glass and handed it to Sirra. 'That I'd live in a slum?'

Sirra grinned, walked around the living room so that her heels
clacked on the parquet, and stopped at the window. She hadn't
offered to remove her shoes and it hadn't occurred to Helena to
ask her to do so. Sirra was the only woman Helena knew who
always wore heels and a skirt. It was as if she were determined to
defy the Icelandic climate with her seventies office-girl look.

'Ach, darling, do you have some ice?' she asked, handing Helena
her glass. 'I like it a little more chilled.'

Helena took the glass with a smile. The wine was chilled to the
ideal temperature – the bottle had been placed perfectly in the
cooler. This was one of those things that she found so sexy about
older women: once they had figured out what they liked, they
could no longer be bothered with any fuss and became refresh-
ingly forthright. It went without saying that ice would ruin the
wine, but this evening Sirra could have whatever she liked. She
would distract Helena's thoughts from the kidnapping case and
provide her with the diversion she needed to be able to sleep
soundly through the night and concentrate her energies in the
morning.

'I've been analysing you,' Sirra said as Helena came over to her
by the window and handed her the glass of white wine, three-
quarters full and with ice cubes that clinked. 'You're some kind of
female Casanova. This flat is designed to seduce women.'

'That's a possibility,' Helena said, somehow pleased that Sirra
had seen through her. It was quite right that when Helena had

furnished and decorated this place, her criteria had all centred on inviting women here to sleep with her. The kitchen was nicely fitted out, but there was only space at the island unit for two people. She had installed a small bar against one wall of the living room, with a wine cooler and a collection of different glasses, so that she could meet a wide variety of requirements for drinks. The only place in the living room to sit was the large, soft sofa, which provided a view of the bedroom with its king-sized bed, a giant vulva painting by Kristín Gunnlaugsdóttir hanging over it.

'Isn't it awkward when relatives come for dinner?' Sirra teased, which made Helena uncomfortable. She had no desire to talk to Sirra about her family. These were two separate worlds; one pleasant, the other unpleasant. Right now her mind was on the pleasant one. She took Sirra's hand and led her to the sofa. Two candles flickered on the table in the half-light and Nina Simone and Lauryn Hill singing 'Killing Me Softly' wove a warm seductive web around them that made any words unnecessary. She sat close to Sirra, raised her glass and they clinked, sipped, kissed gently – and then some more.

Sirra extended one leg over Helena's knee, and she gently ran her palm along its length. Sirra's legs were exceptionally beautiful, which was maybe the reason she dressed as she did. Her legs were bare, although they were so smooth and golden, they didn't look to be. Either she spent time on the sun bed or applied a tan herself – not that Helena was concerned which. All she was interested in was the effect that the silky skin had on her, leading her hands higher, past the hollow behind her knee and along the inside of her leg. Sirra smiled her enticingly beautiful smile that told Helena she was on the right track as she slid further, hands trembling with anticipation that jolted through her like a spark as she discovered that Sirra was wearing nothing beneath the skirt.

16

There were certain patterns that could be read from Guðrún's bank account. Until around a month ago she had gone to the gym practically every day, or at any rate she had gone there and bought something from the kiosk that cost seven hundred krónur; Daníel guessed it had to be a protein shake after a workout. Most days she shopped for groceries, and going by the amounts she spent, this was a couple who ate well. She seemed to go to a coffee house three or four times a week – not always the same one – and at least once a week she bought flowers. Again, she didn't seem to favour a particular place – there were payments to a variety of florists. The first thing that really attracted Daníel's attention was the payment to an airline. Around a month ago she had paid fifty-two thousand krónur to Icelandair. He made a note of it.

There was a monthly payment from Flosi into her account. This was a generous amount and exceeded Guðrún's monthly out-goings, so over an extended period a sizeable amount had built up. Six months ago there had been a healthy three million krónur there. But not now. Daníel scrolled down the list of transactions, pausing at the red lines indicating withdrawals. As well as the usual outgoings, there were a few payments to other accounts; not via a debit card but direct transfers between accounts. These recipients included a Jón Jónsson, who had twice been paid twenty thousand krónur, the second payment having taking place yesterday. A week ago Guðrún had paid sixty-five thousand krónur to someone called Karl Leósson.

Three months ago a new series of frequent but irregular transfers had begun. The first had been for two hundred thousand krónur, then two weeks later a three-hundred-thousand payment, and so on, week after week, right up to the last transfer ten days ago, which had been for half a million krónur. That had left the account as good as empty. All of these payments had been made to a company called Sigurlaug slf, and the suffix told Daníel that this was an unlimited liability company. He would have to ask Flosi in the morning if the name Sigurlaug slf meant anything to him.

Daníel closed his laptop and lay back on the sofa in the little TV corner of the living room. He pulled over himself the duvet Flosi had lent him and closed his eyes, but his thoughts continued to tick over, everything he had just found out becoming part of the mix that he hoped would properly take shape before too long.

Guðrún's life had been quiet and uneventful, with regular habits that had begun to change around three months ago, when she had begun to make increasingly large payments to whatever Sigurlaug slf actually was. In the last few weeks Guðrún appeared to have departed considerably from what had been her usual behaviour for as far back as Daníel had examined her account. The gym had completely dropped out of the picture and there had been flowers only once in the last month. Could that be significant? Could this Sigurlaug slf be a front for some blackmailer who had his hooks into Guðrún and had finally made a move when her money had run out? Or did this company have links to someone who knew that Flosi had fat bank accounts overseas? According to Flosi, apart from himself, Guðrún and Sara Sól, nobody knew about this hidden cash. Flosi dealt with Michael the accountant in Edinburgh personally, so there was no question of a secretary or assistant anywhere who knew anything.

Daníel's thoughts were beginning to drift away from the mix whirling through his mind, spinning into disjointed dreams, when he was startled into wakefulness by the sound of the phone ringing. It was the landline. He quickly sat up, reaching for the earpiece that allowed him to listen in on the call. It was almost midnight, not a considerate time to be calling, so this had to be something interesting.

'Flosi—' a thin female voice said, but Flosi immediately interrupted.

'I can't talk now. I'll speak to you tomorrow.'

'I'll just call back if you hang up,' the woman said, with desperation in her voice.

'Something has come up,' Flosi said quickly, and it was clear that he wanted to end the call as soon as possible. 'Something came up so I can't talk now.'

'You're not answering your mobile, so I had to call the home number. I know I shouldn't, but I must speak to you, my love.'

'Tomorrow,' Flosi said. 'Promise.'

He put the phone down.

Daníel lay back and sighed. The woman had said 'my love' before Flosi had hung up. Flosi and Guðrún's marriage maybe wasn't as perfect as he had wanted them to think. Daníel's list of questions for Flosi in the morning had just got a lot longer.

WEDNESDAY

17

Flosi could hear the policeman pottering about downstairs, but he wasn't yet ready to look him in the eye. He had lain awake half the night; in between bouts of terror at the increasingly horrific images his mind conjured up of what could have become of Guðrún, he had tried to think of some plausible tale he could spin about last night's phone call. He had blocked Bergrós' number on his mobile when the police had started monitoring it, but that hadn't been enough. Although it was a golden rule between them that she should never call his home number, of course that was what she had done, and at the worst possible moment. He knew perfectly well that Bergrós didn't respect the usual rules and limitations.

He felt a painful stab of regret. He had always been able to rely on Guðrún. She was unvarying in her habits and he always knew where he stood with her. He now regretted undervaluing this part of her personality. Bergrós had come across as so exciting and spontaneous in comparison with Guðrún's solid predictability. Bergrós constantly took him by surprise and had set the blood pumping in his veins so hard that he felt he had shed years.

But now he would have given anything to be free of Bergrós' impulsiveness. He'd also have been delighted not to have to explain himself to the policeman waiting downstairs, who had undoubtedly put two and two together and made at least seven.

Flosi tiptoed to the bathroom to pee, taking care to tread lightly; although the house was built of concrete, the thud of footsteps could still carry through the floor. He remembered that from when Sara Sól had been small and he had heard her skipping around upstairs. He didn't flush, but closed the lid of the toilet and sneaked back to the bedroom. He wasn't going downstairs until he had thought up some plausible tale that meant last night's phone call didn't undermine what he had told the police yesterday – that his marriage was as solid as a rock.

And in fact, now that Guðrún was gone, he needed to face up to the cold, hard reality that their marriage was actually a good one. He always looked forward to coming home to her, and to eating her food, to telling her about his day while they listened to the evening news on the radio. He loved the feel of her warm hands massaging his tired shoulders. The only thing he didn't look forward to was the late evening – the snores accompanying the television, the predictability, the monotony. That's where Bergrós had come into the picture. Bergrós offered passion and adventure and unbridled delight. But that didn't mean he no longer loved Guðrún. He would have to find a way to explain this to the policeman downstairs. Because from what he had seen in every one of the cop shows that Guðrún had fallen asleep over, when something happened to the wife, the prime suspect was always the husband.

18

Daníel had woken early, and went quietly to the kitchen, where he sent Facebook messages to his children in Denmark before making coffee. He made a full pot so that there would be enough for Flosi when he came downstairs, but so far there was no sign of him. It was as well for him to get some sleep. He would need all his wits about him for the grilling Daníel intended to give him concerning last night's phone call.

When he had been younger it had annoyed him when people told untruths. He felt that it was disrespectful to his role as a police officer when people he was trying to help lied to him. But these days he simply expected everyone to lie about something. Experience told him that it was somehow hard-wired into people to lie about things of which they were ashamed. Lies didn't necessarily mean guilt, although it could certainly work that way. It was his job to figure out the distinction.

Going by the way the woman had spoken, she was Flosi's mistress, and his reaction showed that this was something he wanted to keep to himself. But yesterday he had been adamant that his marriage to Guðrún was very strong. In Daníel's experience this kind of situation generally didn't add up. People didn't normally look for love elsewhere unless their relationship was flawed, or they were struggling with personal problems. He would have to know what the story was in Flosi's case. This could be a key aspect of the investigation. The police needed to be aware of everyone who could have a connection to the case, and that included secret mistresses.

Daníel refilled his mug and went into the living room, closing the door behind him. He swore quietly as he felt the sticky fingerprint powder on the door handle, and went back to the kitchen for a cloth to wipe it off. The forensics team no longer used this old-fashioned grey-black powder, except when their lenses and lights struggled to make out traces.

He stood still for a moment before closing the living room door, listening out for movement, but there was no sound from upstairs. Flosi was either still asleep or else he wasn't coming down.

Daníel found the number for Kristján, who had been working overnight to set up facilities for the investigation team, and who had also been checking CCTV in the area.

'There are no companies on that street or in the vicinity, except for the filling station and the Króna supermarket, but their cameras only cover their own car parks and don't go as far the road,' Kristján explained. 'So there are no security cameras to check. The traffic cameras are all we have. There's one at Álftanes on Reykjavíkurvegur, on the way out of town, and another at the bottom of Hjallabraut. There aren't that many routes you can take without passing a traffic camera, but so far it doesn't look like there's anything relevant to be seen.'

'Then tell Palli it's his job to sit over it and write down the numbers of every car that went past on Monday, starting from when Flosi went to work, until he came home,' Daníel said. Then thought for a moment. 'Or longer. Let's have every number up to when I turned up at the house yesterday afternoon. And tell him we want the time each one was seen.'

'He's going to be overjoyed,' Kristján said, and Daníel could almost hear him grin.

'Tell him I'll buy him a case of beer if he comes up with anything useful. That should dampen his disappointment and encourage him to pay attention,' Daníel said, smiling to himself at the thought of Palli's expression when he found out what a long and boring job awaited him.

After speaking to Kristján, he sent an email to Helena setting out the schedule for the first part of the day, and then opened the case files in the police's LÖKE database to see what Kristján and Palli had uploaded the day before. They had quietly approached the two neighbours who had a view of Flosi's and Guðrún's driveway, without telling them why they were interested. They had simply asked if they had noticed anything unusual, and as nothing had come from their questions, they had decided not to do anything that could attract any attention in the neighbourhood. It was important not to let it become known that Flosi had called in the police, which was why they were putting so much emphasis on keeping traffic in and out of the house both well disguised and to an absolute minimum, in case it was being watched. In any case, the investigation would be managed from the station, and he would make sure the place was monitored for a call concerning the ransom.

He decided that he would do most of this himself, as dealing with Flosi and those close to him were at the heart of the investigation. Experience told him that the key to the mystery of Guðrún's disappearance was to be found somewhere in the circle of people around her and Flosi.

19

Helena woke to find Sirra already gone. She quickly dismissed any feeling of regret. It was always good to conclude a hook-up with toast and coffee, a couple of kisses, 'have a great day' and 'see you soon'. It was a pleasure to look into each other's eyes after such a night, and a delight to see Sirra's beautiful smile the morning after. But it wasn't remotely necessary, plus it would eat up half a valuable hour of work time. She let the espresso maker pump the coffee while she took a rapid lukewarm shower, stretched her neck muscles under the flow, and tripped with a towel around her waist to the kitchen to take the coffee off the stove before it had a chance to boil over and burn onto the hotplate.

She took her coffee with her to the bathroom and sipped while she dried her short hair, put on face cream and added bronzing powder. Usually these were the only cosmetics she used. She used no make-up and ordinary deodorant was all the scent she needed. She put on dark-blue trousers and a thin, grey rollneck sweater over her singlet, and finally a dark-grey blazer. She checked herself out in the mirror while she finished what was left of her coffee and was satisfied with what she saw. It was amazing what a night with an attractive woman could do for your self-confidence. 'Butch' was what Beta had called her, but she would rather describe herself as neat. She wore simple clothes and no jewellery other than a watch.

She poured the rest of the coffee from the pot and drank it standing at the kitchen worktop while she checked her email. A team meeting had been called for midday, but there was a job list for her from Daniel, and she felt the excitement mount inside her. Accompanied by the gnawing curiosity that came from working on a case that was far from clear. Their work was frequently about gathering information as evidence of events that had obviously occurred – the data they collated was there simply to convince the perpetrator to confess. But this kidnapping was mysterious and more than a little curious. Who on earth would kidnap a person and then demand money for her safe release? It was an enormously reckless plan and not exactly a strategy that any run-of-the-mill, small-time criminal would use to bring in some cash. The ransom was high, so this had to be someone who thought big, someone with extensive plans and the capacity for organisation.

Her job list started with collecting a van marked as belonging to Flosi's company, Garðvís ehf, so that they could come and go from his place without attracting undue attention. Then she was to check the records of a few people to whom Guðrún had made recent payments. Helena rinsed her coffee cup and placed it upside down on the drying rack. This was going to be an interesting day and she was raring to go. Her mind was ticking over like a freshly started computer, ready to take on a complex assignment. She smiled to herself as she left the building, mentally thanking Sirra for her company overnight.

20

Áróra had assembled the two hundred components of the Ikea chest of drawers that she intended to place, completed, in the hall by the time she heard the first of her neighbours leaving for work. Her last sleepless night had been more than a month ago. This kidnapping case had upset her, prompting painful and uncomfortable thoughts about her sister Ísafold's disappearance, emotions she had only just learned how to keep at bay long enough to get some sleep.

She put the chest of drawers together in the living room and wondered about putting a mat beneath it so she could drag it to its new home, but then realised that she had carried the flatpack up the steps, so it could hardly be heavier now that it had been assembled. It was a more awkward shape to carry, but by taking out one of the drawers, Áróra was able to pick it up easily and carry it to the hall. Having spent much of her childhood watching her father train for Highland games, she knew how to use her strength to shift heavy, bulky objects.

She surveyed the results of her work with satisfaction. The chest of drawers looked fine under the window, and placing a green plant pot on top of it would make it both visually pleasing and practical. She recalled from her childhood the mess of hats, gloves, scarves and wool socks that could collect in the hallways of Icelandic homes, so these drawers would be useful as winter approached. Now she needed a thick, absorbent mat to place on the black-and-white diamond tiles, and then she would be satisfied.

She wanted to take a picture and send it to her mother, but she wasn't prepared for the conversation that would follow. She hadn't told her mother that she had bought a flat in Iceland, but the fact would undoubtedly be revealed once her mother realised she was buying furniture for her nest. She knew that Áróra had a flat but assumed that she had rented it, that her spell in Iceland was something temporary and that once Áróra had regained her equilibrium, she would move back to Britain. But Áróra wasn't on the way back to Britain, at any rate, not yet. Not until she had found her sister's resting place. Not while there were so many questions about her disappearance that remained unanswered.

Her enthusiasm for everything else had faded. Even the thought of rolling in a pile of money – as she had often done, quite literally, in the past, when she'd received a hefty bonus from completing a big case – was no longer that attractive. A certain peace of mind was needed to drink a whole bottle of champagne sitting in a bed strewn with banknotes. That peace of mind had been written off the day Daníel had given them the news that Ísafold was considered deceased. The investigation at the apartment where Ísafold and Björn had lived indicated overwhelmingly that her sister had been murdered there. Ever since that moment, there had been a hard ball of tension in her belly, which had pushed her to search and search. Because there was just one thing that would relieve the pain: being able to locate her sister's body.

Suspected of being responsible for Ísafold's death, Björn had vanished without trace. He appeared to have walked out of the airport in Toronto and vanished. Áróra's own search efforts had yielded no better results than those of the Icelandic police and Interpol; after all, her speciality was searching for money, not people. And she had already checked to see if Björn had left any kind of money trail behind him.

Áróra went back to the living room, lay on the mat among the remnants of the packaging that had come with the chest of drawers and did a few leg lifts. Then she turned over and did a hundred press-ups without a break, followed by fifty knee bends. She was bathed in sweat by the time she had finished, although this was nothing like a real work-out. She'd have to go to the gym and lift some proper weights. Her father wouldn't have been impressed if he had known how she had neglected training recently.

She was about to get into the shower when the phone rang. The name on the screen was Michael's, so she answered it straightaway.

'Hi, Michael,' she said, seeing an image in her mind of his cropped head and laughing brown eyes.

'Flosi wants to transfer the money to Iceland and he's prepared to pay the ransom,' he said.

'I'll check out flights,' Áróra replied. 'You've told him that I only travel with registered amounts and he'll have to declare the cash to the authorities in Iceland?'

'I have,' he said. 'I don't think he's in any mental state to take rational decisions right now. Maybe you had better talk it over with him.'

21

Daníel fixed Flosi with the glare that colleagues described as so intense it hurt.

'The most unbelievable details can make a huge difference to an investigation, so I cannot over-emphasise how important it is to tell the full, correct truth,' he said, and saw how Flosi flinched. He rolled in his hands the cup of coffee Daníel had passed him as he came downstairs. It seemed to Daníel that he was trembling. 'Yesterday you were adamant that your relationship with Guðrún is in good shape—'

'It is, that's the fact of it,' Flosi interrupted. 'And now that I look back, I've no idea what I was thinking.'

Flosi twisted his hands as if he were kneading invisible dough.

'What were you thinking, Flosi?' Daníel asked, softening his tone but maintaining the piercing glare. 'You are, as you say yourself, happily married. Yet you have a lover.'

'Yes, yes,' Flosi muttered, finally taking his terrified eyes from Daníel to gaze down into his coffee cup. 'It's not easy to explain, but Guðrún and I were...' He hesitated and grimaced. 'We are. Guðrún and I have become set in our ways, and – how shall I put it? – there was a certain restlessness about me.'

'Restlessness?'

Daníel had no intention of letting him get away with explaining away the hardest part of his situation with some trite phrase.

'Yes,' Flosi mumbled. 'The marriage is good and solid, and I can always rely on Guðrún, but...'

He fell silent. Daníel waited for him to continue. He appeared to have fallen silent. He calmly sipped his coffee, and Flosi did the same, his movements leisurely, but his eyes flickering back and forth over the kitchen floor, as if some respite from this uncomfortable position might be found there. Finally he looked up and laughed foolishly.

'You know what we guys are like,' he said in a feeble attempt to be jovial.

Daníel shook his head.

'No,' he said.

'Aren't you married?' Flosi asked.

'No,' Daníel replied.

'Or, y'know, in a relationship? A long-term relationship?' he asked, and the desperation seemed to take hold of his expression. Daníel decided to let him wriggle a little longer.

'No,' Daníel said. 'I've twice been in long relationships, but I haven't been in the position of living with one woman while seeing another on the side, if that's what you're implying.'

'Yes, well. No,' Flosi gasped, took a gulp of coffee, spluttered, coughed and wiped his mouth with the back of his hand.

'Explain it for me,' Daníel said, softening his tone even further. He adopted an amiable expression that seemed to work immediately, as Flosi sighed and his shoulders drooped. 'If the marriage is so good, why cheat on Guðrún?'

'I suppose the simplest way to explain is that Guðrún and I are close friends and we have a good life together, but there's no passion there any longer. I'm as fit as a fiddle and still have a strong sex drive, but my wife seems to be more interested in the television than in me.'

The words came out in a rush, and Daníel could see him flush pink, starting at his collar line and moving upwards to his cheeks.

'OK,' Daníel nodded. 'And when did you start a relationship with ... What's her name?'

'I don't want to involve her in any way, so I'm not giving her name,' Flosi said, quick and decisive, his self-confidence suddenly regained.

'I see,' Daníel said. He had a keen sense for when it was worth applying pressure and when to hold back. They could trace the call to find out who she was, anyway. But it was important now to establish when this had started. 'How long has this relationship been going on?'

'Well, some months. Maybe coming up for a year.'

'And how close are you?' Daníel asked. 'By that I mean, how much does your mistress know about your circumstances?'

'Everything. She knows exactly what my situation is,' Flosi said. 'I'm completely honest with her.'

Daníel did his best to stifle the grin that came unbidden to his face at this smug declaration of honesty.

'So she knows about your offshore accounts? That you have millions of euros hidden away?'

It took Flosi a moment to realise what Daníel was driving at, but when he understood, he seemed to shudder.

'No!' he said with emphasis. 'No, no, no. Nothing like that. She knows nothing about my financial affairs beyond what's common knowledge, which is that I'm fairly well off. What I mean by "my circumstances" is that she's aware that I'm married and all that. I don't believe that she has anything at all to do with this.'

'Is there any possibility, and I want you to think carefully about this' – Daníel lifted an accusing index finger to underscore the importance of the question – 'is there the slightest possibility that Guðrún could be aware of your mistress?'

22

'Michael said that you're a fixer,' Flosi said, his eyes so beseeching that Áróra almost felt it was a shame to put her cards on the table.

'I'm a financial investigator, which means that I search for lost money. I've helped Michael with all kinds of things over the years. Let's say that I'm usually prepared to bend the rules as far as they'll go, but as I'm a certified financial and secure document courier and can't afford to lose my certification, I only travel with registered and declared cash. So if you want me to collect your euros, then they will have to be declared on arrival in your name. And that means that sooner or later you'll get a bill from the taxman.'

'Yes,' Flosi muttered. 'Of course, of course.' He nodded emphatically, as if stressing that it would never have occurred to him to not declare the money.

'I've no doubt that Michael can find someone to carry the cash, someone who wouldn't declare it. But then you're running the risk of being pulled at customs and the money being seized. It takes weeks of bother to get it released.'

'No,' he said. 'No question. Of course everything has to be legal and above board. The important thing is to have the cash ready when the kidnappers want it. Paying tax is a problem for later on. I'll deal with that then.'

'Good,' Áróra said. 'I'll catch a flight tomorrow.'

She went into the living room, where Daníel sat tapping rapidly at his laptop, the low rattle of his fingers on the keys creating a rhythm with the ticking of the clock.

'What do you think?' Áróra asked, and the rattle of the keyboard stopped as Daníel looked up.

'He'll never pay this ransom,' he said. 'We'll nab these guys when they turn up to collect it. He might as well fill the bag with old newspapers. They'll never get as far as looking inside. But of course I can't stop the man from withdrawing his own money.'

'No,' Áróra said, and went to leave the room, turning back as Daníel coughed.

'We need to stay in close contact,' he said. 'I need to know everything that happens.'

Áróra looked at him thoughtfully for a moment, trying to figure out if he meant Flosi, the money and the kidnapping, or if there was some hidden meaning in his words; about her, about them. She shook her thoughts off as he spoke again.

'It's going to be important for us to have your involvement, because, apart from family, you're the only one who has a real reason to be here, so it's no problem if you're seen coming and going. I'm sure that whoever is behind this is very much aware of Flosi's overseas accounts, so they could easily work out that you're working with his accountant.'

23

When he reached the coffee house on Reykjavíkurvegur, he was out of breath, and despite the bitter wind that had buffeted him as he had jogged up Hraunbrún, he was sweating. He had borrowed a pair of Flosi's tracksuit bottoms and left through the back door and the garden, and gone from there out to the road, in the hope of not attracting attention. Now he would spend some time in the coffee house to check if he had been followed. Anyone watching him could assume that he was a family friend staying with Flosi to support him through this difficult time, and had found time to go for a run, to the shops or to stop off for a coffee, just like normal people did. He would just need to take care that he couldn't be easily tracked back to the police station, or home, as it would be no great challenge to look the building up in the online phone directory to find that he was listed there, along with his profession.

He sat by the window with his coffee and sipped it while he looked out over the street, wearing an expression that he hoped said he was taking it easy, watching the traffic, which streamed past remarkably steadily, considering how late in the morning it was. In reality, all his senses were working overtime as he paid careful attention to every movement outside. The row of shops that included the coffee house was also home to a sports shop, a photocopying place and a mysterious little shop that seemed to sell mostly incense and statues of Buddha; it wasn't seeing much footfall for the moment. A red Honda appeared and pulled up outside the photocopy shop. A man with a sheaf of papers under one arm got out, went into the shop, reappeared minus his paperwork, and drove away. A moment later a woman walked past the coffee house window, and a little later she walked back, this time carrying a bag marked with the sports shop's logo. Cars filtered past, and as far as Daníel could make out, none of them drove suspiciously slowly, or showed any indication that someone might be watching the coffee house. He finished his coffee and sent Helena a text message, asking her to bring the car to the back of the building. Then he got to his feet, and persuaded the surprised proprietor to let him go out through the back entrance.

The commissioner met them just as they arrived at the station and accompanied them up the stairs. She had a grave expression on her face and said nothing more than, 'This is quite something.' To which Daníel and Helena simultaneously agreed that this was indeed a hell of a puzzle. Two adjoining rooms at the end of the corridor on the third floor had been commandeered for them, and Helena opened the door with a key, handing Daníel another.

'That one's yours,' she said. 'There's a new barrel in the lock, and only four keys.'

As the door shut behind them, the commissioner finally spoke to the group that had been brought together in the room, and there was a steely determination in her voice.

'With this investigation we have shorter lines of communication than usual. The head of CID knows about this, but instead of information going through him and the chief superintendent, it comes direct to me. There are four of you in the team to begin with. Daníel, you're running this investigation, and you have Helena, Kristján and Palli with you. Oddsteinn is the prosecutor's representative who is with us on this. Is there anything you want to say, Oddsteinn?'

The commissioner glanced at Oddsteinn, who stood up, his habitually stiff and formal self, and adjusted his tie before speaking.

'Just a reminder that although these are unusual circumstances, we all have to bear in mind that we're working towards a conviction as a final outcome. So everything has to be recorded and the LÖKE database is your best friend as far as that's concerned. I'm available at any time, day or night, if there's any advice you need. Apart from that, I'll do my best not to get in your way until you have a suspect lined up. That's when I'll be breathing down your necks.'

The group broke into a peal of laughter, and the commissioner allowed herself a fleeting smile. They all knew and liked Oddsteinn, who was one of the better members of the prosecutor's team to work with. He came across as unbending and formal, but was nimble and co-operative. The commissioner thanked Oddsteinn for his input before continuing.

'Yes, you have experience of working with the prosecutor's department, Daníel, and you're perfectly able to assess what you need for this investigation. And you'll get whatever you ask for, whether it's manpower or support from other divisions. But while we're figuring out exactly what we are dealing with, the investigation needs to be kept as small as possible to minimise the chance of anything leaking out. The four of you have the keys to this room. Nobody else has access. I repeat, nobody. And I don't have to remind you that you don't discuss this case with anyone not connected with it.'

Helena nodded, while Kristján and Palli muttered something unintelligible. It was clear that they both felt this reminder was unnecessary. The commissioner seemed to notice the looks on their faces.

'We're naturally bound by confidentiality in all of our work, but in this instance that confidentiality extends to anyone outside this room, including colleagues,' she added.

'Áróra Jónsdóttir is in the loop on this,' Daníel broke in. 'She needs to be able to keep tabs. She's not exactly part of the case, but she's able to provide us with important information and she's the key to Flosi's hidden cash.'

Palli raised a hand, like a schoolboy eager to ask an urgent question, and Daníel prepared himself to defend Áróra's involvement.

'What about Jean-Christophe?' he asked, and Daníel, standing beside the commissioner, heard her take a deep breath through her nose, as if stifling a tired sigh. Palli was notorious for nit-picking, and nobody knew if this was a stress response on his part, or if he was simply sometimes slow on the uptake.

'Forensics get the information they need to do their work, and Jean-Christophe and his guys know that this is an ultra-discreet investigation that has to be kept totally confidential. I have impressed on them, as I am on you, that Guðrún Aronsdóttir's life could depend on us keeping things to ourselves.'

For a moment there was complete silence in the room as they all looked up at the commissioner, and Daníel guessed that they were all experiencing the same emotion as he was: a chill that slithered up his back and spread itself out, ice-cold and terrifying, mixed with a nagging suspicion that they weren't equipped to take on this investigation.

'Good luck,' the commissioner said.

24

Kristján had done a good job of setting up their incident room with everything they needed. One room had been furnished with four desks, charging and network cables for their computers and a large whiteboard at the end, while in the inner room was a large table and chairs so they could meet and spread out documents.

Right now, Helena, Kristján and Palli each sat at a desk while Daníel stood by the whiteboard as he summed up the investigation so far.

'I would prefer to be at the scene as long as I can, as I have a strong feeling that the solution to all this lies somewhere in Flosi's background,' he said. 'And while I could have one officer always present in the house for when the kidnappers make contact, I feel it's best if I'm there. I'm gradually gaining Flosi's trust, and it makes things much simpler if we're not constantly coming and going, or getting him to come to the station for questioning. That's a risk we can't take, as we don't know if the house is being watched.'

Helena was satisfied with this arrangement; it meant that she would be the link between Daníel and the boys and would give her an opportunity to prove herself in a management role. She could even be the one running the daily briefings.

Daníel turned to the whiteboard and sketched his familiar diagram, which resembled a lattice of columns and rows, and began to fill them in. They had all seen this before, and while it wasn't exactly necessary to begin with, seeing the diagram gave them the sense that there was an overview of the investigation as a whole – that it wasn't just a hopelessly complex web of minor details, but a simple puzzle that could be solved. The grid would represent their list of tasks as the investigation progressed, and their role was to fill in every single space, with either a cross or a tick.

Daníel wrote *MOTIVE* in large letters at the top of the first column.

'Who could possibly have a motive to kidnap Guðrún and demand a ransom for her release?' he asked in the thoughtful tone he used when thinking aloud. 'Who is so financially desperate that they would go to such extreme lengths? And who could possibly be doing this as a way of punishing Flosi, or even Guðrún herself?'

At the top of the next column he wrote *MEANS*, and carried on thinking out loud.

'Who has the resources to carry this out? If we assume that Guðrún was taken against her will, as the state of the kitchen would indicate, then a certain physical strength is needed, or else more than one perpetrator. That means a vehicle, presumably a van of some kind, and a place where Guðrún can be held, which means premises where unexplained traffic isn't going to attract attention.' Daníel fell silent. He turned to Helena. 'Anything else?' he asked. 'What else would the kidnapper need to be able to kidnap Guðrún?'

'Organisation,' Helena said.

Daníel nodded.

'Yes, it requires some organisational ability. This calls for thought, planning, plotting. This isn't a spur-of-the-moment kind of crime.'

'If they are monitoring the house, then that calls for either tech equipment or manpower,' Kristján added, and they sat in thought for a while. The room was silent.

'They could be,' Helena said. 'We don't know if the house is being watched or not. We just have to assume that it is. We haven't found any cameras or microphones in there, but something, or someone, could be monitoring the house from the outside. There could be a person in a room in some house in the vicinity.'

'The ransom demand threatens to kill Guðrún if Flosi contacts the police,' Daníel said. 'More than likely this is an empty threat. If this a relative or an employee of Flosi's, then it's not likely that this person has the resources to watch the house. However, if there's a criminal group or some such organised gang behind this, it's possible they could be keeping tabs on the house. Until we can be sure, we should assume that's what the situation is.'

'Knowledge of Flosi's money,' Helena said. 'This person must know that Flosi has money that he can put his hands on quickly.'

'Exactly,' Daníel said. 'That's a key point that will be useful to us. Flosi doesn't have that much money here in Iceland that he can withdraw quickly. He said to do that he would have to sell property, which could take weeks or months. Also, he's adamant that two million euros is beyond the credit level his company has access to at the bank, so it's not as if he could simply borrow that kind of money without an explanation. That means the focus is on Flosi's overseas money, and according to him, very few people were aware of these offshore accounts. The fact that the ransom demand stipulates euros and not krónur is a clue, to my thinking.'

Daníel now filled in the top of the final column: *OPPOR-TUNITY*.

'Who was where on Monday afternoon and into Monday evening?' he said. 'I want to see a detailed schedule for everyone connected to this family, and their alibis. Go through Sunday and Monday with each of them. We need to build up a picture of forty-eight hours before Guðrún's disappearance, and where every one of them was, hour by hour, for those two days.'

He filled in the names of everyone connected to Flosi, a row for each. There weren't many of them and there were plenty of blank rows remaining. Daniel put the board marker down and made to leave the room.

'There's your list of jobs,' he said. 'We need to work on this with care, but as fast as possible. I want names, people. More names!'

25

Then there was the other errand Flosi had asked her to run. This was one Áróra should by rights have refused, as she had no desire to get caught up in the man's personal affairs. But there was nobody else, he said. It wasn't as if he could ask his daughter to go and talk to his mistress.

Bergrós wasn't what Áróra had expected. When she thought it over, she didn't know exactly what she had expected, but the woman was nothing like Guðrún. She had thought that Flosi would have gone for someone younger and that the woman who opened the door to the apartment on Grettisgata would be blonde and solidly built, just like both of Flosi's wives, who were to be seen in awkward family pictures on his living-room wall, with Sara Sól at different ages, in various sulks.

Bergrós was petite, with frizzy dark hair that fell to her shoulders in perfect disarray, and her skin was scattered with dark freckles. Her moss-green eyes flickered like those of a wild animal, and Áróra could see right away that her body was tense, as if ready to react, under the patterned Indian gown that reached all the way to her sandalled, red-lacquered toes.

'I have a message for you from Flosi,' Áróra said. 'Could I come in for a moment?'

Bergrós hesitated and her green eyes narrowed as she looked Áróra up and down.

'What sort of message? And who are you?'

'Flosi is in a difficult situation at the moment and he asked me to tell you that for the next few days he can't contact you. My name's Áróra, and I'll explain. But wouldn't it be better if we sit down?'

Bergrós began to fidget, and Áróra wasn't sure if she had heard more than half of what she'd said to her.

'Difficult situation? How so? And what do you mean by a few days? I've tried to call him and he practically hung up on me, and his voice was so strange...'

Áróra saw that the best option would be to take matters into her own hands. She stepped into the doorway, took hold of Bergrós' arm and pointed the way into the apartment, speaking in a calm, measured voice.

'Flosi asked me to come and talk to you and he sends you all his love. I'm carrying out a small assignment for him. He asked me to talk to you because he trusts me. Let's sit down in the kitchen. Do you have any tea?'

She would have preferred coffee, but judging by the trembling she could feel through Bergrós' arm, the last thing she needed was anything that might agitate her even more.

The flat was small but packed with an astonishing amount of furniture, most of it old, made in dark wood, which oddly suited Bergrós' colouring. There was just about space in the kitchen for two chairs and a little table under the gable window. Áróra half pushed Bergrós into one of them. The spire of Hallgrímskirkja could be seen from the kitchen window, and for a moment Áróra was reminded of the childhood memories connected to this church tower, the sound of the bells in the cold, still air, and a morning throwing snowballs with her sister during some visit to Iceland.

Áróra picked up the kettle and filled it at the kitchen tap, while Bergrós jumped to her feet, opened a cupboard and took out a couple of packets of tea. Áróra took them, checked the wording, chose the one that seemed to be caffeine-free, dropped them into cups and poured boiling water over them. When she turned round with the two mugs, Bergrós was in tears.

'He's dumping me, isn't he?' she sniffed, her voice an octave higher than before, as if her vocal chords had been stretched. 'He's dumping me and he's sent one of the staff to do his dirty work.'

Áróra was on edge by the time she left Bergrós' apartment an hour later. It was as if the tension she had sought to allay in Bergrós had transferred to her. All the same, she felt she had managed to calm the woman down, convincing her that Flosi was experiencing some temporary difficulties and would be in touch as soon as these problems were behind him. Without explaining what these difficulties were, she said that they were connected to Flosi's wife, Guðrún. She knew that Flosi was hoping to keep Bergrós separate from all this, to shield her from visits from the police, but as Daníel had issued an absolute blanket ban on any mention of the police in connection with Flosi, she had to leave out that part. But it seemed unlikely that Bergrós had anything to do with it. She seemed to be a quivering heap of indecision.

Áróra started the car and headed for Weights. This was the place she had chosen after trying out every gym in Reykjavík. It wasn't exactly a gym, more a large garage with some exercise machines and some good weights that the owner allowed selected friends to use. Her father's name had opened the door for her. He was still famous with a certain group, having been Iceland's strongest man two years in a row and twice Highland games champion. Áróra opened the boot to find that she had forgotten her bag with her training gear. She had been fool enough to take it inside a couple of days ago to wash her stuff. But now she badly needed a release for the tension, so she took off her trousers and her sweater where she stood by the car, and put her shoes back on. These had soft soles and would be fine for lifting.

She nodded to two of the guys who were lifting weights and neither of them seemed to notice that she had turned up in her knickers and a singlet. She picked up a rope and began skipping to warm up, immediately feeling the tension slide away.

She liked this place. Most days there would be two or three guys lifting weights, selling steroids or munching pizza. She knew the type; they reminded her of her father and the men in the group around him. These were musclebound giants with Viking tattoos and plaits in their chest-length beards. She was the only woman who trained at Weights, and didn't lift the kind of weight the guys did, but heavy enough that they liked watching her take the weight all the same, and they'd nod with the kind of approval that warmed her heart, as if her father was there among them, watching her nurture her strength.

26

Helena looked at her list of jobs and decided to start with the task that linked everything together: producing a timeline of the two days in Guðrún's life before she was kidnapped. Statements had been taken from Flosi and Sara Sól, and she was using the list of transactions from Guðrún's bank account to fill in the gaps.

There wasn't a lot to go through for Sunday. According to Flosi, they had been at home all day. He had made a quick trip to the bakery around midday, they had finished tidying the garage, Guðrún had watered plants and knitted, while he had checked some work files on the computer, and then Guðrún had cooked chops and prepared a salad, before falling asleep in front of the television while Flosi had watched a nature documentary, finally waking her up so they could go to bed. Nobody but Flosi had seen Guðrún that Sunday, but that hardly mattered as plenty of people had seen her on Monday.

Guðrún had slept late on Monday, as she did every morning, according to Flosi. He had left for work around eight so as to be there for eight-thirty, and he made a habit of taking Guðrún a cup of coffee before leaving the house. She had sat up in bed as he arrived with the coffee, he kissed her goodbye as he left, and he said that he had assumed she had drunk her coffee in bed as usual, before getting up. Before midday a van had arrived to collect the stuff they had cleared out of the garage and took it all to Sara Sól's home.

Flosi knew little of Guðrún's daily routine, but said that he knew she vacuumed the hall every day and most days would put some clothes through the washing machine. There wasn't a great deal of clothing to wash, and the better garments went to a dry cleaner. Helena saw that there was a card transaction from

Monday at the laundry along their street; she would send Kristján to check what time Guðrún had been there. There was also a seven-hundred-krónur transaction at the Vellir gym – one of the places she visited regularly, but hadn't called in at for a month. Then there was a substantial amount spent at a fish shop. Helena guessed that this had to be the langoustine that Guðrún had been busy preparing when she had been abducted.

There were regular transactions for groceries, the laundry and the State Alcohol Monopoly; they appeared every week, or more frequently. The transactions Daníel had highlighted were the unusual ones, and the direct transfers.

These included fifty-two thousand krónur to Icelandair roughly a month ago. Jón Jónsson had twice been sent twenty thousand krónur, four months apart, and the second payment had taken place on Monday, the day Guðrún had disappeared. Karl Leósson had received sixty-five thousand krónur a week before. Helena looked up the ID numbers for both men and checked them against the phone directory, finding out that Jón Jónsson was a delivery driver and Karl Leósson a pest-control specialist.

Then there was Sigurlaug slf, to which Guðrún had begun to make payments roughly three months ago – these were large amounts, generally more than two hundred thousand krónur each week for several weeks. These were the only transactions in Guðrún's list that looked genuinely dubious. Helena opened the Tax Authority website and looked the company up. Its listing told her that Sigurlaug was an unlimited liability company in the 'other education activities' category and registered to a woman called Sigurlaug Sigtryggsdóttir.

Helena's phone rang, and seeing that Daníel was calling, she answered right away. He had only just left, so he could hardly be at Flosi's house already, especially as he meant to jog half of that distance.

'Another name for you,' he said, sounding out of breath, and

Helena immediately got to her feet and picked up a board marker. 'Bergrós Skúladóttir. She's Flosi's mistress. She has an unregistered mobile so it wasn't possible to trace her through her call, but Flosi asked Áróra to go and talk to her, to explain that he's in a spot of bother at the moment.'

'She didn't mention to her that—'

'Of course not,' Daníel interrupted sharply. 'Áróra is no fool.'

'No, of course not,' Helena said, writing the mistress's name on the board. 'You want me to go and talk to this Bergrós?'

'Let's hold back on that,' Daníel said. 'Áróra went to see her and said that the woman doesn't seem to know whether she's coming or going. She's tiny and Áróra reckons she's not in any condition to organise a kidnapping. Besides which, she seems not far off being a nervous wreck. We need to prioritise who we start on, and we need a solid pretext so that we don't have any leaks. We'll figure out a reason for you to pay her a visit tomorrow. But now you can go over to Garðvís ehf and fetch the van. And take the opportunity to chat to Flosi's staff while you're there.'

'Okey doke,' Helena said, picking up her keys. She would use her own car to go to Garðvís, and would park somewhere in the vicinity.

'Could you look up Sigurlaug Sigtryggsdóttir – date of birth in seventy-three – and her company, Sigurlaug slf, and see what you can find,' she said to Kristján as she left, and he nodded. Palli didn't look up, He sat with his chin resting in his hand, rocking gently to the music he was listening to on his headphones while he watched traffic camera footage and noted down an endless list of car registration numbers.

27

Garðvís ehf was a considerably larger company than Helena had expected. The offices were above a warehouse in the Vatnagarðar business area. Inside, once she had climbed a narrow set of spiral stairs, a beautiful view over the sound was presented to her. There were no cruise liners at the quay now that summer was behind them and Iceland's waters were as foul as the gloomy weather that battered the windows of the office.

'Good morning,' said an older woman in a business suit who strode towards her with an outstretched hand. 'Unnur. Flosi said that you were on the way to collect a van.'

Helena introduced herself as Flosi's cousin and accepted the set of keys the woman handed her. She was clearly the efficient type who did nothing slowly, as she seemed ready to spin around and go back to her desk before Helena had an opportunity to talk to her.

'I couldn't sneak a coffee while I'm here, could I?' she asked quickly, spying a substantial espresso machine at the far end of the open-plan office.

Unnur lifted a questioning eyebrow and nodded.

'Of course,' she said, indicating that Helena should come with her to the machine.

'I've a terrible chill in me today,' Helena said apologetically, but her sweetest smile wasn't enough to elicit the slightest glimmer of one on this efficient woman's face.

She took a cup from the shelf next to the machine and placed it under the spout.

'How do you like your coffee?' she asked, and Helena leaned forward to look at the options the machine offered.

'Just an espresso,' she said and made another doomed attempt to melt the woman's frosty exterior. Unnur pressed the right button and the machine began the noisy process of grinding and brewing coffee.

'Is this a big company?' Helena asked, trying to sound as if she was making conversation while she waited.

'There are ten of us here working full-time. Then there's Flosi's daughter Sara Sól, who is becoming more involved.'

Unnur stared at Helena inquiringly, as if she were having doubts about her reason for being there. Helena pretended not to notice her watchfulness, and continued to chat.

'All ten of you just for this? Importing gardening stuff?'

The disapproval on Unnur's face made her want to bite her tongue. More than likely her inquisitive tone had sounded false and condescending.

'People often ask,' Unnur said patiently, 'if it's possible for this many people to work full-time with gardening goods in a country where the summer is only three months. But, of course we do more than just that. We have products that are in demand at different times of the year – snow-clearing equipment, fertiliser, a considerable product line related to animals and farming – and a substantial part of the company's activities relates to distributing US goods on the UK market. There are two staff handling just that side of things.'

Helena quickly nodded to indicate that she had taken all this in, and looked around with interest.

'I see,' she said. 'I hadn't realised that the company was so big.'

'We have two full-time drivers making deliveries here.'

'Ah, OK,' Helena said, rattling the keys. 'And I'm taking the van off one of them, right?'

'We actually have three vans. We've just acquired an extra one.' Unnur hesitated, and a courteous note of inquiry appeared in her voice. 'Flosi said that it's important,' she said, and Helena knew that now would be the moment to drop a few words of explanation about her need to borrow the van, to provide a little information about herself, and a word of thanks. But she let the thanks be enough.

'Thank you so much, and apologies for disturbing you. It'll just be a couple of days.'

She knocked back her coffee, smiled again, handed the cup to Unnur, and saw that this time, for courtesy's sake, she forced a tiny sliver of a smile.

28

Helena sat at Daníel's side at the kitchen table, noting down Flosi's explanations for payments from Guðrún's account. He seemed to have everything at his fingertips. Jón Jónsson was a van driver they called in whenever something larger than would fit into Flosi's jeep needed to be moved. They had been clearing out the garage and had got rid of a substantial amount of unwanted stuff. Jón had made one trip to the waste disposal facility and another to Karen and Sara Sól. Most of the stuff had been left over from Sara Sól's childhood. That had been collected on Monday morning.

'I suppose Karl Leósson must be Kalli the pest control guy,' Flosi said, pushing his reading glasses higher up his nose and peering at the statement Daníel showed him.

'That fits. The man is a pest control specialist,' Daníel said. 'Have you needed to use his services recently?'

'Sure. Kalli comes twice a year to replace the traps around the house and dose them with poison. It's a big house and there are quite a few traps, including some by the garage. Guðrún was absolutely adamant that she didn't want any mice getting in. A bit on the hysterical side, from my point of view, but I didn't interfere.'

'And this flight ticket?' Daníel said, tapping the payment to Icelandair and pushing it in front of Flosi.

'Ah,' Flosi said. 'I completely forgot to tell you about that. Guðrún saw some special offer online and went with one of her friends for a weekend to New York at the beginning of this month.'

'But there's no other sign of that in her transactions,' Helena said. 'Not a single payment to a restaurant or any shops.'

Flosi shifted awkwardly in his chair.

'No. I told her not to use the card unless absolutely necessary, and I gave her plenty of dollars to take with her.'

'In cash?' Daníel asked.

'Yes. I had some foreign currency. That's not forbidden these days, is it?' Flosi said, a truculent look on his face, and Daníel noticed that Helena made a note on her pad.

Daníel looked down at the sheets of paper in front of him and saw that they had come to the big question. He had notes from Kristján, who had looked up Sigurlaug Sigtryggsdóttir. She was forty-seven, lived on Langholtsvegur and appeared to offer her services as a life coach to individuals and companies – presentations about mindfulness and positive thinking.

'Was Guðrún seeing a life coach?' Daníel asked, but before Flosi could answer they were interrupted by the doorbell ringing, so it was difficult to be sure whether Flosi's look of surprise was in response to the question or the doorbell. Daníel glanced at Helena and tipped his head slightly, so she stood up, left the kitchen and shut the door behind her. 'Helena will answer the door,' Daníel said, and repeated his question.

'Not as far as I know. But if you mean her friend Sigurlaug, then they see a lot of each other. But her coaching is mainly about lifting a glass,' Flosi said, forcing a laugh, although Daníel could sense its hollowness.

'So Sigurlaug Sigtryggsdóttir is a friend of Guðrún's?'

'Yes, they've been friends for years. She's the friend she went with to New York.'

'Are they close?' Daníel asked. 'For instance, could this Sigurlaug know something about Guðrún that you wouldn't?'

The question left a look of confusion on Flosi's face that Daníel had come to recognise, the one that told him Flosi was uncomfortable because he didn't know where this might lead.

'Do you mean you might get something out of talking to Sigurlaug? It probably wouldn't do any harm, but I doubt she knows anything that I'm not already aware of.'

'Do you know any reason why Guðrún would be paying money into Sigurlaug's account?'

'What? No. Just some stuff between friends, isn't it? Sigurlaug could have paid for a meal or something that weekend and Guðrún might have settled up. Those two do like a long champagne lunch...'

'These are payments to Sigurlaug's company account, that's her unlimited liability company,' Daníel said. 'Could Guðrún have been paying for coaching sessions?'

'It's not something I know anything about,' Flosi said. 'Payments, you said? So more than just one?'

Flosi craned his neck to see the statement, and it was obvious that he longed to snatch it from Daníel's hands.

'Yes,' Daníel said. 'And some substantial amounts. Altogether it's around three million krónur over the past three months.'

Flosi stared back at him, his eyes wide, dumbfounded as if unable to believe what he was hearing.

'You're not aware of Guðrún purchasing anything from Sigurlaug – coaching, services, or any items?' he said, and Flosi shook his head. 'Could Guðrún have been lending her money?' Daníel continued, and Flosi's jaw dropped.

Finally regaining the power of speech, he said, 'I don't think so. Sigurlaug's well off. And I'd have thought Guðrún would have spoken to me about that kind of amount. I simply don't understand this...' he said, as the kitchen door opened and Helena appeared in the doorway.

'Sara Sól is here,' she said. 'She rang the bell because she brought her mother with her. It seems they mean to cook you dinner, Flosi.'

29

'I had to tell her,' Sara Sól said.

Flosi nodded as he hugged her. 'Of course, my love,' he said, patting her back. This was how he had always calmed her when she had been tiny. As a brand-new father he had read in some magazine that the rhythm of patting an infant's back was the most effective way to calm them down. It was reminiscent of the mother's heartbeat, the rhythm that accompanied them from day one, living with this beat all the way from being nothing more than a bundle of cells, before their own heartbeat had formed. He had followed the magazine's advice and kept an old-fashioned alarm clock that ticked loudly by Sara Sól's cot, and had patted her back when she was restless. It had worked, and he continued using this approach. Not that it was needed much these days. A heartbreak last year and a dispute with a fellow student who had failed to contribute to a group project had led her to seek solace in her father's arms. And again now.

'Mum saw I wasn't feeling right and she kept asking me what the problem was, so I couldn't keep it to myself any longer,' Sara Sól sniffed, while Karen held Flosi's arm and squeezed encouragingly.

'I had to come here with her and do something to support you,' Karen said. 'Of course, there's not that much I can do under such terrible circumstances, but at least I can make sure you're properly fed.'

She heaved a shopping bag onto the kitchen worktop and began taking items from it.

'Thank you, Karen,' Flosi said.

He wasn't sure how much of an appetite he would have, but her concern for him gave him a warm feeling deep inside. Karen went confidently to the cupboard and selected a pan, and Flosi felt a moment's discomfort. Guðrún wouldn't be overjoyed at the sight of Karen rooting through the kitchen she had made such an effort to make her own. But he pushed these concerns to the back of his mind. Strife between two women who had made this kitchen their own at different times was of no importance right now. What was important was to find Guðrún and bring her home – and Karen was prepared to support him.

'Thank you,' he said again, and took a seat at the kitchen table where, just now, the police officers had sat facing him, with a flood of questions and allegations that Guðrún had recently transferred a stack of money to Sigurlaug's account. He would have to take a look at her account himself, as this sounded very strange.

He heard Daníel in the hallway say goodbye to his female colleague, and a moment after the door had closed behind her, he appeared in the kitchen. He came across as a genuinely sweet person. His light-grey eyes were so gentle that Flosi felt there was a real sympathy behind them when they talked. But when the female officer joined him and they sat side by side, formal and serious, writing down his words, Daníel came across as detached, a more distant and cold persona, although Flosi could see that he watched his every movement, impressed every word on his memory – ready to use against him.

'You're eating as well, aren't you?' Karen said, glancing at Daníel, who nodded and thanked her.

That was what had always been so wonderful about Karen, her ability to get to grips with circumstances and make the best of them. Karen made everyone welcome, whether they were hungry, wanting a place to stay or in need of help of some kind. Now Flosi regretted having let this irritate him while they had been married: the distant relatives sleeping on mattresses on the living-room floor, the enormous casseroles she produced 'in case someone drops by', and the weekends she spent helping people she barely knew move house or giving their garden a makeover.

Daníel stood by the island unit and watched Karen dice onions and chop herbs, and Flosi was suddenly filled with apprehension. What if Karen were to tell Daníel something that would cast him in a bad light? What if she were to tell him that he had betrayed her, and had moved her and Sara Sól out so that he could move his new woman in – just because he had been tired of her, fed up with her being busy all the time, with Sara Sól's gymnastics training that she had made him sit and watch, and her laughably old-fashioned domesticity. Then there was Karen's figure, if he was completely honest with himself. Carrying a child had stretched a few things and she hadn't done a lot to keep herself in shape. On the other hand, Guðrún had been young, pert and lively, and in her presence he found himself shedding the years. But now he was back where he had been before, cheating on wife number two in favour of the excitement of younger flesh. Until she had disappeared. Until she had been abducted. It wouldn't be long before the police began to suspect him. Perhaps he was already at the top of the list of suspects. He took three deep breaths, deep down into his belly, just as he had taught Sara Sól to do when she was small, whenever she lost control of her emotions and needed to calm herself.

Then he heard it. Karen wasn't talking about his infidelity and betrayal to Daníel. Instead she was describing how well Flosi had treated her and their daughter after the divorce, how they had split everything they had built up together, how he had bought her out of both the house and the company, and on top of that had supported her with generous maintenance payments for Sara Sól.

Flosi felt himself choking with gratitude. He hoped that this would give Daníel a positive image of him, show him that he was in fact a decent guy who didn't belong on a list of suspects – because as long as the police had him in their sights, they would be losing valuable time in the search for whoever had really stolen Guðrún away from him.

Flosi felt the emotion choke him, and his eyes filled with tears as Sara Sól came into the kitchen, having wiped away her own tears and washed her face, and immediately set to preparing a salad. She never did this with Guðrún, because Guðrún never wanted any help in the kitchen. But now the two of them were there, his former wife and his only daughter, preparing a meal. If it hadn't been for Daníel standing there with a smile on his face, this could have been an image from his former life. Now he realised what was really important: the women in his life. He hadn't always treated them fairly. But now he wouldn't fail them. He wouldn't put the business or money ahead of Guðrún, but would do every single thing in his power to bring her back, safe and well.

30

This was the oddest family dinner Daníel could remember having been present at. Karen had laid the table in the dining room and had confidently fetched candlesticks and table mats from the sideboard, and now the candles cast a mellow light on the people gathered around the table. Flosi seemed to be numb, but allowed himself the occasional smile, ate his chicken and said little. Karen sat at the end of the table, his former wife, concerned and glowing with pleasure as she spooned a little more rice onto Flosi's plate and handed him the salt before he asked for it. Sara Sól's eyes carefully followed her parents' every movement, and she seemed to feel out of place, like a teenager in a social situation she wasn't able to completely understand. He himself was out of place, someone who clearly didn't belong, but who provided the gathering with some kind of a stamp of approval. The reason they sat there together was that Guðrún had been abducted, because a crime had been committed.

After dinner Flosi stood up and helped Karen clear the table, and just as Sara Sól was about to get to her feet and help, Daníel reached out a hand to touch her arm, so she remained seated. He waited for a moment, until the clatter of crockery from the kitchen told him that the former couple were washing up, before speaking.

'Have you had any sense that your father and Guðrún have been going through difficulties in their relationship?' he asked, leaning forward and looking into Sara Sól's eyes. People found it harder to avoid giving an answer when the questioner looked into their eyes.

Daníel had expected that Sara Sól would be reluctant to say anything about her father's private life behind his back, so her direct answer took him by surprise.

'Yes,' she said. 'And it's been like that from day one. To be honest, they've never been right for each other.'

Daníel's eyebrow lifted.

'What do you mean by that?'

'Ach, well. She's not what you might call the sharpest chisel in the box, and Dad's this super-smart businessman. And she's never liked me, which has caused some tension for Dad.'

'Can you give me an example?' Daníel asked, and Sara Sól was silent for a moment.

'For example, my room,' she said. 'One day Guðrún packed up all my stuff and moved it to the small room, so that she could use my old room as a space for sewing in. Not a word to me or Dad.'

'But you've been living with your mother since your parents split up?' Daníel probed cautiously.

Sara Sól didn't seem inclined to hold back. 'But this is my child-hood home. She could at least have asked.'

Daníel nodded. 'Presumably that put your father in a difficult position?'

'That's right,' she replied. 'Of course, he had to take her side, so there wouldn't be a massive row, but he understood my point of view perfectly; he felt Guðrún should have asked before taking the room for herself.'

'Understood,' Daníel said and dropped his voice. 'Have you ever been aware of any violence in your father's relationship with Guðrún.'

Sara Sól grimaced, and Daníel expected her to storm out in anger. But she appeared to understand that it was worthwhile staying calm.

'Not at all,' she said with a firmness in her voice. 'Absolutely not. If you're thinking along those lines, then you're misunder-standing Dad's brand of male chauvinism.'

Daníel smiled and again fixed his eyes on hers.

'How so?' he asked.

'Ach, people see him as being old-fashioned, and of course they're right. He likes to have his wife at home, running the household, keeping the place neat and tidy, and all that. Of course he can be bloody-minded. But he's never laid a finger on Guðrún, or on Mum. Never. He's the type who puts women on a pedestal. Going to the gym and the hairdresser, keeping herself looking good and cooking him cordon bleu dinners has been a full-time job for Guðrún. And as far as he's concerned, that's the way it should be. He treated her like some sort of princess. He'd go out and warm the car up for her if she was going somewhere, carried heavy stuff for her, opened doors, all the stuff that American men do.'

Daníel digested her words for a moment.

'Your father is good to Guðrún, so these difficulties can't have been down to that sort of thing,' he said.

Sara Sól shook her head. 'No,' she said. 'But maybe I'm making too much out of it. At any rate, Dad has been a lot happier lately,' she added.

Since the new mistress appeared on the scene, Daníel thought to himself, but decided to turn the conversation to the relationship between Karen and Flosi.

'How do your mother and father get on?'

'Just fine,' Sara Sól said confidently – she was maybe a little over-emphatic: her voice suddenly lifted. 'You can see them together right now. They genuinely support each other when there's something that needs to be dealt with. Dad organised my grandmother's funeral together with Mum, and I can tell you that she'll haunt the place until all this has been resolved.'

They looked up as Karen appeared bearing a tray loaded with a teapot and cups, placing it on the table.

'The apple cake is warming up,' she said, and vanished back into the kitchen.

Sara Sól leaned close to Daníel and whispered,

'I think Mum's still in love with him, even though she wouldn't admit it. They're good friends, and if it wasn't for Guðrún, I think they could get back together again.'

Flosi came into the room, placing a bowl of whipped cream on the table as he sat down. There was still a distant look on his face, and it didn't escape Daníel that Sara Sól also noticed this. It was clear that she was living the dream typical of the child from a broken family – believing her parents could pick up their relationship again – so she was obviously unaware of her father's latest infidelity. Her suspicion that her mother was still in love with Flosi was also interesting. It meant that mother and daughter each deserved a row on his whiteboard down at the station.

31

Flosi sat up in bed with his laptop on his knees and went through Guðrún's bank transactions. He couldn't understand it. The account was almost empty. He had been aware that the amount that he transferred to her every month was on the high side, considering what she spent on food, household stuff and herself. But he was pleased that she had a nest egg building up in her account. It allowed her to splash out on expensive luxuries when the mood took her. She could buy furniture, and she could pamper him with decent presents on his birthday. He had been overjoyed with the new set of golf clubs last year, and no less with the look of pride he saw on her face as she knew that her choice had hit the spot.

He felt the sob that was never far away rising, ready to take hold of him again, and he swallowed a couple of times. He looked around and saw Guðrún everywhere. She had redesigned the bedroom as soon as she moved in, and he had been delighted with the result. Karen had just bought furniture that seemed to be fashionable and lined it up somehow, and had never achieved this wonderful warm style that Guðrún had a talent for. Everything she touched took on a new beauty and comfort, as their bedroom had. He liked the feel of the warm carpet on his feet when he got up in the mornings, and the floor-length blackout curtains ensured that there was always darkness, even at the height of summer. He had wondered whether the spreading palms in pots belonged in the bedroom, but they had now become essential as Guðrún had been convinced of the myth she had read somewhere that plants produce oxygen during the night, so people sleep better near them. The bed was scattered with plenty of pillows that made it easy to make himself comfortable sitting up, as he was now, peering at the laptop screen, checking every single transaction.

He had to confess that his dwindling interest in Guðrún over the past few months had meant that he had practically stopped keeping an eye on her, an example of which was that he hadn't checked her account for a long time. He'd had no idea that she had been paying these large amounts to her friend Sigurlaug. The police had their suspicions about this, but it could hardly be related to the abduction. There had to be some other explanation. Sigurlaug had to be investing the money for Guðrún, or something like that.

All this gave Flosi a chill of discomfort. Guðrún told him everything. She even chattered about flowers and handicrafts, stuff he didn't want to hear, so he was astonished that she had managed to keep her mouth shut about handing her friend around three million krónur. Could it be that Guðrún had kept part of her life a secret from him, just as he had from her, with Bergrós?

The thought had just formed in his mind when the phone rang and without answering it, he knew it would be Bergrós. He knew the cops would be listening, but to hell with them. They knew by now that he had a mistress, and they could hardly suspect that Bergrós could have anything to do with it. That would be ridiculous.

'Flosi,' she said the instant he replied, and he could hear she was in tears.

'There, there, Bergrós,' he said. 'What's the matter?'

'What's the matter?' she almost screamed down the phone, and her voice took on the piercing tone that was the only unattractive thing about her. 'The matter is that you've shut me out, you're ignoring me. I'm going crazy wondering what you're doing, why you don't come and see me, why you don't call.'

'I sent Áróra to explain everything to you—'

He didn't manage to finish the sentence before she cut in and he instinctively moved the receiver a little away from his ear.

'Who the hell is this Áróra, and why can't you tell me properly what's going on?'

'That's just it, my dear Bergrós,' he said. 'I can't explain precisely what's going on, but this is a very serious matter and I have to say that I need some space to re-evaluate my life. Hopefully this will all be over in a few days and then we can meet and talk things over.'

The silence on the phone took him by surprise, considering how upset she had been a moment ago. Then he heard her sniff and realised she was still crying.

He could hear it more clearly as she spoke again. The piercing quality in her voice had disappeared, replaced by a tone that was somewhere between resignation and despair, which stung him deeply.

'If you're busy re-evaluating your life then no doubt you're re-evaluating our relationship. And what happens to our baby then? The child that's growing inside me?'

THURSDAY

32

Áróra's eyes were sore from lack of sleep as the aircraft took off, giving her a view over Reykjanes. It was getting light, and as the aircraft rose higher in the sky she noticed more and more tracks cutting through the lava fields below like a complex network of arteries that had formed completely organically. She wondered how many of these roads she had driven along, checked carefully, the drone flying behind her as it filmed a wide strip of lava to each side, in a search that was probably entirely hopeless. Deep inside, she didn't believe that she would one day actually stumble across her sister's remains, which Ísafold's boyfriend Björn had hidden before absconding to Canada. But the police hadn't come up with any better theories, plus she didn't have any brighter ideas of her own, so she had spent the summer going up and down these tracks around the city, and had expanded her search to the Reykjanes area. There were still many of these rutted tracks to explore, and she felt again the feeling of urgency that had powered her this far. There was so much left to check, and she was wasting time on this journey when she could be searching for her sister. Michael could have found another courier to fetch Flosi's euros, but nobody else would search for her sister. But was that really true? She felt a warm glow as she thought back to the material she had seen on Daníel's desk. Like her, he was still pondering what had become of Ísafold.

Once the aircraft was over the sea, she pulled down the window shade and closed her eyes. Leaving Iceland was more of a wrench than she had expected. Conflicted emotions drifted through her thoughts, and she attempted to pin them down. It wasn't exactly confusion that she felt, rather a kind of shock that came with leaving Iceland. This was a country of which she had never been all that fond, but which attracted her like a magnet. Áróra took a long breath and let this feeling settle in her belly, where it grew and became clearer. It wasn't anxiety, nor a need to reach a conclusion. The feeling that took root inside her and which swelled as Iceland became more distant was a guilt-drenched sorrow. She had failed her sister. She had given up on persuading her to leave Björn, to leave the violence. She had failed to respond to her call for help. It was a mistake that was difficult to live with. All she could do now was find her sister and ensure that she was buried respectably. That was what she was determined to do, regardless of how long it might take or what it might cost.

33

Daníel had admonished Flosi for keeping important information to himself. He stressed how vital it was to be open, however annoying it might be.

This was the reason he wanted to be present in the house, close to Flosi; to be on the scene as the heavy protective layer on the surface gradually melted away and the secrets below floated free. This was part of every police investigation. People hid things, and lied, and took decisions themselves, deciding that certain parts of their lives had no bearing on the crime, instead of telling the whole story and leaving the police to decide what might or might not matter.

This was just the kind of thing that mattered. Flosi expecting a child with another woman opened a whole new dimension to the case.

'Think hard, Flosi,' Daníel said. 'Is there any possibility that Guðrún knows that another woman is expecting your child?'

Flosi appeared not to consider the question for even a single moment before making a reply – he had begun to shake his head even before Daníel had finished speaking.

'No,' he said. 'We've kept the relationship totally secret. I even have Bergrós' number stored in my phone under a false name, look.' He handed his phone to Daníel, 'Leonid' there on the screen. 'Leonid works for me in the export department, and I've told him never to call me. It's such a trial to understand what he's saying through that Russian accent, y'see, so he'll never call. I have his number stored simply as L, just in case I need to get hold of him, and I use his full name as an alias for Bergrós.'

Flosi seemed almost proud of this subterfuge, as if this alias could be enough to prevent Guðrún from ever finding out about his infidelity. Daníel spun the phone round in his hand, tapped the messaging app, and opened a string of messages from 'Leonid'. He scrolled through them and opened one that had been sent a month before.

Longing to see you, my darling, the message read. Daníel handed the phone back with the text showing on the screen.

'It only takes two clicks to find that,' he said, but Flosi still shook his head.

'Guðrún never looked carefully at my phone,' he said. But then he seemed to begin to doubt himself; Daníel could see beads of sweat forming on his forehead. 'You don't think that...' he muttered, as if to himself. 'You don't think Guðrún could have known about Bergrós? You don't think this could be linked to the abduction?'

Daníel wanted to say something encouraging to Flosi, something that would quell the churning desperation behind his controlled appearance, which threatened to burst out at any moment. Instead he turned the conversation elsewhere, to practical matters.

'Would you be so kind as to call Sigurlaug, Guðrún's friend, and ask her to drop by this afernoon as you need to speak to her privately.' Flosi sat up straight on the sofa, appearing relieved to have a task to carry out, something to concentrate on. 'And not a word to her on the phone about Guðrún's disappearance,' Daníel added. 'And it goes without saying that you make no mention of the police. When she arrives I'll introduce myself as a friend of yours.'

34

Palli was still engrossed in traffic camera footage and didn't look up as Helena appeared in the incident room. She wanted to ask where Kristján was, but was reluctant to break his concentration. He appeared to have developed a routine, as at intervals he paused the replay and marked a cross against one of the numbers on the long list on his pad. He was clearly viewing this footage a second time. Helena thanked her lucky stars that this job hadn't been given to her. This kind of monotonous precision work wasn't her favourite. It was just as well that the IT division usually looked after checking traffic camera recordings, but in this instance it was essential to keep as much as possible within the team.

She sat at her desk, opened her laptop and continued to set up the timeline around Guðrún's activities on Monday, up to her disappearance. Flosi had gone to work around eight, leaving Guðrún in bed with a cup of coffee in her hand and that morning's *Fréttablaðið* open on her knees. Once she was up, she had called the van driver and dispatched him with a van full of stuff to Sara Sól's home. After that there was no indication of what she had been doing, before turning up at the laundry further along the street at around one-thirty. The owner knew Guðrún well and had told Kristján that she brought shirts and blouses to be cleaned every week. At three minutes to two the CCTV at the Vellir gym showed her go into the changing room, re-appearing moments later for an energetic workout. At twenty past three she was visible at the reception area, where she bought a shake and sat on a sofa while she flipped through a glossy magazine as she sipped her drink, apparently relaxed. At twenty-five to four she stood up and left the gym, and presumably headed for the fish shop, as the fishmonger Helena had spoken to yesterday recalled that she had been there 'mid-afternoon-ish', but couldn't provide a more exact time.

After four on Monday there were no indications of where Guðrún had gone; she had probably gone home with the carton of fresh langoustines, and they knew she had been busy preparing dinner when she had been abducted. Flosi had arrived home at seven-twenty, by which time the bread had burned in the oven, so they could assume it had been there well past its usual forty-minute baking time. So it seemed likeliest that between six and seven that evening, someone had appeared in the kitchen, snatching Guðrún away from preparing dinner. Her car was in the drive and there were no signs of a break-in, and both Flosi and Sara Sól had confirmed that the back door was generally unlocked.

Helena shared the timeline document on the system with the CCTV clips from the gym, the statements made by the laundry owner and the fishmonger. Then she picked up her phone and called Daníel.

'Just seen your docs,' he said. 'Can you chase Palli for me? But gently. No need to upset him.'

'Will do,' Helena said.

'Then I'd like you to be here this afternoon when Sigurlaug comes to see Flosi,' he said. 'You're one of the staff from his wholesale business, and I'm an old friend of his. He'll tell her himself that Guðrún has disappeared and a ransom has been demanded. It'll be interesting to see her reaction, and to see if she has anything to add to all this.'

Helena agreed and listed for him all the institutions she had checked. Guðrún hadn't appeared on any passenger lists leaving the country, she hadn't been admitted to A&E, nor to the women's refuge, and Kristján had made plenty of progress on checking guest lists for all the hotels in the south-west part of the country, which CID had helped them collect.

'Forensics sent me a message earlier to let me know that there's information listed on LÖKE about the analysis they did on the ransom demand, but nothing that's any use. In short, it was printed on a standard printer, on standard paper and the only prints are Áróra's and Flosi's.'

'Disappointing,' Helena agreed. She had hoped that the letter would have given them something to work on.

'One more thing,' Daníel said. 'Can you invent a reason to pay Bergrós a visit, as one of Flosi's staff? What came out of their conversation last night is that she's pregnant, and he's the father.'

Helena's heart skipped a beat. This was big, something that could make all the difference to the investigation.

'That's piling on the pressure,' she said.

'Exactly,' Daníel said.

35

Getting to meet Bergrós was no easy matter, as she demanded to know who Helena was, and became agitated at the prospect of another of Flosi's staff coming to speak to her, instead of the man himself. That supported Helena's hunch that she genuinely had no inkling of Flosi's true situation. Helena had made an appointment to meet her at eleven, and Bergrós had said that she would be at home, but nobody answered the bell. Helena had called her phone three times and was about to try the neighbour's bell and be asked to be let into the building so she could go up and hammer on the door, when Bergrós appeared, hurrying along the street.

'So sorry. I thought I'd just nip out to the bakery, and then I couldn't find a parking space when I came back,' Bergrós panted as she rooted through the deep pockets of her woollen coat for her keys.

She wasn't carrying a bag from a bakery, and Helena also found it strange that she had gone by car, considering there were several bakeries within walking distance, and the weather was fine. It was cool, but with no wind, and birds could be heard singing in the gardens along the street. But pregnant women could suffer cravings for the oddest things at any moment. The pregnancy was precisely the reason for Helena's presence.

Bergrós opened the door and Helena followed her up the staircase and into the little attic apartment. Helena declined coffee and made her way to the kitchen, planting herself on a stool and waiting for Bergrós to sit down as well. But Bergrós appeared to be flustered, her movements sharp and quick, and her voice had a brittle quality, as if it was about to crack. She was beautiful, with a chiselled face and high cheekbones, but everything about her

seemed chaotic: her hair, her multi-coloured clothes, her movements as she flitted around the kitchen, and her voice.

'So you're pregnant by Flosi?' Helena said without any pre-
amble, and finally Bergrós' agitated fluttering stopped, and she
stood still and stared. Helena felt that her green eyes were striking
sparks.

'How do you know?' Bergrós asked and now her eyes were cold
and sharp.

'Flosi told me,' Helena replied. Technically this wasn't true, but
there was no way to explain that Flosi's phone was being tapped
without giving the whole game away and admitting that she was
a police officer. Bergrós slumped onto a stool and buried her face
in her hands. Helena could see that her whole frame was wracked
with gasps.

'Hey, hey. There, there,' she said, getting up and gently patting
Bergrós' back. 'It can't be that bad.'

Bergrós snapped upright and looked up, the tears suddenly
gone, the fiery green spark returned to her eyes.

'How am I supposed to know how bad things are when nobody
tells me anything?' Her bafflement turned to anger. 'All Flosi will
tell me is that he needs to re-evaluate his life. This Áróra – and I
don't have a clue where she fits into all this – won't tell me anything, and then there's you, who seems to know all about Flosi's
private life.'

Helena sat down again and used Daníel's strategy of waiting a
moment before saying anything. With angry people it was best
not to reply right away, but to let their rage settle. Sometimes the
time it took to draw a few breaths was enough for people to cool
down and regain control of their emotions.

'I'm just a colleague he trusts. Sometimes I do some deliveries
for Garðvís.' Helena was astonished at how easily the lie came to
her. 'Flosi asked me to stop by and ask if there was anything you
needed, and to let you know that you can call on me and Áróra if

you need help with anything,' she went on in a low, gentle tone. A few moments passed before she saw that Bergrós had regained something of her delicate equilibrium, but she was still unsteady.

'There's nothing I need,' Bergrós said. 'Except Flosi. Will you ask him to come and talk to me?'

'I'll do that,' Helena said. 'And I'm sure he will the moment he's able to. But in the meantime, you can always come to me.'

She picked up a pen from the kitchen sideboard and wrote her phone number on a corner of a copy of *Fréttablaðið*.

'We are in love,' Bergrós said, apologetically. 'This isn't just an affair. We're expecting the baby after Christmas. I'm five months pregnant and I know he loves me and our baby, but he's been dragging this out for five months or more now, saying he's almost ready to divorce Guðrún and come and live with me.'

'I see,' Helena said straightening her back. In reality, she didn't understand at all. This didn't chime with Flosi's account of his relationship with Guðrún. According to him, Bergrós was just an adventure, a diversion from a passionless but otherwise excellent marriage. A child certainly changed everything, not least because Sara Sól had said that her father had dreamed of having more children.

Helena had heard enough, and got to her feet. She would have to call Daníel and let him know that he could add a tick in the *MOTIVE* column, against Flosi's own name. Bergrós went with her to the door, and Helena took her hand as she said goodbye.

'Ask Flosi to come and talk to me,' Bergrós said again, holding Helena's hand tight.

'I promise.' Helena hesitated. 'Hopefully this will all become clear in a few days, and Flosi will be able to come and see you himself.'

'These problems of Flosi's are something to do with a money scam, aren't they? Something to do with the Russians?'

While she very much wanted to, Helena knew she couldn't

question Bergrós any further without raising her suspicions. She got back in her car, and after sending Beta the nurse a text to suggest a salad lunch, pondered Bergrós' words. What made her think Flosi's problems were down to a financial scam? And who were these Russians she had mentioned?

36

Flosi felt his head was ready to burst. It wasn't exactly a headache, but a pounding in his head that pulsed with the rhythm of his heartbeat, so he could practically feel the veins in his temples swell with each contraction of his heart. This had been the second time today that the policeman had sat opposite him with that diffident expression on his face, demanding in his own understated way that Flosi answer a whole string of personal questions. As they came, the pulsing in his temples had increased, until he had finally yelled at the policeman.

'What business is it of the police, and what does it have to do with Guðrún's disappearance if I'd wanted more children or not? And how the hell can you imagine that Bergrós could have anything to do with Guðrún being abducted? She's at least thirty kilos lighter than Guðrún. You can really imagine Bergrós overpowering her and whisking her away just like that? What kind of bullshit is this turning into? How about you coppers do something to search for Guðrún instead of sitting on your backsides and giving me a grilling? I'm not extorting money from myself!'

The policeman said nothing for a moment, continuing to watch Flosi with his searching gaze, except that now, after he had raised his voice, Flosi felt that the expression on the man's face was not so much diffident as pitying.

'I know it's difficult,' Daníel said at last, and then there was a long pause during which Flosi felt all the breath had been knocked out of him, as if his body was a punctured balloon and the air was leaking out of it. He no longer had the energy to curse or shout. But the pressure in his head was still there, with a rhythmic pulse in his temple.

The policeman finally spoke again.

'The way we work is that we consider every possibility, and then rule them out one by one. If we approach things from the other end, there's the risk of becoming too focused on a single theory, which could lead the investigation into a dead end.'

Flosi nodded, even though he wanted to shake his head.

'But you concentrate endlessly on me and my personal life, when you should be checking out which foreign crime gangs have been active here...' He hadn't finished speaking when Daníel held up an index finger, indicating that he had something to say.

'We are looking into all that as well,' he said, to Flosi's relief. 'We have put out feelers in every possible direction, even outside the country, so we certainly aren't only focusing on you and your family. But the fact of the matter is that you, your daughter and your mistress all had good reason to want Guðrún out of the way, and in reality we can't be sure that the abduction hasn't been orchestrated as a distraction from another crime.'

Flosi felt a shudder of horror.

'What do you mean?' he gasped. 'You mean that Guðrún could be dead?'

Daníel shook his head.

'I've no reason to believe that's the case,' he said. 'There was nothing about the state of the house to indicate that. But one must keep an open mind. You are expecting a child you've long desired with another woman, who could be tired of having to share the father of her child with Guðrún, and Sara Sól, your sole heir, could see your assets being split in two by an impending divorce. So it's possible to conclude that Guðrún had been getting in the way of you all.'

'What total crap,' Flosi muttered to himself, while his thoughts whirled through his full-to-bursting head. 'Sara Sól doesn't need to be concerned, because to start with she doesn't know about Bergrós, and secondly, Guðrún and I had a pre-nuptial agreement.'

'Had?' Daníel asked, eyebrows lifting.

'Have,' Flosi said, wishing that he could punch himself on the jaw. It was no surprise the police were suspicious considering he constantly referred to Guðrún in the past tense. He couldn't understand what was going on inside his own head. He could feel the pulsing growing stronger and stronger, until it became painful. It wasn't just in his temples, but deep inside his brain, where his thoughts were fogged and he no longer understood anything, least of all himself.

37

Áróra had never seen Michael at such a loss. She had always felt that this broad-shouldered Scot was the completely imperturbable type. Generally he was cheerful, always looking for positive solutions. There was hardly a millionaire Michael hadn't helped find a place to keep his cash safe, somewhere offshore. But he and Áróra didn't always agree. Sometimes their interests lay in different directions, as her work was mainly about finding hidden money and his was mainly to do with hiding it. It was remarkable that they had worked together so many times before. Occasionally Michael had clients who needed to track down money hidden by bitter colleagues or betrayed spouses. Áróra was grateful for these assignments and his recommendations, but always backed away when Michael tried to tempt her into working for him permanently.

Now, though, Michael seemed dispirited. He sat and turned his phone over and over in his hands, and had a couple of times seemed about to say something but hadn't been able get the words out. They were in a restaurant in Kensington he had chosen and there was plenty of time before her evening flight to Iceland.

'What is it, Michael?'

He sighed, about to speak, but looked relieved when the waiter appeared to take their drinks order. As soon as the waiter was gone, Áróra repeated her question.

'Shall we talk about it after lunch?' Michael suggested.

Áróra shook her head.

'Out with it,' she said. 'Something's bugging you, so let's hear it.'

Michael shifted in his seat and leaned forward, his voice low, almost a whisper.

'I'm afraid that I may have involved you in something unfortunate,' he said, and his eyes flitted around the room, as if he was making certain they weren't overheard.

'Unfortunate?' Áróra said with a grin. 'That's a very English way of putting it.'

'In that case, I'll translate it into plain Scottish for you. I'm scared as fuck because I've managed to drop you into a pile of shit up to your knees.' Áróra laughed, and Michael smiled and sighed. 'And I'm afraid that I'm going to have to ask you to dig even deeper into this.'

'Tell me more,' Áróra said once the waiter had delivered their drinks and taken their lunch order.

'This account of Flosi's in Panama,' Michael said, running a hand over the stubble on his scalp. Áróra nodded encouragingly. 'Usually Flosi doesn't touch it. The funds there don't go through any of the accounting I do, and of course they're not declared. Flosi said that he'd declare the cash as income when he decided to move it all to Iceland.'

'I know how it works,' Áróra said. 'Let's skip the teaching your grandmother to suck eggs stuff, shall we?'

Michael laughed awkwardly.

'Yeah, I know,' he continued. 'Flosi has maybe told you, but he – or to be more precise, we, because I helped him back then when he wanted to set up this account – have used this for the commission he gets from companies when he distributes their products, mainly machinery, to retailers in Iceland and the UK. These are healthy amounts of money, and I have to admit that I hadn't checked this account for a few years. I just expected these commission payments to pile up steadily.'

'But what...?' Áróra was curious, not least because of the awkward expression he wore. His broad, dark face was stiff with tension; it was a look she hadn't seen before.

'But now, when I took a look in there to withdraw these two

million euros for the ransom, there was something of a surprise waiting for me.'

'What surprise?'

'Now there are significantly higher amounts than just those commissions in the account,' Michael whispered, dropping his voice as the waiter swept over to them, bringing chicken for Michael and an English breakfast for Áróra.

'So you thought you were taking part in a small-time swindle, and now you've found out that you're unintentionally involved in some massive scam,' Áróra teased, and felt her mouth watering at the aroma of bacon. She picked up her knife and fork, ready to make a start, but put them down when she saw Michael's expression. He seemed not far from tears, swallowing a few times, his Adam's apple bobbing up and down his muscular throat. Áróra felt goose pimples break out as she realised that he wasn't nervous or stressed – he was terrified.

'It's no joke,' he said in a low voice. 'Your average Joe doesn't keep this kind of money hidden away.'

38

To Helena's mind, Beta was the personification of robust health. She sat in the lotus position on the sofa, lifting the environmentally-friendly bamboo bowl to her chin as she spooned up salad with an eagerness that bordered on greed. Her naked body still glistened with sweat, and she undoubtedly needed to replace some of the calories they had burned off in bed. She was a joy to the eye, and Helena delighted in allowing her eyes to rest on Beta's breasts while they ate.

'I'll bring the salad next time,' Helena smiled.

'Yes, well. About that,' Beta said, putting her bowl aside, chewing her last mouthful and dabbing at her lips. 'I don't think there's going to be a next time. This is our last salad lunch. And our last of anything.'

'Really?'

Helena put down her salad bowl, even though she had only eaten half of the contents.

'Yeah. This isn't doing what it should for me,' Beta said, and her smile was so lovely that Helena felt that what she was saying didn't fit with the look on her face.

'Wait a minute. Has something changed?' she asked.

Beta nodded.

'I'm the one who has changed,' she said and her smile broadened, as if there were some secret behind it. It was as if some inner memory instinctively brought forth this happiness that made her face glow.

'Going steady? In love with someone?'

'Actually, no,' Beta said. 'But now I'm ready to be. Right now I'd be ready for a little romance. This arrangement – you know, salad lunches and hook-ups – isn't doing it for me anymore.'

Helena felt an odd burning sensation rush up her throat. This was a bizarre conversation to have so soon after the intimacy they had shared only a short while ago.

'I'd be prepared to change the arrangement,' she said, completely at odds with her own convictions. She longed to keep *the system* unchanged. She wanted to be able to call on Beta and meet her at short notice, as they had done up to now. But naturally there could be some flexibility – some way to take into account what Beta might be looking for. 'I'd be happy to go out on dates, y'know, dinners and movies or something.'

But Beta's smile stayed where it was and she shook her head.

'I don't think so,' she said. 'You're fantastic just as you are, but you aren't the type I'd date.'

'Oh.'

Helena was at a loss to know how to respond, so she muttered some apology.

Beta laughed.

'It's perfectly fine,' she said. 'No apology required. I'm not even remotely bitter. I just don't see that I could fall for you beyond, you know.' She waved her hand to give her words emphasis, and Helena suddenly became aware of her own nakedness. She snatched up a blanket from the sofa and wrapped it around herself, stood up and went to the bedroom, from there to the bathroom, and locked the door behind her.

She sat on the lid of the toilet for a while, surprised by the hammering of her own heart, strong and fast, as if she had been given a shot of adrenaline as powerful as a punch in the face. It was a feeling she hadn't experienced much since leaving rapid-response shifts. She got to her feet, stood under the shower and her skin and lungs contracted under the ice-cold blast, so that she let out a low unintended cry.

When she went back to the living room with a towel around her, Beta was gone. The environmentally-friendly bowls stood side by side on the coffee table, Beta's empty apart from a scrunched-up serviette and a wooden fork, her own still half full of salad that she now couldn't bring herself to finish.

39

Helena was late and when she finally arrived, her dark hair was damp and she smelled of soap. She had presumably taken a shower, either at home or at the station, but Daníel didn't have an opportunity to ask why, as his phone rang. It was Palli.

'I've been through the traffic CCTV twice, and there's nothing to be seen,' Palli said. 'Not a thing.' There was a bitterness in his voice, as if he wanted Daníel to be aware of the endless valuable hours that had been wasted. 'I've matched all the numbers against the database and there's nothing except the usual traffic offences, driving under the influence, all that shit. Nothing that's even slightly suspicious.'

'All right, my friend,' Daníel said. 'I owe you three-quarters of a case of beer for that.'

He felt it worthwhile mentioning the beer at this moment, as Palli wouldn't be delighted by the next assignment waiting for him.

'Hey, what do I have to do to make it a full crate?'

'Go over the CCTV again, with your attention on something other than the cars.'

'What do you mean?'

'Watch the recording again, but this time watch out for anything other than cars,' he said, and Daníel ended the call ahead of the expected string of expletives. He went into the kitchen, where Helena was talking to Flosi. Daníel had already briefed Flosi on the story he was to tell Guðrún's friend Sigurlaug, as well as what not to say. He would have liked to have been able to prepare Helena in more detail, but there was no time, as the doorbell rang and Flosi grimaced as he tucked his shirt into his trousers.

'OK,' Daníel said. 'As we discussed. Helena, you're one of Flosi's staff at the wholesale business, and you know what's happening. Your role is to make it possible for Flosi to continue to run the business by running errands and ferrying paperwork back and forth.'

Helena nodded and Flosi went to the door.

Daníel heard an exchange of words in the hall and waited a moment before going to join them and extending a hand to the visitor.

'Daníel,' he said. 'Flosi's cousin.'

'Sigurlaug,' the woman said, her handshake warm and firm. She looked to be approaching fifty, but had retained her youthful figure, accentuated by her tailored suit, and her hair and make-up were impeccable. 'It's best to say that I'm primarily Guðrún's friend, although Flosi and I are naturally good friends as well.'

'I'm a distant relative of Flosi's. I worked for him for a while when I was a youngster, so we've kept in touch ever since,' he said, and this explanation appeared to take Sigurlaug by surprise as she looked Daníel up and down. Flosi took Sigurlaug's arm and steered her to the kitchen.

'Coffee?' he suggested, and she nodded.

Daníel followed, prepared to jump in if Helena's introduction were to go wrong. He wasn't sure how good a performer she would turn out to be. But there was no need, as Helena wasn't in the kitchen. The back door stood half open, swinging in the breeze that chased a few russet leaves around the floor.

Daníel went to the door and closed it, scanning the garden for Helena, but she was nowhere to be seen. Flosi acted as if nothing were amiss and began making coffee, while Sigurlaug sat at the table and Daníel's phone pinged as a message arrived.

He opened the short text message that Helena had clearly sent in a hurry.

I know her. She knows I'm a cop.

40

Sigurlaug's reactions left Flosi stunned. She appeared to make all the appropriate responses to the news that Guðrún had been abducted – initially disbelief, then astonishment and finally concern. All the same, he couldn't help feeling that she was playing a part. Or maybe he was doing her a disservice. People reacted in all kinds of ways to bad news, and he couldn't say that he knew Sigurlaug well enough to make up his mind about what she was actually thinking. She was a bag of nerves, that much was certain.

'You mustn't go to the police,' she said. 'If they're going to ... to...' She hesitated and Daníel took the opportunity to put in a word.

'Flosi isn't going to the police,' he said. 'My cousin and I have discussed this at great length, and we reckon this is the best way to handle things.'

'You must pay the ransom,' Sigurlaug said, and now Flosi could see how agitated she had become. There was a tension that ran all the way along her jawline. 'Do exactly what the kidnappers say. You mustn't take any risks.'

'Of course not,' Flosi muttered, and Daníel nodded in agreement, giving him a rapid wink of one eye to tell him to start asking the questions they had talked through beforehand. 'But have you noticed anything unusual about Guðrún's behaviour recently?'

Sigurlaug started.

'What do you mean? What sort of unusual?'

She folded her arms across her chest and leaned back in her chair. Flosi noticed that Daníel watched her with interest.

'Just ... well, has she been acting oddly? Frightened or nervous?'

Sigurlaug shook her head and frowned.

'I don't know what you mean by that. She can hardly have been aware herself that she was about to be kidnapped?'

Flosi was lost, not knowing how Daníel wanted him to respond, but instead he stepped in.

'We were wondering if there was anything in Guðrún's life that you might know about, but which Flosi wouldn't,' Daníel said. His voice was soft and deep, and it seemed to have a calming effect on Sigurlaug. Flosi heard her sigh heavily.

'Such as what?' she asked, staring at Daníel, who returned her glare steadily.

'I don't know. A lover, maybe?'

Flosi snorted in disbelief, and so did Sigurlaug.

'Of course not,' she said and levelled a glance at Flosi that he felt contained an element of accusation. 'Guðrún isn't wired to be unfaithful.'

Flosi's imagination was running at full speed. Did Sigurlaug know about his relationship with Bergrós? Was that what she was implying? Because if Sigurlaug knew, then there was a good chance Guðrún did too. And how did that fit into all this? And what the hell was Daníel doing asking if she had a lover? Despite everything that had coursed through his mind since Monday, that was one thing that hadn't occurred to him. Sigurlaug was quite right that Guðrún would never cheat on him. Or would she?

Flosi stood up and felt faint. He was confused and upset, and most of all he longed to burst into tears, but he wasn't going to do that in front of Sigurlaug, so he rushed out to the hall and paced back and forth with quick steps. All the while he took deep breaths, right down into his belly to help gain control of his emotions before going back to face Daníel and Sigurlaug in the kitchen. He could hear their voices, speaking in low tones.

He was startled by the doorbell ringing. He rushed to the door, somehow expecting Guðrún to be standing there, in person, telling him that it had all been a misunderstanding, just a terrible nightmare, and that in a few moments he would wake up and discover that the worst days of his whole life had just been a couple of hours of bad dreams, and everything would go back to where it had been before. But it wasn't Guðrún at the door, it was Karen. She was carrying shopping bags and smiling at him, and the familiarity of her smile and her concern, and the fact that she appeared to have come to cook him a meal were somehow all too much for him, and he fell into her arms and wept.

At that moment Sigurlaug appeared in the hallway and squeezed past them on her way out.

'Isn't it wonderful, having a spare to fall back on?' she hissed and her heels clicked as she strutted out to her car.

Flosi looked up and wiped his face, Karen's hands still on his shoulders, and wondered whether or not Daníel, who was now also standing in the hall, had heard Sigurlaug's parting remark.

41

'How did you say you knew her, this Sigurlaug?' Daníel asked.

Helena looked uncomfortable, standing in Flosi's back garden. Through the windows they could see Flosi pacing back and forth, in conversation with his former wife, who was busy in the kitchen.

'Uh, we've dated. Sort of.'

Helena buried her hands deep in her pockets and stared at something in the distance, beyond next door's garden. Daníel followed her gaze but there was nothing to be seen. She was staring into the distance so as not to have to look at him.

'So what do you know about her?'

Helena's expression became even more perplexing.

'Look, when I say we dated, that's maybe an exaggeration,' she said. 'I know very little about her. We haven't talked all that much.'

'Where did you meet?' Daníel asked, and Helena glanced at him quickly, and then down at the waterlogged lawn, pushing the toe of one shoe into the soft earth.

'Through an app,' she said, still looking at the ground, before drawing a long breath, clearing her throat and looking up. 'Fuck it. I'll be straight with you. I don't know her at all, but we've fucked loads of times. We have a mutual hook-up arrangement. I didn't even know her name was Sigurlaug. On the app she calls herself Sirra and there's no name on the doorbell at her house.'

'It didn't ring any alarm bells when you saw her address on the system?' Daníel asked.

'No. I hadn't read Kristján's report on Sigurlaug. Sorry.'

Daníel wanted to break into his usual lecture on the importance of every member of the team staying constantly abreast of every item of information that was uploaded onto the system. But of all people, Helena was the last one who deserved that kind of dressing down. Although things had gone wrong this time, she was normally the most reliable of them all, if still a little inexperienced and not as intuitive as she might be.

'So when you saw her coming, you decided to make yourself scarce so she wouldn't see you?'

'That's right. She knows I'm a cop.'

'Fair enough,' Daníel said. 'That's clear. I'll put it in writing and make sure that Oddsteinn knows, so that all the formalities are in order.'

Their eyes met, and he knew that they were thinking the same thing. If this Sirra was linked to the abduction and had also been watching the house, then the attempt to disguise Helena in a vehicle belonging to Flosi's company wasn't going to be convincing. Sigurlaug could have recognised her from a distance and become aware that Flosi had gone to the police.

'I don't think so,' Helena said, as if responding to his unspoken thoughts. 'I don't see her as a kidnapper.'

'Nor do I,' Daníel said, although both of them knew that a feeling for people wasn't of much value in a police investigation. They needed things to be proved, or in this case, disproved.

'How about,' she began, 'I drop by her place this evening and look around?'

'No,' he said.

'A quick look round for signs of anything out of the ordinary, that someone might have stayed there. Anything unusual.'

'No,' he repeated. 'You have to keep away from her now, until we can be sure she doesn't have a connection to the investigation.'

Helena looked at him, hesitating.

'What?'

'It's just that ... the one evening Sirra and I arranged to meet recently, which was actually on Tuesday night, she wanted to come to me. That's unusual, because she always prefers us to be at her place.' Helena fumbled in her pocket for a moment. 'Look, here are the messages from Tuesday when I suggested we meet up. "Happy to hook up but it'll have to be at your place".'

This was certainly interesting. Could Sigurlaug have been blackmailing Guðrún in some way? That would explain the payments from Guðrún's account, which Sigurlaug had just now explained as money Guðrún had let her have so it could be prudently invested on her behalf. Guðrún wanted some money of her own, independent of her husband's wealth. It had sounded plausible the way Sigurlaug had explained it. But maybe it wasn't true. Perhaps Sigurlaug had been squeezing money out of her, and once Guðrún's account had been emptied, she had abducted her so that she could extort money from Flosi. Daníel thought the options over for a moment while Helena watched him. This was how it sometimes was between them, when she could almost hear him thinking.

'What if Guðrún is bound, gagged and drugged in Sirra's spare bedroom?' she said.

'Sirra certainly encouraged Flosi to pay the ransom, and she was a touch too emphatic about it,' he said, and they stared at each other. He was ahead of her in dismissing the thought. 'Nah,' he said, and Helena said the same thing a second later.

'Nah.'

It was too far-fetched to imagine that Guðrún's friend could have forced her out of the house and into her own place, keeping her there against her will. On the other hand, everything about Sigurlaug was beginning to lend weight to another theory that was gradually taking shape in his mind, and when the phone in his pocket rang and he saw Palli's number on the screen, he knew before answering the call that what he would tell him would support his line of thinking.

'Fucking hell, Daníel,' Palli said. 'You're a genius. Just try and guess what I've just seen on one of the traffic cam recordings?'

42

Áróra re-arranged the blanket so that it hid the chain snaking from the steel bracelet on her wrist to the briefcase on the business class seat at her side. These days, when she travelled with money, she always booked a seat for the cash as well, as it was difficult to sit with someone beside you when the briefcase had to be on your knees for the whole flight. The spare seat at her side also meant that she escaped the usual questions from people who were invariably curious about the contents of the case shackled firmly to her hand.

Once they had collected the cash from the safety deposit box at the bank and driven to the airport, accompanied by a security guard Michael had brought along, airport security had taken over and led her through the fast-track route. She handed over the documentation that accompanied the money, and the briefcase had been X-rayed in a special machine so the chain didn't have to be released from her wrist. In fact, the chain couldn't be released. Only Michael knew the code to the lock built into the steel bracelet, and he would give Flosi the numbers over the phone that evening, when Áróra had reached her destination.

One of the cabin crew brought her a drink and leaned over, asking if there was anything else she could bring her, an extra cushion, or anything to make her more comfortable – she had noticed the briefcase, because the blanket had slipped once again and it was visible to anyone passing along the aisle. Áróra courteously declined, and draped the blanket back over the case. It would be a relief to arrive at Flosi's house and be rid of it. But there was something else that was making her uncomfortable. The large amounts passing through Flosi's account were highly suspicious, and she wondered whether to tell Daníel about them right away, or to do some of her own digging first.

Michael had given her viewing access to the accounts on the condition that she kept anything she saw totally confidential. The fact that he had allowed her access to a client's account was a real concern for Áróra, as this alone indicated just how serious he judged the situation to be. Although Michael was an expert in helping people keep their money out the taxman's sight, frequently breaking laws in the process, he normally fiercely defended the interests and confidentiality of his clients. But these were unusual circumstances, and it could well be in Flosi's own interests for them to identify the source of the cash that had flowed through his account in Panama; there might be something there that could link to his wife. It was clear that Flosi had more secrets than he had let on about.

At Keflavík airport a security guard met her at the airbridge and accompanied her to customs, where she registered the money entering the country and provided copies of her identification documents. Flosi could expect a hefty bill from the taxman next year, as well as some tough questions about the origins of this money, and why he hadn't declared it before as income.

She looked around the arrivals hall. Daníel had told her that he would send a plain-clothes police officer to fetch her. She scanned the waiting faces, and her heart took an extra beat when she saw Daníel himself standing near the front of the crowd, his eyes already on her before she had seen him. He smiled quickly as their eyes met, and a smile immediately crossed her face as a little rush of warmth went through her.

43

The moment Sirra opened the door, Helena regretted going against Daníel's instructions. Sirra was surprised to see Helena, and clearly less than delighted. The sizzling look that Helena usually got from her was noticeably absent, while her eyes were dull and puffy, as if she had been weeping.

'What..?' She looked Helena up and down, as if she had somehow forgotten they had arranged to meet. 'I wasn't expecting you,' she said.

Helena did her best to put on a cheerful, carefree front, as if she had casually decided to drop in – which was, however, something completely at odds with the agreement between them.

'Thought I'd check on you,' she said with a broad smile.

Sirra's smile in response was faint.

'But you always text.'

'Yeah, but I was in the area and thought I'd stop by. A spur-of-the-moment thing. Aren't you going to invite me in?'

'I'm not exactly in the mood for company right now,' Sirra said, but stepped aside to allow Helena to enter.

The apartment was almost dark, apart from a small lamp that glowed next to the large living-room window overlooking Laugardalur valley. If Helena had been inclined to guess what Sirra had been doing just before she knocked, she would have imagined her sitting under the dim lamp, looking out into the autumn gloom with the melancholy expression that seemed to have settled on her face.

'Anything wrong?' Helena asked, taking her arm.

Sirra placed her hand over Helena's.

'Nothing in particular,' she said, forcing another smile. 'Just feeling down somehow.'

'OK,' Helena said. 'I'm here if you need to talk.'

'Wouldn't you like a beer now that you're here? You're not on call, are you?'

'No,' Helena said quickly. 'A beer would go down well.'

Sirra disappeared and began bustling around the kitchen. Helena heard the fridge open and the clink of glasses, and took the chance to check out the corridor and the rooms leading off it. There was a double bed in one, with a rolled-up duvet on it, but not in a duvet cover, as if a guest might be expected. Helena didn't know if this was normal, as she had never looked into this room before. Normally they went straight to Sirra's bedroom, and sometimes they hadn't got further than the sofa in the living room.

Helena went quickly into the little bathroom off the corridor, quietly shut the door and opened the cupboards. They were mostly empty, with no toothbrushes or gels to be seen. Sirra kept her own cosmetics in the en-suite bathroom leading off her bedroom, but guests staying over could be expected to use this one. But there were no signs of any guests. Helena flushed the toilet and let water run from the tap into the basin for a moment before returning to the living room.

Sirra had switched on more lights and sat on the sofa with a glass of white wine in her hand, and in front of her stood a tall glass of beer with nuts in a little dish next to it. Sirra did everything in style. She would never serve a drink other than as if in a bar. And she would never dream of asking anyone to drink beer straight from the bottle, as Helena habitually did at home to keep washing up to a minimum.

'How are things?' Helena said as she sat next to Sirra. 'What's bugging you?'

Sirra smiled, and this time it reached her eyes. She seemed to be returning to her normal self. Maybe a visit was what had been needed to cheer her up.

'Ach, I don't know,' Sirra said. 'Probably this autumn weather.

The trees turning that rusty colour. Maybe I ought to take myself south to the sun sometime soon.'

'Not a bad idea,' Helena agreed, and an image came unbidden to her mind of her and Sirra side by side on sun loungers, cocktails in hand, Sirra's body glistening with sun-tan lotion.

They finished their drinks in silence, clinking glasses twice, but Sirra seemed to have no desire to talk. Daníel's trick clearly didn't work every time. It wasn't always enough to sit quietly, waiting for the other person to fill the void. For that the silence needed to be awkward, even uncomfortable. But there was nothing uncomfortable about sitting and enjoying a drink without saying anything.

When Sirra broke the silence, it was to give Helena an oblique hint that it was time to go, saying she wasn't in the mood, that she needed to be by herself. Helena got to her feet and Sirra stood up to see her to the door. In the hallway Helena noticed a huge, brightly coloured bunch of flowers that had been placed against the mirror on the sideboard. She hadn't noticed it on the way in. Sirra's discomfort had taken all her attention.

'Fabulous flowers,' she said, and Sirra smiled at the sight of the red-gold lilies arranged above a sea of green.

'Yes, a friend brought them for me,' Sirra said, picking up a leaf that had fallen from the bouquet onto the sideboard.

'Friend?' Helena said, lifting an eyebrow.

'No, not like that. Just a friend,' Sirra said, and a shadow crossed her face, as if the sadness that had been banished for a moment had returned to her eyes. Helena hugged her. Sirra pressed her close, quickly, and just as quickly let go.

'You know where I am,' Helena said. 'Just to talk if that's what you need. About whatever.'

Now Sirra laughed, although there was no joy in her laughter, and there was even a sharpness in her eyes.

'I remember you saying at the beginning that you didn't go in for drama. That you didn't want any emotional entanglements.'

'Yeah. But all the same,' Helena said. 'You know where to find me.'

She could hear how empty her own words sounded, and as she walked to her car, she could feel a flush of self-reproach that made her throat and cheeks burn. This hadn't been a good day for female relationships. First there had been Beta's rejection, and now Sirra's strange demeanour, which, much as she would have liked to ignore her detective's instincts, Helena found rather suspicious.

44

'I had a massive sense of hopelessness this morning when the plane took off over Reykjanes,' Áróra said as she sat at Daníel's side and looked out of the window. There was nothing but darkness out there on this stretch of the road where the lights seemed to have stopped working and only the reflectors near the verge lit up as the headlights caught them. 'I've searched so many tracks, and there are so many more. All that wild land. All that jagged lava. The sea all around.'

'True,' he said. There wasn't much more he could say. He knew exactly what she was talking about. Early in the summer she had told him that she had bought a drone to search areas alongside these tracks around the city.

'Thank you for not giving up,' she said, turning towards him.

His eyes left the road for a moment as he glanced at her, and he was relieved to be behind the wheel. It gave him a pretext to look away again. Otherwise he would have stared at her and given himself away. This weird eagerness, this longing, that sometimes took hold of him in her presence made him shiver.

'No thanks needed,' he said. 'I'm just sorry that there's nothing that can tell us more about what happened to your sister, or where that bastard Björn is hiding.'

'It doesn't matter,' she said. 'I know the investigation has hit a dead end. I'm just so grateful that you haven't given up on it. I saw the paperwork at your place when I went to fetch your stuff.'

'She's in my thoughts every night,' he said, and immediately regretted the sincerity in his voice. He quickly switched to a tone that was more neutral, more 'police'. 'It's difficult to accept when there's no conclusion to a disappearance.'

Áróra hummed something in reply and they sat in silence, the only sound the rattle of the studded tyres of Flosi's car, which Daníel had borrowed to fetch Áróra from the airport. He'd have to remember to tell the man off for switching to winter tyres so early in the autumn. It wasn't as if he lived in some remote wilderness.

Unusually, he was the one who finally gave up and broke the silence between them; normally he used it to make people talk. Few people could stand to be quiet for long around others.

'We're starting to get some kind of an overview of this case concerning Flosi,' he said. 'It's not certain that Flosi's going to need all the cash that's in that case.'

'Really?'

'Guðrún has been spotted on traffic CCTV around dinner time on the evening she disappeared, walking along the street away from the house, alone.'

'Wow.'

'Exactly,' Daníel said. 'She's walking up to Reykjavíkurvegur, and that's where she disappears from sight. She could have got in a car anywhere, at any point, along that stretch of road between Álftanesvegur and Fjarðarkaup supermarket.'

'So this is just a family affair?'

'Yes,' Daníel sighed, either from relief or disappointment, he wasn't sure which. 'It looks like that. It's going to be the divorce from hell.'

45

Michael had called Flosi and given him the code to unlock the case from Áróra's wrist and open it. When Flosi had finished stacking the bundles of notes in the safe in his bedroom, he signed a receipt for the cash, and Áróra could breathe more easily. It was always a relief when the cash she carried had been delivered into the right hands.

But her relief wasn't just that she had handed over the money. It was also positive that Guðrún had been spotted walking nearby. That meant she didn't need to tell Daníel about the mysterious financial traffic through Flosi's account. Since the abduction was clearly a family affair that looked to be about to be resolved, there was no need to get the police involved in Flosi's financial affairs. This wouldn't stop her conducting her own investigations, but they would have to wait, because for now it was important to update Flosi on the latest developments. She meant to be there to provide him with moral support, but when they were back in the kitchen she could sense Daníel's hesitation, how his eyes flicked at intervals in her direction as he explained the situation, and she felt that she was there no less to support him than Flosi.

'We've finished examining all the CCTV footage from the district on the evening Guðrún disappeared,' Daníel began, and glanced quickly in Áróra's direction, as if he were seeking backup – as if hoping that she might provide some input that would make things easier for him.

But Flosi spoke first.

'And?' he demanded. 'What's on there?'

Daníel hesitated again.

'There's a ... Well ... Guðrún can be seen walking along Hraunbrún and onto Reykjavíkurvegur. She was alone.'

'What ... how?' Flosi began, and the expected flood of questions dried up for a moment, before he groaned and started again. 'And the kidnappers? Can't they be seen?'

'No. She was alone, and then she disappears out of shot and could have got in a car somewhere. That's assuming someone had come to collect her.'

'Abduct her, you mean? So why was this place a shambles? I thought she had been kidnapped from here,' Flosi said, pointing at the kitchen floor, staring for a long moment from beneath frowning brows, clearly thinking back to that fateful Monday evening and the puddle of white wine, the burned bread, the broken glass.

'You and Guðrún have a pre-nuptial agreement,' Daníel said, 'that sets out that in the event of a divorce, Guðrún would leave the marriage with practically nothing.'

'Of course I would never leave Guðrún penniless. What are you insinuating? And what does our pre-nuptial agreement have to do with all this?'

Flosi's voice rose in volume, but he seemed confused rather than angered.

'Perhaps Guðrún had become concerned about her situation – maybe she had found out about your mistress.'

'I've told you already that Guðrún knew nothing about Bergrós. It's just not possible. And I don't see why you're so interested in her. She has nothing to do with all this, nothing at all.'

Áróra again noticed the enquiring look in Daníel's eyes and put a hand on Flosi's arm, and with that he became a little calmer.

'It seems,' Daníel said in a low, mild tone. 'It seems that Guðrún abducted herself.'

This seemed to take some time to filter through to Flosi's consciousness. The wrinkle in his forehead deepened while he fought to gain control of his thoughts, and then his eyes filled with tears.

'So, taking this new information into consideration,' Daníel said. 'Do you have any idea where she might have gone?'

Flosi ripped a sheet from a roll of kitchen paper and dabbed at his eyes. Then the skin of his forehead became smooth again and his mouth opened as if he had something to say, and then closed again as his expression hardened.

'No,' he said in a firm voice, getting smartly to his feet and leaving the kitchen.

Áróra watched him go along the corridor and turn to take the stairs, and a moment later the bedroom door upstairs could be heard banging shut.

FRIDAY

46

Áróra stood and stared out of the window at the street lights across the road shivering in the wind so that the cones of light they cast moved across the pavement like lapping waves. It was getting on for three in the morning. She had slept for an hour, but once she was wide awake had been unable to stop thinking about her sister, Ísafold. There was a gnawing guilt that came with these thoughts. If only she had responded the last time that Ísafold had asked for help. If only she had been a better sister. She tried to dampen down the negative emotions by thinking of Daníel, the documents she had seen on his desk and the prospect that he would find a lead that would tell them something about Ísafold's disappearance. But it was hopeless. She knew from experience that there was no point lying awake in bed, as the longer she lay there, the more her negative thoughts would pursue her. It was better to get up, get herself a snack and study the maps. The map of the Reykjanes area had been very much on her mind ever since she had started to search early in the summer.

Now it was three o'clock and she had eaten two slices of toast spread with cheese, drunk a foul-tasting mug of herbal tea that was supposed to have a relaxing effect, and had spent a good while poring over the map. Seeing all the crosses on the roads and the tracks she had already checked with the drone gave her the feeling of having made some progress, so she tried to concentrate on the thought of how much of Reykjanes she had in fact already covered, because looking at the tracks she still had left to search filled her with impatient trepidation. Supposing Ísafold was there, at the next one? She could be alone there now, abandoned to the most miserable conditions death can offer, the autumn storms battering her body and washing away evidence.

The tea did nothing to take the edge off her nerves. The impatience inside her demanded activity, movement, focus. She could sit over the map until morning and check the weather forecast in the hope that the wind would be light enough in the next few days to fly the drone. Or she could use the inspection access Michael had given her to take a look at Flosi's offshore account. Although his financial affairs weren't directly connected to the abduction, it could still be interesting. Maybe she would find herself something to work on. Maybe she'd be able to re-awaken her delight in being a financial bloodhound and again enjoy rolling in cash.

She went to the bathroom and took a lukewarm shower, dried her hair, pulled on a singlet and tracksuit trousers, and went back to the kitchen to put more water in the kettle. She put five spoonfuls of coffee in the cafetière and decided that working from home would call for a decent espresso machine. That made her smile for a moment. This was the first time that she had envisaged some kind of everyday life in this flat, unconnected to Ísafold. Up to now she had looked on it as a temporary place to live until her sister were found. But maybe the idea of settling in Iceland wasn't so crazy after all. Here she was, halfway between Europe and the States, and Iceland's business regulations weren't as strict as those in the EU, so this could be a good place to be based.

47

The rest of the world was shut out completely – that was until Áróra heard the first sounds of a neighbour's car starting up, presumably to go to work, as she saw it was now seven-thirty. She had been so engrossed in her work that she hadn't noticed time passing. She stood up, stretched her arms high over her head and reached forward, hands on the floor to stretch her back, and followed that with forty knee bends, then stretched again and did another forty. She wanted coffee, but the cafetière was empty even though she had no recollection of having refilled her mug. Her concentration on Flosi's offshore account had given her a fairly clear picture of what seemed to be going on there.

The bulk of the traffic that had filled the account was payments from all kinds of smaller businesses that were mostly registered in Britain, plus some in the Nordic region. She had traced some of them and found out that they included night clubs, health resorts, massage parlours, laundries, garages and restaurants. Altogether, there were 193 such companies. The amounts varied, but a large number of payments from each company across every month meant that each month's total was a healthy figure. The commissions earned, and which Flosi had allowed to build up over a long period, were still just a fraction of what was now in the account.

But there were also outgoings. The largest amounts went to a company called INExport Inc, registered in the US, which meant its annual accounts weren't available to Áróra. So she concentrated on the other two; these were registered in Iceland: Tækjakistan ehf and Garðlager ehf, both of which appeared to be well managed and respectably profitable. None of the names of the directors listed in the company registry were familiar to her, and searches for those names revealed nothing of interest. She looked up the companies on the internet, and saw that both were registered as having phone numbers and email addresses.

Áróra picked up her spare phone – the one she kept taped to the back of her bedside table, and which she hadn't used since arriving in Iceland. She had to think for a moment before she remembered the PIN. When it was finally live, she used it to connect to the internet, hiding her IP address, and emailed both Tækjakistan ehf and Garðlager ehf with an enquiry about buying a robot lawn mower. It maybe wasn't the ideal time of year to be pretending to be looking for garden implements, but she couldn't think of any other pretext for contacting these companies. Now she just had to hope that whoever read the emails would click the image she had embedded of a robot lawn mower, which would activate software that would give her a back door into the user's computer.

48

Helena stood at the whiteboard, making efforts to keep her hand-writing legible as she noted down the points that Daníel, Kristján, Palli and the commissioner came up with. Oddsteinn from the prosecutor's office sat in one corner and seemed more absorbed in his phone than what was going on in the room. Helena always felt nervous around the commissioner, even though she had never been anything but friendly towards her. There was just something about her rank that made Helena nervous. All the same, the commissioner would be the last person to pull rank. She was lively and approachable, and always wore a black uniform shirt, the same as any other police officer. Helena's hand shook a little as she rubbed out with her thumb and replaced a badly formed A in the words *offshore account* on the board.

'Guðrún was one of only a very few people who knew about Flosi's offshore savings,' Daníel said. 'It's no coincidence that the ransom demand is in euros.'

Helena wrote *Guðrún knew about the euros* on the board, and realised that she would have to write in smaller letters if everything relevant to the case were to fit on the board.

'Flosi was tired of the marriage,' Daníel said. 'And he had been having an affair for some time.'

Helena wrote *affair* on the board.

'And the man's mistress is pregnant,' the commissioner added, and Helena wrote *Bergrós pregnant*.

'Flosi had long wanted more children,' Daníel said. 'So this must have been exciting news for him, making it tempting to divorce Guðrún and take up with the mother of his child instead.'

'It's not certain that Guðrún was aware of Bergrós and the child,' the commissioner said thoughtfully.

'My impression is that it's highly likely,' Daníel said. 'I thought that her friend Sigurlaug insinuated it when she and Flosi met.'

'Is there any way of being sure?' asked Oddsteinn, who up to now had sat in silence.

Helena shook her head.

'It's something that Sigurlaug could be able to confirm. But Sigurlaug doesn't know that Flosi has involved the police in this, and it's best to keep it that way, as, if our thinking is correct, they're definitely in touch.'

The commissioner nodded her agreement, and Helena breathed more easily.

'Flosi and Guðrún had a pre-nuptial agreement to the effect that he would keep any assets he brought to the marriage,' Daníel said. 'That includes the company and the house. Guðrún brought no assets to the relationship and they have not acquired any significant assets or property jointly, so there's a financial incentive for her.'

Helena wrote *Pre-Nup* on the board.

'According to what's been filed on LÖKE, she wanted her own flower shop,' Palli said, and although his remark felt slightly off-topic, this was a valid point and Helena picked it up.

'That's right,' she said. 'Flosi and his daughter Sara Sól were both against the flower shop dream, so we could say that even though Guðrún may not have been aware of the infidelity and the child, she must have been frustrated that her ambition had come to nothing.'

'It supports her motives,' the commissioner said, nodding.

Helena felt a warm wave of gratitude, similar to when she had been a child and the teacher had praised her for working so hard.

'Then there's the CCTV footage,' Palli said. 'She's seen walking alone and uncoerced away from her home.'

Helena had just finished writing *left home* on the board when Kristján spoke for the first time.

'Considering she left the house of her own volition that evening, there's the question of why the kitchen was such a shambles,' he said, and Helena wrote *staged abduction* on the board, adding a question mark to it.

'All of the indications concern personal aspects of Flosi's life,' Daníel said. 'There's nothing at all from either the analysis unit here or from colleagues in other Nordic countries to suggest that organised crime gangs are involved in anything of this nature.'

The commissioner stood up and made for the door.

'Fine. Good work. Please keep me informed,' she said as she left the room and shut the door behind her.

Helena could sense her shoulders relaxing. Daníel stood up and went to the board. He took down the picture of Guðrún that had been at the top, and replaced her with Flosi.

'I think we should now work on the basis that Guðrún staged her own abduction as a way of extorting money from her husband prior to an impending divorce. So the real victim in this case is Flosi.'

49

It was just before ten when Áróra arrived outside the premises of Tækjakistan ehf, having driven around in circles in Grafarholt, which was where Garðlager ehf was supposed to be located. The site turned out to be not even at the weathertight stage of construction yet – just concrete walls with boarded-up gaps that would become windows. Áróra put her foot down and headed for the next company on her list.

Nobody seemed to have yet turned up for work at Tækjakistan. From the outside, it looked very small, just part of one of the long buildings in the Smiðja commercial district, like an afterthought tacked onto a garage that occupied most of the place.

Áróra got out of the car and walked over to the door, only to find it was locked and there were no lights on inside. She took a quick look through a window and saw that the interior was in keeping with the outside: just an office chair and a counter on which stood two computer screens. Áróra went back to the car, started the engine and drove a circuit around the district, returning to park on the far side of the street between two cars that looked to be waiting to be fixed.

She didn't have to wait long for a sign of life at Tækjakistan. A gleaming black Range Rover drove up to the building and pulled up right in front of the window, and out got a young man who loped to the door and opened it with a key. He was tall and burly, and his clothes were in a style that didn't match the car – his tattered jeans flapped around his legs and he wore a black T-shirt with a band logo under a baggy hoodie. Áróra started the engine, inched the car forward so that the Range Rover no longer interrupted her view, and she watched closely through the window.

Inside, the man shook off his hoodie and draped it over the

back of the chair, sat down and lifted his feet onto the counter. Then he took something out of a drawer. Áróra couldn't make out what it was, but after a while, judging by his movement, she realised that he had to be holding a controller for a computer game. He appeared to have turned up for work to play a computer game.

Áróra listened to the radio while she waited, starting the engine at intervals to clear the mist from the windscreen and to warm herself up. The man sat in more or less the same position for almost two hours, until he finally put the controller aside and stood up. He put on his hoodie, went out and locked the door behind him, first hanging up a big sign, handwritten in letters so large that Áróra could read them from across the street: *Gone to lunch*. He got into the Range Rover and drove away, and Áróra waited a moment before following.

She was surprised to see him turn into the next street and pull up in front of an Asian restaurant. It had been such a short distance that it would have been quicker to have walked, although the weather was on the blustery side. She waited a few minutes after the man had disappeared inside, and then followed him.

She saw as she walked in that he was sitting with a plate piled high with noodles – there must be quick service in this place. There were five dishes on offer. Áróra chose curried chicken with noodles, and decided when she saw the size of the portion that she would have to leave half of the noodles, otherwise she would be asleep soon after lunch. Even now, every time she looked down at a plate of food she felt she could hear her father's voice emphasising the need for protein – the essential building blocks for muscles, Vikings, Valkyries, and troll girls like her. 'Troll girls need protein,' he had always said, 'meat, fish and eggs. Meat, fish and eggs.' A passion for body building was what they had always had in common – or being 'power-crazy' as her mother had always called it – and Áróra had always been grateful for the positive body image he had managed to implant in her. Many tall women became hunched, as if trying to pull themselves into a more acceptable female size. But her father had championed their troll-and-Viking blood, assuring her that Icelandic women were the biggest and strongest in the world. It wasn't until Áróra had been approaching twenty during a summer holiday that she realised that while many Icelandic women were certainly on the solid side, most of them were shorter than she was.

Áróra ate fast, ready to get to her feet and follow the man, but he seemed to be in no hurry. He ate a leisurely lunch while checking his phone, and stood up to fetch a second helping. Áróra got up as well, and got herself a coffee in a hefty mug that was included in the price of lunch. It turned out to be thin and sour, so she pretended to take the occasional sip while she waited for the man to finish his lunch.

50

Daníel hadn't been able to assess Flosi's mental state that morning, as he had come downstairs and left the house, calling out that he was going to work. It had been so early that Daníel hadn't been up, and while he tidied up the sofa and the bedclothes, he thought to himself that it was probably good for Flosi to focus more on normal life today. The last week had been a strange one for him, to say the least.

When Flosi returned from work that afternoon he was in an odd mood, and his demeanour was one Daníel hadn't seen before. It went without saying that his frame of mind would be changed, now that he knew Guðrún was probably not in any danger and that there was a strong likelihood she was behind the extortion attempt. It would be understandable, in fact, to see his fear replaced by anger. But his cheerfulness took Daníel by surprise. Flosi marched in, flung his coat over the banister and amiably clapped Daníel on the back.

'So how are things going for the guardians of law and order?' he asked with a grin.

Daníel smiled courteously in return.

'Not bad,' he said, and was about to ask Flosi to come and talk to him in the living room, but he had already headed for the kitchen, where his former wife, Karen, was laying the table for the takeaway she had brought with her. Daníel had been about to order pizzas when Karen had appeared with her arms full of food.

Daníel heard an indistinct exchange of words from the kitchen, but then Flosi's voice rose, and he could hear he was telling Karen that she had no need to be dogging his footsteps.

'I can buy my own KFC,' he bawled as he marched out of the kitchen and encountered Daníel.

'Could we talk, Flosi?' Daníel said.

For a moment Flosi seemed to be undecided, thinking it over, but then followed Daníel into the living room.

When Flosi was seated at the dining table, Daníel opened the message ready on his phone and tapped *send*.

'I've just sent you a picture of a ransom demand that arrived in the mail today, postmarked on Monday,' he said. 'I took a picture of it before it was sent to be analysed. You can enlarge it to see what it says, but the gist is that you're to leave the money in an open sports bag on Miklatún on Monday afternoon, and then Guðrún will be released.'

Now there was none of the despair Flosi had displayed over the last few days.

'Absolute bullshit,' he said and laughed as he shook his head.

Daníel looked at him enquiringly, but was unable to fathom his mood.

'We need to discuss the next steps,' he said calmly.

But Flosi got to his feet, a determined look on his face.

'After dinner,' he said. 'Since Karen took the trouble to bring those chunks of chicken all this way, we'd best eat them.'

Daníel sat still in the living room for a while as he thought over the change in Flosi's behaviour. This determined, headstrong version was probably closer to Flosi's normal self than the broken, confused man Daníel had seen so far.

51

'It was good of Karen to bring us something for dinner,' Daníel said as he took a final mouthful of chips dipped in cocktail sauce. He had barely nibbled at his food, unlike Flosi, who had put away what had looked like a double portion, leaving a heap of chicken bones gnawed clean in front of him.

'Yeah. I was maybe a bit abrupt with her earlier,' Flosi said, wiping his mouth. 'I'll buy something nice for her tomorrow.'

Karen had left immediately after the angry exchange of words with Flosi, and Daníel wanted to say that maybe it would be an idea to call her, apologise and thank her for bringing food, but he stopped himself before saying anything. It wasn't his job to teach Flosi manners, to tell him that he shouldn't buy his way out of his mistakes.

'There are two ways that we can respond to the ransom demand,' Daníel said. 'One is to ignore it: give no response, and see what happens. The outcome could be another demand, maybe a threat, and finally Guðrún would give up and reappear. For her it's not a realistic option to stay hidden away for long. When she shows up, we would have some difficult questions for her to answer.'

Flosi said nothing, muttered to himself, leaned back in his chair and patted his belly in satisfaction. Daníel was astonished by his apparent lack of concern.

'The danger with this approach is that if we're wrong and Guðrún is genuinely being held by criminals, then we are putting her in danger.'

'I don't think you're wrong. Guðrún kidnapped herself. That's the only theory that makes sense.'

Daníel looked at Flosi thoughtfully. He no longer seemed to

be giving any thought to the possibility that Guðrún could be in danger. This was a complete change from his previous attitude, when he constantly had tears in his eyes at the idea of Guðrún's fate. Now there was a coldness to him, almost a lack of concern about the whole thing. It was as if a burden had been lifted from him – which could be seen as normal, but Daníel had expected more sorrow and anger over his wife having betrayed him.

'Even though we are working on the assumption that Guðrún staged her own abduction,' Daníel said, 'there's still a possibility that she was genuinely kidnapped. So we need to be cautious. I'll stay on duty here over the weekend and we'll continue to tap the phones.'

'Yes, yes. That sounds perfectly sensible,' Flosi agreed, apparently without needing to think it over.

'Our other option is to allow the handover to take place on Monday, as the ransom demand sets out. You leave the bag in the park at Miklatún, and the Special Unit stakes out the whole area. Either nobody comes to fetch the bag, or someone turns up to collect it and we grab them, whether it's Guðrún in person or someone acting for her. That seems to me the less risky option, taking into account the remote possibility that Guðrún really has been abducted by criminals. In that case, we arrest them and work on a new basis.'

'That sounds good,' Flosi said, and stood up. 'But we're hardly going to fill the bag with cash, are we?' he asked.

Daníel shook his head.

'No. We put ten kilos of old newspapers in the bag, but it would be handy if you could put a few bundles of euros on top, because the demand stipulates that the bag has to be open. That's presumably so that the contents can be seen from a distance. I could get the cash through the police if you prefer.'

'No, no need for that,' Flosi said. 'Of course I can put forward the money. This is my problem, after all.'

He left the room, and Daniel heard him jog up the stairs. He seemed to have shed years.

Daniel got to his feet and emptied the bones, paper plates and the pile of crumpled serviettes into the bag the food had been delivered in. He dropped the bag into the bin, and had just wrung out a cloth to wipe down the table when he heard a cry from upstairs.

He rushed into the hall and was about to run up when Flosi appeared on the landing, his face white and terrified.

'The money's gone!' he called out, his voice quavering. 'The safe is empty.'

SATURDAY

52

By the next morning Flosi had become much more subdued. Even from his footsteps on the stairs Daníel could hear that he was not as agitated as he had been the evening before.

'I'm going to go to work and then I'll try to catch up with Sara Sól,' he said as he came into the kitchen, freshly shaven, a cloud of aftershave about him and the knot of his tie tight at his throat. 'She's not answering my calls and that tells me that she took the money. She has a key to the house and comes and goes as she pleases. That was yet another bone of contention between her and Guðrún.'

Daníel handed him a cup of coffee. Flosi took it, sipped, burned his tongue and swore, taking the next sip with more care and a loud slurp.

'She has to be doing this to get attention,' he said as he sat at the kitchen table. 'She used to do the same when she was little – hiding my shoes so I couldn't go to work, or my phone so I couldn't answer calls when I was supposed to be spending time with her.'

Daníel wanted to make the point that two million euros in cash was a slightly bigger deal than a pair of shoes, and that Sara Sól was no longer a child but a grown woman, but he kept quiet. It would be ideal for Flosi to go to work and spend some time with his daughter. Daníel had other ideas about where the money had gone, but he wasn't about to say anything to Flosi without being certain.

They munched their breakfast cereal in silence and for the first time it occurred to Daníel what a strange partnership this had become. There could hardly be two men so dissimilar, but in spite of that they had got on well over the past few days.

'This should all be resolved on Monday,' Daníel said. 'Then you'll be free of me.'

'Hopefully it'll all be sorted out quickly,' Flosi said. 'Not that I'm in any hurry to see the back of you. You're...' He cleared his throat awkwardly. 'You're a calming influence. So it's been good to have you around. And Guðrún would say that you're well house trained.'

Daníel laughed.

'Thanks. Maybe I can get a reference from you if I manage to reel in a woman one day.'

'How come you're single? Do you spend all your time on people's sofas as part of your job? No time to find yourself a girl?'

'No, the situation isn't that bad. I've had my eye on someone particular for a few months now. Made a few moves, but the interest doesn't seem to be working both ways.'

'What the hell?' Flosi said. 'You need to make more of an effort. Faint heart, and all that. It's always worked for me to splash out. Smart dinners, presents, travel. Most women like to be pampered.'

'That wouldn't go far with this one, I reckon. Apart from that, she should be the one treating me. She's considerably better off financially than I am.'

Flosi scowled.

'Is this one of those career women?' he asked.

'Well, I can't say I really know,' Daníel said, which was quite true. He had little idea of how Áróra managed her work, whether she was ambitious and genuinely had a passion for what she did, or if she had gone down this route purely for the money. 'She's a good bit younger as well,' he added. 'So I reckon my chances are slim, to be honest.'

'Rubbish!' Flosi said. 'They all have some kind of Daddy complex – no little girl ever gets all the approval she needs from her father. That's where we older guys can score.'

Flosi stood up, leaving the crockery where it was, leaving Daníel speechless. In a couple of sentences Flosi had managed to combine both some shrewdness, which Daníel felt was somewhere on the borderline between Freudism and feminism, with crashing chauvinism. He had no idea why it had occurred to him to share something so personal. This had begun as an everyday conversation, but had become something that was out of order at a professional level. In future he'd keep this kind of thing for his confidante. Lady Gúgúlú knew all about the wreckage of his two previous relationships, and over the preceding months had heard much about Daníel's thoughts concerning Áróra.

He heard Flosi shut the door behind him and got to his feet, putting the cups and bowls in the dishwasher and wiping down the table.

When the doorbell rang, he went to the door and opened it for Helena and Kristján.

'Ready?' Helena asked, and he nodded, taking his jacket from its hook.

'Let us know right away if anything interesting crops up,' he said to Kristján, who headed for the living room sofa. Then he followed Helena out.

'I've a feeling this is going to be an interesting day,' she muttered.

53

Her headache was a real killer and the painkillers she had knocked back with her morning coffee hadn't properly taken effect yet. She had gone to sleep late, and several times the tension in her body had startled her into wakefulness. More than likely the stress of this investigation was starting to take its toll. Yesterday would have been an ideal time to make use of *the system* and spend the evening with a beautiful woman to take her mind off work. But with both Beta and Sirra out of the game, everything had somehow gone wrong, and it was clear to her that she would have to rethink how she approached relationships.

Daníel said little on the way, and Helena was in no state to hold much of a conversation. It wasn't until they pulled up outside the house that Daníel gave a long whistle and Helena quickly noticed what had elicited such a reaction. A newish motorhome was parked in the drive, next to a generously proportioned caravan.

'Someone's keen on camping,' Helena said, and for a moment she felt a stab of regret that summer was over and she hadn't spent any time around a campfire listening to the sound of guitars being strummed. It was a ridiculous notion, as this wasn't the first summer she hadn't taken time off – in fact it was the third in a row. It had been so long since she had taken a summer holiday that she couldn't remember the last one.

Daníel didn't bother with the doorbell, instead knocking firmly on the smoked glass of the front door. They saw Sara Sól come to answer.

'Your father has gone to work and is expecting to meet you there,' Helena said as the door opened, noticing that the girl's face was swollen from weeping. Her eyes were red and her cheeks puffed and flushed. Helena would have liked to have taken her words back, but Daníel's warm, sympathetic voice took over, and Helena promised herself that this was what she had to practise – along with cultivating patience.

'I imagine you know why we're here,' Daníel said softly.

Sara Sól nodded and sniffed.

'Yes. Mum's in the living room,' she said, moving aside to let them in.

Helena hesitated for a second as she stepped into the hall, where it would have been normal to take off her shoes, but there was not an inch of space anywhere, neither to move nor to leave a pair of rain-soaked shoes. The only space was the tiny triangle the door needed to swing open, as if it were a giant windscreen wiper, shoving slush aside. The rest of the hall was a continuous stack of shoes, and the walls were hung with coats, jackets and sweaters, which hung on top of each other so that the walls or any cupboards that might be behind them were completely hidden.

'How many people live here?' Daníel asked, looking around in amazement.

'The two of us,' Sara Sól said dryly, gesturing for them to follow her along a passage that was narrow, because both sides were stacked high with plastic boxes full to the brim with stuff. At the end of the passage there was a large living room that could at one time have doubled as a dining room, but by the window next to the kitchen was a pile of stuff, mainly clothing, some of which seemed to have price tags still attached.

'Mum's a compulsive shopper,' Sara Sól said, as if to answer the questions that Daníel and Helena hadn't asked. In a corner sofa at the far end of the living room Karen sat hunched, holding out a Bónus supermarket carrier bag full of euro notes.

54

As there had been no alert to let her know that her Trojan horse email had been opened, Áróra decided it was time to hurry things along. She went to Tækjakistan's little cubbyhole in the Smiðja district, in the hope that the man she had watched eat his lunch the day before had made it to work.

It turned out that he had. He sat with his feet on the desk as he played a computer game. Judging by the sounds coming from the computer, this was a battle game. The noise was so loud that he didn't seem to notice when Áróra entered the shop, and he jumped with surprise when he saw her approach the counter.

'What? Can I help you?' he asked, his attitude far from welcoming.

'Yes,' Áróra said, smiling amiably. 'I'm looking for a lawn robot, one of those mowers that mows your lawn automatically—'

The man hardly let her finish speaking before he cut in.

'We don't have anything like that.'

'Really?' she said in mock surprise. 'I was told you did, so I sent an email yesterday—'

Again, she was interrupted.

'No. Nothing like that.'

'Don't you have stock here?' Áróra asked, craning her neck to look around, as if peering behind the man towards the narrow door behind him. More than likely it was just the toilet, but it would be interesting to know if there was more to Tækjakistan than this cubbyhole.

'Why are you asking?'

There was a sudden suspicion in the man's eyes.

Áróra forced a laugh in response.

' I was just wondering if you had a stock here so you could take a look and check what mowers you do have.'

'There's no stock here,' the man said shortly. 'This is just an office.'

As she had suspected, this place was just a step up from a brass-plate company.

'Oh,' she sighed. 'Do you know where I could find a lawn robot?'

She looked innocent, eyes wide, hoping that coming across as helpless would prompt a response.

The man groaned and removed his feet from the desk.

'What make are you looking for?'

'Well, I don't know. My husband asked me to come and check it out, and he was sure you'd have them in stock,' she said, flutter-ing her eyelids as she gazed at the man. 'Could you take a look at the email I sent yesterday? There was a picture of the type of lawn robot he's looking for.'

He sighed, shook the mouse and clicked a few times. Áróra shifted along the counter so she could see the screen, and saw him open the message and then click on the attachment that opened a perfectly innocent picture.

The man looked sulkily at the screen and shook his head.

'Nah. Don't know what that is,' he said. 'Haven't a clue who sells these things.'

'OK, thanks anyway,' Áróra said sweetly, sending him a dazzling smile.

The smile was still on her face as she emerged onto the street, as she was satisfied with this piece of work. Sometimes it was useful to play the helpless blonde. She could go home, brew some strong coffee and get to work, because she now had access to Tæk-jakistan's computer.

55

'I thought Flosi would look after me for ever,' Karen said, dabbing at the tears running down her cheeks. She seemed to weep effortlessly, as if deep inside her was a silent well that had been filled to overflowing. Sara Sól wiped her nose and sniffed repeatedly, and an occasional sob could be heard in her throat as she sat opposite her mother and looked at her in despair. 'When I say me, I mean that we'd look after each other like we always had. I just couldn't understand that he was no longer as fond of me as I was of him.'

Daníel nodded and she looked over at him enquiringly for a moment.

'You're separated, aren't you?' she asked, and he nodded wordlessly. 'I can see you understand exactly what I mean. The heartache. The loneliness that grabs at you at the weirdest moments.'

Daníel understood perfectly. Each time he had separated, it had been his decision, but that did nothing to alleviate the sorrow that inevitably followed.

'I suppose the simplest way to say is that after we split, I lost control of my life,' Karen continued. 'I consoled myself by buying all kinds of things that would make me feel better, make me happier. And it always worked, but only for a little while. Then my heart would start to ache, and the same thing would happen again. I'd go and buy something, like a set of golf clubs, telling myself I'd feel better if I played golf.'

'You only went in for golf when Dad started playing,' Sara Sól broke in. 'She joined the same golf club as him,' she added by way of explanation, glancing at him and Helena, and her tone of voice was such that Daníel wouldn't have been surprised to see her roll her eyes.

'That may well be,' Karen said quietly.

'Admit it,' Sara Sól said. 'You've never stopped loving him.'

Karen didn't reply but a weak, apologetic smile crossed her face. Daníel cleared his throat.

'You said the other evening that Flosi had been completely fair about the separation, and you weren't left badly off,' he said.

Karen dabbed at her face, and sat up straight on the sofa.

'That's right,' she said. 'We split everything down the middle, and he paid maintenance for Sara Sól, plus he always put money in her account as well.'

'Which I saved up and used to buy you out of the house,' Sara Sól said, her voice somewhere between sharp and emotional.

'Yes. This house, which I bought after the divorce, was pretty heavily mortgaged a couple of years ago. So Sara Sól offered to buy me out.'

'And now you're up to your ears in debt again,' Sara Sól said. This time there was no accusation in her voice, only despair. 'Because you still spend and spend and spend.'

Karen sighed and pushed another carrier bag of money across the table to Daníel, who took it and handed it to Helena.

'Flosi upset me last night,' Karen said, and the tears again flowed down her cheeks.

'I understand,' Daníel said, recalling the angry exchange that he had half heard coming from the kitchen.

'And I know Flosi well enough to be sure that he hadn't changed the combination on the safe.'

'My date of birth,' Sara Sól said. 'He uses my date of birth as his PIN for everything.'

'So you took the cash to get back at him, or because you needed the money?' Helena asked, her tone gentle, but Daníel could tell from her question that she had the report she would have to write in mind. This was a mandatory question: *What reasons did the accused give for the theft?*

'Ach. I don't know what I was thinking,' Karen said, no longer bothering to mop up the tears. 'I just knew about all that money up there. And he was so horrible to me … It was just a moment's madness on my part.'

56

Sara Sól went with them to the door and followed them outside. They paused to say goodbye standing between the motorhome and the caravan. The rain had stopped, but the wind came in gusts, apparently from every direction; it was so strong that Helena was terrified that it might snatch some of the money from the two carrier bags in her hands.

'Is there any chance that this doesn't become a major issue?' Sara Sól asked, looking at Daníel. It was clear that she had more hope of a positive answer from him than from Helena.

'I'll talk to your father,' Daníel said in a voice so gentle that it was as if he were speaking to a child. He never ceased to take Helena by surprise. He seemed to have some sympathy for everyone, regardless of how unpleasant or annoying they were. She longed to model herself on him and his mild understanding of all kinds of people, because she knew that this made him a good detective, but she simply wasn't able to. She was unable to put herself in someone else's place as easily and naturally as he did.

They got into the Garðvís van, Daníel behind the wheel while Helena put the bulging carrier bags in the passenger-side footwell and clamped them between her knees.

'It's a strange feeling to have two million euros in a couple of Bónus bags,' she said. 'Shouldn't we call in an escort for this?'

Daníel shook his head.

'No, that'll attract too much attention. It's best if we get this back as unobtrusively as possible and discuss with Flosi whether he wants her charged, or if he wants to just treat it as a family matter. I'd guess he would prefer to avoid taking this to court and laying that burden on his daughter. She has enough problems, poor thing.'

'You're so nice,' she said, putting her sunglasses back on, even though it was a gloomy day. 'Every time I see this Sara Sól I want to give her a good shake. I don't get how you manage to be so reasonable with everyone.'

She felt woozy as the van pulled away, and could have done with an ice-cold Coke right at that moment.

'It comes with experience, my dear. Let's talk again in twenty years,' Daníel said, shooting her a grin.

'I don't know,' Helena said. 'If anything, I feel my shell growing harder the longer I'm a cop.'

'I mean life experience, not just professional experience.'

'That doesn't add up,' she said. 'I know old cops who are still wankers. And a couple of young ones who are nice like you.'

Daníel smiled again.

'Life experience isn't counted in years,' he said. 'Unfortunately, it seems that people only learn by dealing with hardship. The good times don't help us to grow up.'

'Shit. You're so deep,' Helena sighed. The painkillers hadn't made any kind of dent in her headache, so tonight she would have to find the relaxation she needed.

'Every time life punches you to the ground,' Daníel continued, 'it knocks away some of the arrogance and the illusion of self-importance, and that makes it easier to understand the circumstances others find themselves in.'

57

It occurred to Daníel that Helena wasn't her usual self, but he decided against saying anything. This was the first time that he had noticed her being anything less than fully alert when she turned up for a shift. He knew she was aware of his opinions of those who reported for duty on a major investigation on anything other than top form, and in general she wasn't the type to let him down. She was reliable and precise, and normally the one to let others know that they weren't firing on all cylinders. Something must have upset her, unless it was the tension around this investigation that was affecting her. For his own part, it had been a relief to discover that Guðrún had probably staged her own abduction. From that point, the focus could be on tracking her down, then digging deep for the reasons behind her actions before initiating a legal process.

But beneath the surface he was troubled by a slight doubt – that things weren't what they appeared to be. He knew himself well enough to know that this doubt would stay with him until he and Guðrún were sitting opposite each other as she recounted her version of events.

Maybe it was this doubt that was also troubling Helena. While it was tiny, this uncertainty over whether or not Guðrún had done this herself, it stung, nagged and irritated. And along with it came the mental image of Guðrún as a captive, terrified – her life in danger if they weren't able to conclude the case properly.

'There's an overwhelming likelihood that she did this herself,' he said, as if he was speaking to himself rather than to Helena. She grunted her agreement. They were outside the house and he stopped the car in the street, waiting for a moment, eyes on the rear-view mirror, but there was nothing to be seen. There was no sign that they had been followed, so he steered the car up the drive.

Helena got out of the car with the bags in her hands and headed straight for the front door. Daníel took his time, following a few steps behind, ready to react to any kind of attack or ambush by criminals determined to snatch the cash. But everything was quiet. This was just his nerves at work. He had never before been this close to such a pile of money.

Flosi was sitting on the stairs in the hall and looked up as they came in. His face was puffed with weeping. Yesterday's good spirits had vanished.

'Has something happened?' Daníel asked, but both Flosi and Kristján, appearing from the living room, shook their heads.

'Nope,' Flosi mumbled. 'Just reality catching up with me, I suppose,' he said. 'I think it's all just starting to sink in properly. I'll go and lie down for a while.'

He stood up, and Helena handed him the bags.

'Money,' she said.

'Ah. Yes,' he said, taking the two Bónus bags, and Daníel was struck that he seemed completely unperturbed at the fact that the two bags contained more money than many people would earn in a lifetime.

'Karen took the money,' Daníel said.

Flosi absently nodded his head.

'Yes. I spoke to Sara Sól. I agree with her completely that we can keep this within the family,' he said, then turned and made his way up the stairs.

'You're welcome,' Helena said.

Flosi paused halfway up the flight, turned and looked down at them.

'Of course, yes. Thank you. I'm very grateful that you recovered the money,' he mumbled.

Daníel could see that Helena was itching to give him a piece of her mind, so he spoke before she had an opportunity.

'I suggest that after Monday you ought to pay this money into an Icelandic bank account and pay the tax,' he said, slipping into the authoritative tone that suited him, but which he was careful not to use too frequently. 'I think you'll have to agree that this money has caused enough harm already.'

There was plenty more he could have said. He could have explained the importance of taxes. He could have presented an entire lecture going through the reasons why the wealthy have a responsibility to repay the society from which they have profited. He could have pointed out to Flosi the irony that the man was calling on his services, those of the police force, which was funded by taxpayers, at the same time as he was evading paying millions of krónur in tax. But he held back.

There was something in the expression on Flosi's face, as he stood on the stairs, hunched as if gravity was exerting an extra-strong pull on him, that made him unable to feel anything but sympathy for the man.

Flosi nodded a couple of times, muttered something unintelligible, and turned to continue his way up the stairs. As he did so, he looked as if he were struggling to cope with the weight of the bags of money.

58

Judging by its accounts, Tækjakistan was an interesting company. Áróra went through the figures and wrote down a few notes as she tried to work out how it operated. There were outgoings, connected to the Range Rover and the salary of the sulky guy behind the reception desk. It also paid an astronomical rent for its poky cubbyhole of an office to a company called Kuzee slf. According to the registry of companies, this was owned by a man called Leonid Kuznetsov. A quick check through publicly available documents showed that he was a Russian citizen with an Icelandic residence permit. The other invoices paid by Tækjakistan were all to Flosi's company, Garðvís ehf, and the company's only revenue appeared to be from Flosi's offshore accounts.

No more was to be gleaned from Tækjakistan's accounts and there was little else to be found in the company's computer. The email in- and outboxes were empty, indicating that mails were deleted immediately, and the browser seemed to be used only for porn and computer games. She signed out of the connection and switched off the spare phone that she had used to connect to the internet. She had, however, been able to find out from the national registry that this Leonid, who looked to be Tækjakistan's landlord, lived just a stone's throw from her.

The weather was grey but dry. To be on the safe side Áróra put on a raincoat and wound a thick scarf around her neck. It was a short walk and she had no idea what she might find out, but a dose of fresh air would at least clear her mind.

She walked briskly down to the slipway, past the harbour and the shore, and turned into the Shadow District. Leonid's taste for housing seemed to be similar to hers: his apartment was in one of the large corrugated-iron-clad houses on Lindargata. She twice walked past the house, and then stepped into the porch where she checked the names beside the doorbells and saw that the door at the side of the house, which seemed to lead up a set of stairs to the middle floor, was marked *L Kuznetsov*. Now that she had located exactly where Leonid's flat was, she could go home to fetch the car and park it somewhere with a view of the door. That would give her an opportunity to watch anyone coming and going, and to see if any interesting visitors turned up. It was obvious that Tækjakistan was a front company, and now she needed to find out if Leonid was genuinely the landlord. At any rate, the whole thing smelled fishy.

Áróra had hardly stepped onto the pavement when she heard footsteps behind her. Before she could turn around a hand took hold of her shoulder, and a moment later she felt the impact as she was slammed against the wall, held fast by an arm pressed hard against her throat.

'Are you following me?' yelled the sulky guy she had spoken to earlier in the day, his face flushed red with agitation. 'Who are you?' he demanded, without lowering his voice.

She was furious with herself for not having been more cautious. He must have appeared from Leonid's doorway, and no doubt he had seen her from the window of the apartment, walking back and forth along the street.

There were two options open to her in such a situation. She could wait for him to relax the pressure so that she could speak and pretend to know nothing, telling him that it was pure coincidence that she had been at Tækjakistan that morning and then snooping around the landlord's place later in the day. But that wasn't a tempting prospect. She wouldn't buy that story herself. The other option was to free herself and run for it.

She knew that she would have to react fast. It wouldn't be long before the adrenaline rush would fade and her adrenal glands would start to pump out the hormones that would rob her of any strength. She could almost hear her father's voice pronouncing the self-defence lecture that he never tired of repeating to his daughters: *Use all the strength you have. Don't hesitate. If you hesitate, you're in danger.*

Áróra raised her hands to the man's face and jammed her thumbs hard into his eyes, so that he backed far enough away for her to ram a knee into his crotch. That was enough to loosen his grip as he doubled up, then she took the opportunity to smash a knee into his face. Then she ran. First as if the devil himself were on her tail, and, once she could be sure that he wasn't tailing her, she slowed down and puffed as she jogged gently the rest of the way home.

She wondered if she should feel guilty for having hurt the man, but swatted away any such thoughts. He had attacked her instead of approaching in a civilised manner and asking what she might be looking for. That told its own story. People who reacted like that had things to hide.

59

They had just finished the case meeting in Flosi's kitchen, and Daníel was about to tell Helena and Kristján to go home and get some rest when his phone rang. He answered without checking the number on the screen and was surprised to hear the commissioner's serious tones.

'A body has been found, just now,' she said. 'A group of tourists on a trail run of some kind found something on the beach below the south-coast road, west of Thorlákshöfn. The rescue squad is being called out to help the police recover the body, as the shoreline is rocky there. There's a CID squad leaving for the scene now. You ought to get yourself over there and check it out, in case it's the woman you're looking for.'

Daníel put his shoes back on as he ended the call.

'Kristján, you're on duty here. Helena, you're coming with me.'

He hurried out to the car and started the engine, with Helena close behind him.

'What's going on?' she asked.

'A body,' he said. 'Seems it's a woman.'

'Fuck,' Helena said.

'Yep.'

That tiny nugget of doubt that had lurked and nagged deep in his thoughts had now grown huge. He quickly thought through all their procedures from the moment they had floated the theory that Guðrún had staged her own abduction. It was as if Helena could hear his thoughts.

'We've done everything by the book,' she said. 'We continued to work on the assumption that she could be held captive. We kept the police involvement secret. Made sure nothing leaked out. Waited for events and prepared to nab the kidnappers on Monday.

Even though we reckoned Guðrún herself would collect the ransom, or someone acting for her, we still carried on as if she had been abducted by a criminal gang. We've done everything right.'

'I know,' Daníel said, but Helena's words still reassured him. It had been worth going through all this, being prepared.

They were heading along Reykjanesbraut, past IKEA. He put his foot down to beat the lights. Helena held on tight to the handle above her seat so as not to be thrown to one side as Daníel swerved past one vehicle after another at a thoroughly illegal speed. Garðvís could expect complaints over the way its driver handled the van, and there would undoubtedly be a few speeding fines on the way if any speed cameras were to catch them. But he didn't have time to worry about that now.

'We can't be certain it's her,' he said. 'There's no indication at all that it's Guðrún.'

60

Daníel knew better than anyone that death never appeared twice in the same guise. All the same, the vision that greeted him left him at a loss. This was such a desolate place, and the sight of it filled his heart with an aching emptiness. It was dusk when they arrived, which limited what they could see, but he guessed that even in broad daylight, there would have been little to observe.

Not far from the south coast road was a track that hugged the shoreline. They drove along it listening to instructions from the Selfoss police until they saw their lights, then they parked at the side of the road and walked the rest of the way.

Everything was grey, with a hint of drizzle in the air, dulling the flashing lights of the police cars, weakly mirrored in the wet ground. The floodlights that the CID team and the rescue squad had set up repeatedly tripped a fuse in the generator, shutting themselves down again and again, providing alternating spells of dark silence and noisy brightness, against the backdrop of the booming waves at the foot of the cliff.

Tape had been strung between the posts of an electric fence and closed off a large area from the track to the edge, where there was a drop of a few metres to the sea. Daníel could see Baldvin and Gutti at the edge of the cliff, looking down at the shore below.

'Helena Úlfarsdóttir and inspector Daníel Hansson from CID,' Helena told a uniformed officer.

'Quite a team they're sending from Reykjavík,' he said as he let them past the yellow tape. 'We're about to move her. Looks like a middle-aged woman.'

'Hell,' Daníel muttered from between clenched teeth. He fought to hold back the fear that his doubts had triggered inside him, and which now threatened to break out with full force. What if this was Guðrún and she had been murdered by the kidnappers because of a procedural error on his part? Maybe because he had come to the wrong conclusions? Had they relaxed things too early, once they had decided that Guðrún had staged her own abduction, instead of pushing the investigation with even greater urgency? Had the kidnappers seen the police and carried out their threat? Had they not been cautious enough?

Beyond the tape barrier stood a group of ten or so people in bright rain anoraks and jogging trousers, speaking to two police officers, who conscientiously made notes of everything they said. Some of the group had their head torches switched on, which seemed at points to dazzle the two officers, and two of the group had started jumping around, either to keep themselves warm or ready to continue their run.

This was something to which Daníel could never become accustomed, that life could go on moments after death had called. Before long the wild runners would continue on their way, the police officers would go home to their partners and children, as would the rescue squad, the forensics people and the divers. Without doubt, most of them would have something to eat, watch a little television, kiss their sleeping children where they lay in their warm beds, before going to their own beds and sleeping soundly. But he and Helena, or Baldvin and Gutti, would have to inform someone of this death, and see that someone crushed beneath a burden of grief.

'The commissioner said that if you recognise her, then it's your case, otherwise Gutti and I will be looking after this one,' Baldvin said as Daníel came to stand beside him at the cliff edge.

'Yes,' Daníel said. 'If she's linked to the case we're working on, then you can leave us to it. Our team will get some additional manpower to deal with it.'

'What's that? Is this some top-secret thing you're working on?' Baldvin asked, chewing so energetically that Daníel guessed it had to be nicotine gum.

'You could say that.'

They stared down into a sea that was so dark, nothing could be seen except for a dinghy that hovered offshore, occasionally flashing the narrow cone of a searchlight beam across the surface of the water.

The generator chattered for a few seconds and then the floodlights flashed into life and bathed the sea below them in brightness. And this little illuminated world filled with colour, the grey gloom dispelled and the protective clothing of the rescue teams in the dinghy reflected a dazzling orange. It was calm and there was little wave movement, just a languid rush and retreat at the foot of the cliff beneath them. A little way off, the dinghy edged closer to the corpse floating in the clear green sea. The swell gently lifted the body, so that its arms moved like wings in the dark-red slick of blood around the woman. The movement was reminiscent of someone lying in the snow, playing at making snow angels.

The forensics team photographed everything from the clifftop, and finally the diver slipped from the dinghy into the water and approached the body with a stretcher just as the faint clatter of a helicopter could be heard approaching.

Daníel had spent long enough over the past few days carefully examining the family pictures on the walls of Flosi's home to be able to make out, without the slightest doubt, and even at this distance, that the body floating like a bloodstained angel in the sea below was Guðrún.

SUNDAY

61

Áróra's back was so stiff that she had to move cautiously so as not to groan with pain. Either being slammed against a wall by the guy from Tækjakistan had left her bruised, or else these were over-stretched muscles, the result of giving him a dose of his own medicine. It was a long time since she had been in a real fight. Her exercise routine over the last few years had been centred around weights, and that meant careful, precise movements.

Daníel had explained to her that they had decided it was best to wait for the body to be brought to the city and for the pathologist to complete the initial examination and compare the remains to photographs of Guðrún before they informed Flosi of her death.

It was almost seven on Sunday morning when they stood ready on the steps outside Flosi's house. Kristján answered the door and let them in. He had done as requested and woken Flosi, who waited for them in the kitchen in his pyjamas, with a mug of coffee in his hands. Áróra was shocked at his appearance. It was as if he had already heard the bad news. His complexion was grey and he was unkempt and unshaven, and looked dispirited.

'I have bad news for you, Flosi,' Daníel said as they entered the kitchen. It was as well to get straight to the point. Áróra knew there was nothing that could soften such a blow.

'Well, then,' Flosi said in a low voice, and went to the kitchen table and sat down.

Daníel took a seat next to him and Áróra sat at his other side, ready to provide support and comfort, to be the family friend who would help Flosi in his dealings with the police – or something along those lines, as Daníel had suggested.

'A body was found in the sea west of Thorlákshöfn last night,' Daníel said gently. 'There will have to be a formal identification, but I can confirm that it's Guðrún. You have my deepest condolences.'

Flosi looked down into his coffee and his head rose and fell a few times, as if he were nodding.

'According to the pathologist who carried out an initial examination, she hadn't been in the water for long, and the only injuries to be seen so far appear to be serious trauma to the head caused by heavy blows, so until the post-mortem has been carried out, we will assume this to be the cause of death.'

Flosi didn't look up, but continued to nod his head as he stared into his mug.

Áróra laid a hand on his arm.

'My condolences,' she said quietly, her voice strangely hoarse, stinging her vocal chords as if she had been screaming at the top of her lungs. She knew her body would continue to give her reminders of yesterday's scuffle over the coming days.

'Is there anything you want to ask us?' Daníel said, and Flosi shook his head. 'OK. That can come later,' Daníel continued. 'And you're welcome to ask me or any of us. Anything at all, at any time.'

'Thank you,' Flosi mumbled.

'Should I call anyone for you?' Áróra asked as gently as her sore throat would allow. 'A relative or a friend? Or maybe a priest?'

Again Flosi shook his head.

'Sara Sól is here,' he said. 'She stayed overnight. I need to tell her about this.'

Daníel watched Flosi for a long moment, and Áróra could see from the look in his eyes that Flosi's reactions had taken him by surprise. Maybe this subdued response was something unusual.

'Of course, there's no need to conceal the police involvement in this case any longer,' Daníel said. 'But Kristján will remain here in case the kidnappers make contact. He's here to support you, and you can go to him for anything you want to discuss. You have my number as well and can call me at any time.'

Flosi finally looked up and Áróra saw that his eyes were puffed, as if he had been weeping before their arrival. But now his eyes were dry and numb, as if the only thing he wished for was to be able to go back to sleep. He got slowly to his feet and went to the kitchen door, standing beside it. His demeanour suggested that he wanted to show them out. He wanted them to leave. Áróra understood this perfectly. When she had lost her father in her teens, her sister Ísafold had sought solace in their mother's arms, while Áróra had wanted be alone to sob into her pillow.

Daníel's hand was on the door handle when Sara Sól came down the stairs.

'What's going on?' she asked, glancing from her father to Daníel and back.

'It's Guðrún, my love,' Flosi said. 'She's dead. They found her body in the sea last night.'

Sara Sól sat on the stairs, crumpling as if all the strength had been drained from her legs.

'Was it the kidnappers?' she asked. 'Did the kidnappers throw her into the sea?'

'Going by what the pathologist has told us after the initial examination,' Daníel said, 'and this could change following the post-mortem, it's out of the question that she could have hit her head falling from the rocks. It appears that she received a blow to the head that was the cause of death, and the body was then disposed of in the sea. A large floor mat was also recovered from the water and as it was heavily bloodstained, it supports this theory. It still has to be confirmed that the blood on the mat is Guðrún's, but it seems likely it was used to transport her.' Daníel paused, looking at the father and daughter in turn. 'A small amount of blood was also found on the rocks at the shore, which supports the theory that she had been thrown off the rocks at precisely that point, just south of Laxaslóð.'

'Laxaslóð?' Sara Sól echoed, her glance suddenly sharp and her interest sparked. 'Laxaslóð near Thorlákshöfn?'

'That's right,' Daníel said. He was intrigued and stared at Sara Sól.

Flosi also appeared to have lost the ability to stay on his feet and sank down onto the steps too.

'So how could she have abducted herself, if she's been found murdered?' Sara Sól asked, her voice rising, tense and agitated.

It occurred to Áróra that the calming presence of a priest would be more use to Sara Sól than to Flosi. He seemed to have accepted that this whole affair would inevitably end badly. But Sara Sól had clearly been more hopeful of a better outcome.

'We don't know,' Daníel said gently. 'We don't know what the sequence of events could have been. But we will do everything we can to find out.' He coughed, and then he spoke again, his voice even softer. 'Can I ask you, Sara Sól, how you're familiar with Laxaslóð? Do you know the area?'

'Only because of our summer house,' she said.

'Summer house?' Daníel asked, and any trace of gentleness had disappeared from his voice. 'What summer house?'

62

Daníel sighed with relief as he closed the door of his apartment behind him. He dropped his bag and pulled off his clothes on the way to the bathroom, where he stepped into the shower and let the hot water beat a tattoo on his head as if this could wash away all the events of the last few days.

There was no longer any need to hide the police involvement in the case, so a patrol car was now stationed outside Flosi's house and the phones were still being tapped. He had left Kristján on duty there, with instructions to be discreet. Flosi would need space to mourn. When Sara Sól had come down the stairs just as he and Áróra were about to leave, she appeared to have been more upset by the news than Flosi.

After Daníel had explained everything as clearly as he could and managed to extract information from them about the summer house, without letting his irritation show, Sara Sól had burst into tears and demanded to know if there was any doubt that the dead woman was in fact Guðrún. She had levelled accusations at the police for not having searched effectively, demanding answers that he was unable to give her about what had actually happened. In fact, her reactions had been normal, more or less what would be expected when people were informed that a loved one had died under suspicious circumstances.

But Flosi had been oddly calm. He had been subdued, nodding repeatedly as he and Áróra spoke, an occasional tear escaping from the corner of his eye to run down his cheek. He asked nothing, blamed neither himself nor the police out loud, but simply sighed deeply and continued to nod his head. It was as if he had expected such news, and this troubled Daníel deeply. He knew from long experience that people can react in different ways to bad news, but he had got to know Flosi pretty well over the last week, and this was not the reaction he would have expected from him.

What had the wretched man been thinking, not mentioning the summer house? If it hadn't been inappropriate at that moment, Daníel would have given him a furious piece of his mind. How often had he made it clear to Flosi that he should tell him everything, that he shouldn't hold anything back? But that hadn't seemed to make any impact. Flosi let fall information reluctantly, and only when pushed into it.

Daníel got out of the shower, wrapped himself in a towel and went into the living room, without caring about leaving wet footprints on the parquet. He could clean that up later. He opened the doors to the garden and went out onto the decking, the cool outside air fresh against his body, still hot from the shower, so that steam rose from him. He looked out over the garden and realised that the grass still seemed to be growing. He'd have to mow it one more time this autumn to stop it becoming overgrown. He glanced at the untamed patch by the rocks at the end of the garden that both Lady Gúgúlú and the invisible inhabitant that she assured him lived there seemed to protect.

The stalks of dandelions poked up from the unkempt grass; seedheads that had already distributed their loads over his lawn waved sarcastically at him in the breeze. He would have to put down weedkiller for the dandelions next spring if he were to prevent the garden from becoming a mess.

The vapour had stopped rising from his shoulders and he shivered. Now he was cool enough to dress. In the bathroom he applied deodorant and aftershave and looked at himself in the mirror. He looked tired, but rest wasn't an option. A long list of jobs awaited him. He would need to discuss an examination of the summer house with Helena and expanding the team with the commissioner, and he would have to speak to Palli about co-operating with the cybercrime and electronics department so they could get information on mobile phone activity around the summer house and along the south coast, as well as checking traffic cameras in the areas, assuming there were some. He would have to liaise with Kristján – ask him to handle communication with the pathologist and to keep a close eye on Flosi; and he needed to talk to forensics about the investigation of the site where the body had been found.

On top of that, he was going to call in at Flosi's company, Garðvís ehf, to talk to people there about the summer house and Flosi himself. His reactions to this morning's news had earned him a place on the list of suspects.

63

Helena had fallen fast asleep on the back seat of her car, parked outside the summer house, while she waited for the forensics team to arrive. She had curled up beneath a down anorak and a dreamless hour had passed in a flash. She sat up at the sound of a car in the distance and wiped the mist from the inside of the windscreen. It was the forensics van driving along the track to the summer house.

It halted next to the police car.

Jean-Christophe emerged, along with a young woman Helena didn't recall having met before, and she went over to meet them. Jean-Christophe looked dubiously at the few metres of yellow crime-scene tape that Helena had strung across the track between fence posts.

'I didn't have enough tape to go right around the place,' she apologised. 'But there's nobody around but us.'

The young woman slid open the door of the van and took out white overalls, which she and Jean-Christophe quickly put on.

'Why hadn't this place been checked?' he asked, and Helena was relieved that he'd come straight to the point – asking what everyone had to be thinking.

'Because although this is the family's summer house, it's registered as the property of Flosi's company. We haven't had reason to look into the company's property,' Helena said. 'Plus, they didn't have the sense to tell us about the summer house until now.'

Jean-Christophe grunted, pulled up his hood and tucked his foot protectors under one arm as he hung a camera from one shoulder.

'Have you taken a look inside?' he asked.

'Yes,' Helena replied. 'Nothing to see. Everything's in order, all spick and span. I don't think this should take long.'

He grunted again, pushed his glasses higher up his nose and stooped under the yellow tape. Helena watched him walk along the track towards the summer house, and then turned to his colleague.

'I don't suppose I could be in luck and you've brought a flask of coffee with you?' she asked hopefully.

The young woman shook her head.

'No,' she said. 'We were supposed to be off duty, so when the call came, we just threw everything in the van and headed over here.'

Helena sighed. Her thoughts wavered between her initial impression: that there was nothing to be found here, so she would soon be on her way and could find breakfast somewhere on the road back to town; and the other option: that the place could provide some information relevant to the investigation – which was what she actually hoped. But that would mean the forensic team would be there for longer and she wouldn't be able to get away. If that were the case, she would call the police in Selfoss and ask them to send them breakfast – and coffee.

64

Flosi's colleague Unnur was in her sixties, but spry and deft in her movements. The thick heels of her shoes clicked as she marched rapidly across the car park outside Garðvís, and as Daníel extended a hand, he had to admire how immaculately she was turned out this early on a Sunday morning. Her hair looked as if she had come straight from a salon, and once back inside, she took off her coat and he saw that her dark-blue suit was freshly pressed.

'What exactly are you looking for?' she asked, suspicion in her eyes as they followed the officers who had accompanied Daníel up the spiral staircase leading to the office space.

'We need to take all the computers Flosi works on – plus notebooks, diaries and anything else he uses on a daily basis. If there are any communication devices belonging to the company, such as work phones, then we need those as well. We would appreciate your assistance in locating all this.'

'Does Flosi know about this?' Unnur asked, her suspicious gaze now turned on Daníel.

He smiled encouragingly.

'Yes,' Daníel said. 'Flosi is aware of this.'

He had informed Flosi earlier that morning that the investigation was being ratcheted up to a new level, and now there would be searches carried out at Garðvís, the summer house and his home, and in a different manner to before. Daníel wasn't sure that Flosi appreciated what this entailed, but that didn't matter. He had no say over where they searched or what they took away for further examination. Daníel had both warrants and manpower to carry out these searches, an additional seven officers added to his team, plus the forensics division had called in more staff.

'Is this something to do with Leonid?' Unnur asked.

'Leonid?' Daníel said. 'Who's Leonid?'

The name rang a bell at the back of his mind. He was sure that Flosi had mentioned him as one of the staff.

'Oh, it doesn't matter,' Unnur said and the suspicion in her expression was replaced by an awkward look. Her eyes dropped to the floor and then glanced around, as if looking for something that she could point to that would draw attention away from the question.

'Who is Leonid?' Daníel repeated.

'Ach. Don't mind me. Please don't think I disapprove of foreigners, or anything like that. I'm not asking because he's Russian. That just came to mind because nobody here really knows what he does. Even Thorbergur, who works with him in the overseas department, isn't certain what his job is. He doesn't really deal with anyone here except Flosi. It must be because he doesn't speak any Icelandic and his English is pretty poor.'

'I see,' Daníel said. 'No, this isn't about Leonid, as far as we know. We just need to take items that concern Flosi personally.'

She nodded and made her way behind the officers who had already gone up another narrow, steel spiral staircase that shivered and rang under their feet. Flosi's office was clearly marked and they had already found it and were stacking up documents on his desk. The computer was in a box along with notebooks and other items.

'What happens now?' Unnur asked. 'When will you bring all this stuff back?'

Daníel smiled and asked a question of his own instead of answering hers:

'I understand you were at work here yesterday?'

'I was,' Unnur replied. 'I work to two o'clock on Saturdays.'

'Did you notice if anyone came here to meet Flosi? Friends? Family? Customers?'

'Yesterday? Nobody came to meet him yesterday,' she replied with conviction.

'You're absolutely sure?'

'Totally,' Unnur said. 'He came in here and asked after Sara Sól, as if he had expected her to be here. He had hardly sat down to start work when his office phone rang and soon after that he went out.'

'Really?' Daníel felt the pricking of goose bumps down his back. 'We are talking about yesterday, Saturday?'

'We are,' Unnur said. 'I thought it was odd, considering he has been away from work for so long, that he should rush off like that.'

The goose bumps were accompanied by his heartbeat picking up pace and the trepidation that had been lurking inside him forced its way to the surface.

'He came to work on Friday, didn't he?'

'No,' Unnur said. 'Yesterday was the first time I've seen him since Monday.'

Daníel swallowed twice to clear the pressure he felt at his throat. The invisible hand of fear seemed to have grabbed him by the neck. Could he have been wrong? Could he have miscalculated so catastrophically?

65

Daníel stood in the car park outside Garðvís, waiting for a forensics team to collect the van. This was the new company van that Garðvís had bought a few weeks ago, and which didn't yet bear the logo; and this was the van Flosi had taken the day before, after his short spell at the office. Daníel felt like standing against the wall and banging his head against the yellow-painted concrete. He should have had Flosi tailed. There should have been a plain-clothes officer in an unmarked car right behind him the whole time. He called Helena's number and she answered on the first ring:

'Helena.'

'Hæ, it's me.' He hesitated for a moment before continuing. 'Flosi didn't go to work on Friday, as he said he was going to. Yesterday morning he turned up briefly, took a work van, left his own car there, brought the van back late in the day and went home in his own car.'

'Fuck,' Helena said.

'Exactly,' Daníel agreed. 'Any news from the summer house?'

'Jean-Christophe is in there with the video camera,' she said. 'He can't be much longer. There was nothing to be seen when I did a walk-through. This should just be a pro forma check.'

Daníel sighed.

'Let's hope so,' he muttered. 'We *should* certainly hope so.'

He ended the call, swallowed a few times and cleared his throat energetically to free himself of the tightness there and to allow himself to breathe properly. Then he made a call to the station and requested that the patrol car outside Flosi's house be replaced with an unmarked car, and for Flosi to be followed if he were to leave the house.

He watched the forensics team haul the van onto a trailer and asked them to put covers over the wheels. He wanted samples taken from them and compared to the terrain both at the summer house and along Laxabraut leading off the south coast road where they had seen some tyre tracks running towards the sea. One of these sets of tracks had to be from the vehicle used to carry Guðrún's body and drop her into the water below the cliff.

When the forensics technicians were gone and the officers who had accompanied him had returned to the station with everything that had been removed from Flosi's office, Daníel wondered if he ought to go to the station as well and wait for Helena's conclusions from the summer house. It was Sunday, and staff had been called in to examine the van, but that would take time. From what Helena had said, they were just starting to work on the summer house. He could think anywhere – and the best place to think was at home, where the coffee was a hundred times better than what could be had at the station.

He drove home as if in a daze, trying to dismiss the feeling that he had made a mistake, and making an effort to think logically. Emotions, guilty feelings and self-reproach served only to cast a shadow on his thoughts. He would have to reach a decision on how to approach Flosi, and there could be no ill-thought-out measures. They would need enough solid evidence to obtain an arrest warrant, which they could slap on the table if he were to react badly when asked to account for his whereabouts on Friday and Saturday.

As soon as he stepped out of the car at home, he could hear the yells – piercing high-pitched howls of pain:

'Stop! Stop, please!'

He ran, following the sound around the corner of the house and towards Lady Gúgúlú's garage, which had been converted into a flat.

The doors were unlocked, so he burst in. The guy who straddled

Lady Gúgúlú, delivering one punch after another, didn't even manage to turn his head before Daníel had taken hold of him, put his arm in a lock and slammed him to the floor.

66

At least half an hour must have passed since Jean-Christophe had finished filming the exterior of the summer house and the plot around it before going inside, and then finally appearing in the doorway, asking for the Luminol. The young woman – who had introduced herself, but Helena had already forgotten her name – had been ready with the can and the sprayer in her hands, and made her way smartly up to the house.

It was odd that Jean-Christophe's flawless Icelandic pronunciation only gave way to a French accent when he used slang or a foreign word. Helena walked back and forth on the road alongside the yellow tape and giggled at his pronunciation of Luminol with a long oo-sound. She was cold and she was still sleepy, but didn't want to close her eyes again in the car, as it wouldn't be long before Jean-Christophe would appear and give her a decision on whether the summer house could be crossed off the list of jobs, or if it needed to be painstakingly searched.

She didn't have to wait long. He emerged and came towards her with a determined stride. She waited, taking in the serious look on his face. He stooped under the tape, stood up straight and looked her in the eye.

'There are clear indications of blood having been cleaned away,' he said. 'A lot of blood.'

He opened the forensics department's van and took out a black bag and a pair of shoe covers, and asked her to follow him. Just short of the door he handed her the shoe covers and told her to step precisely in his footsteps. She did as he instructed and followed him to the door, where they carefully wiped their feet on a mat placed there for that purpose. Then Jean-Christophe led her inside the summer house. From the entrance hall they went into the main area, which was a combined living room and kitchen with a dining area in a conservatory to one side, although this had been closed off and the blinds pulled down.

'Wait here,' Jean-Christophe said to Helena as she stood by the kitchen units. He followed an invisible trail to the window in the north wall, pulled the curtains across and returned the same way, then reached for the switch and turned off the lights. For a moment the living room appeared completely dark, but after a while chinks of light could be made out sneaking past the edges of the curtains.

'Spray,' Jean-Christophe said to the young forensics technician.

Helena heard the sound of the spray and immediately a large blue patch on the living-room floor glittered, its edges irregular as if liquid had flowed there, and in places there were lines across the patch as if it had been wiped. Jean-Christophe pointed to the traces that stretched beyond the illuminated patch.

'These are cleaning marks,' he said. 'This is where blood has been wiped away.' Then he pointed to an area where a triangular section seemed to have been cut into the patch. 'This is where the corner of the rug was.'

The glimmering brightness was reminiscent of the burning heart of a fire, and then it faded and died away, leaving just an impression behind, like Northern Lights that appear without warning and vanish just as quickly. Except that the emotion this light show left did not tug at the heartstrings; instead it triggered a sorrowful horror. Guðrún had died in this place.

67

The police officers who came to fetch the thug had been keen to take a statement and wanted to call an ambulance when they saw Lady Gúgúlú's face. But Daníel managed to talk them down from all this as Lady Gúgúlú wouldn't hear of a trip to A&E or having the guy charged. She threatened first that this would end their friendship and then that the hidden people would be unleashed to persecute him if he didn't stop going on about doctors and statements.

'It was just a misunderstanding,' she said again and again. And Daníel gave way, asking the boys from the station on Flatarhraun to have the thug, now howling as he sat in handcuffs in the back of the patrol car, cool off in a cell for as long as they could get away with, and to give him as severe a talking-to as possible before releasing him. This wasn't a satisfactory conclusion, as far as he was concerned, but he told himself that right now Lady Gúgúlú needed a friend more than she needed a policeman.

He went back into Lady Gúgúlú's garage, where she sat in a chair, trembling as if she had suddenly become very old. He took a stool, moved it across to her and sat down.

'Look into my eyes,' he said, watching to see if the eye that wasn't closed by the swelling reacted. 'Do you see me clearly, or is it misty?'

'Darling, don't worry about me,' she said. 'I always see you exactly the way you are.'

'Headache? Faintness? Ringing in the ears?'

'No, darling. I'm just fine. Apart from being *skide-fuld*.'

Danish slang seemed to come as naturally as English to her.

'Were you knocked unconscious at all? Spark out? Did everything go black, or did you see stars?'

'I always see stars when you're near me, darling.'

'Be serious,' Daníel said. 'Do you think you were hit hard enough to give you concussion?'

'No.'

Daníel sighed. She probably wouldn't tell him even if she had. He examined her throat but could see no marks there, but in any case bruising wouldn't appear right away.

'Did he have you by the throat?'

'No.'

'I'm asking because there's a danger of a stroke after being in a chokehold,' Daníel said, but Lady Gúgúlú seemed oblivious.

'Stop fussing, darling,' she said. 'I just need a nap and a shower. Then I'll be fine.'

'I'm going to get my first-aid box and fix up that cut on your cheekbone. You can take a shower while I fetch it. But not too hot. That'll make the cut bleed more.'

He jogged through the garden and glanced at the rocks and the unkempt patch around them.

'Shouldn't you keep a better eye on your own people?' he snapped at the rock as he passed. If something supernatural really lived there, then it would understand what he meant. Lady Gúgúlú was a stalwart guardian of the rock and the area around it, but this obliging attitude didn't appear to work both ways. The old tales about the helpfulness of the hidden people didn't seem to have much basis in reality.

He put cheese and ham between slices of bread from the freezer and put the sandwich in the grill. As soon as it was ready he put it on a plate and picked up the first-aid box and a bag of frozen peas before making his way back out to the garage. Lady Gúgúlú appeared from the bathroom in a cloud of steam, swathed in a towel and minus the wig, making the injuries to her face even more stark.

'You'll have to help me get the false eyelash out of my left eye,' she said. 'It's caught up in the swelling.'

She sat in the chair.

A yelp of pain escaped her as his fingers pushed through the swollen area around the eye to take hold of the eyelash.

Daníel shushed her. 'Shall I just pull it?' he asked.

'No, just draw it towards you steadily and the glue will dissolve.'

He managed to remove the false eyelash and wrapped an antiseptic wipe around the tip of a finger, eased it back into the swelling and applied it to what he hoped was the eyelid. The wipe came out black with mascara.

'A&E would have done a neater job,' he said, holding the bag of frozen peas to the eye. 'Keep that there,' he said, and moved on to apply wound closures to the cut on her cheekbone.

'I always thought my left side was my better one,' Lady Gúgúlú said, and Daníel couldn't help smiling. She clearly hadn't had her sense of humour knocked out of her.

'Do you know that guy?' he asked.

'No,' she replied. 'He was at my show last night. I mean yesterday evening. We went to a party together afterwards, and then he desperately wanted to come home with me. He whispered in the taxi that he was going to fuck me senseless. But when it came to getting down to it, he turned crazy and violent.'

'You ought to have him charged,' Daníel said. 'That's assault.'

'Ach, no. He'll figure things out for himself, poor lad,' Lady Gúgúlú said, 'I could feel his boner as he was punching me.'

Daníel got to his feet and handed her a couple of painkillers.

'Eat the sandwich and drink two glasses of water,' he said. 'You'll feel better when you wake up.'

68

The pain in Áróra's back was finally dispelled by a hot bath, so she decided that it had been nothing more serious than a few muscles overstretched by the previous day's altercation. She would have to get herself back to fighting fitness by starting kickboxing again, which she had trained in for much of her life. It would be useful if she was going to concentrate on investigating money laundering. In that line of business watchdogs like the sulky guy would occasionally show themselves, and it would boost her self-confidence to know that she was fit enough to take his kind of aggression.

After the depressing visit to Flosi earlier in the day she had spent most of the morning tracking and then figuring out an overview of the flow of money in and out of his offshore accounts. The turmoil of transfers, payments and invoices in every direction was intended to complicate matters, thus concealing the flow of finance, which would attract attention if the payments were fewer and larger. In the last few years she had become increasingly aware that when this kind of obfuscation was generated, very few of those involved had the full picture of what was actually going on. Each of them looked after their own part of the game, either for profit or because they'd been intimidated into doing so.

But once you looked beyond the tangle, there was generally a fairly straightforward pattern behind it all. If she were to make a guess at what lay behind this confusion that Flosi was involved with, her impression was that this horde of small companies – clubs, health spas, massage parlours, laundries and more – could easily be used to pass on the proceeds of crime, which were then paid into Flosi's offshore account and from there went into Tækjakistan.

This company, with its cubbyhole of an office and a single salaried employee who spent every day playing computer games and taking long lunch breaks, when he wasn't rounding aggressively on anyone he thought was being too nosy, was clearly a front company with no other purpose than to be a conduit for the proceeds of crime. Garðvís, which was a genuine company, issued hefty invoices and Tækjakistan then paid them, which was how the cash was put into legal circulation, mixed up with the money Flosi's company earned from its usual activities. Overall, this was a largely standard money-laundering operation.

The question was whether the flow of cash ended with Garðvís, meaning this was Flosi's criminal operation, or if his company was a link in the chain that passed the money on. If that was the case, then there was every likelihood that Flosi was involved with people who would have no scruples about abducting his wife – and even murder her if he didn't do as he was told.

Áróra had dried her hair, applied moisturiser all over, lacquered her nails and put on discreet make-up and mascara. She wondered about lipstick as well, but decided that was taking things too far. She was only calling in on Daníel to tell him what she had discovered about Flosi's finances, and somewhere inside it felt a little wrong to be working on her appearance in the shadow of Guðrún's death. While Áróra hadn't known her, she could sympathise with Flosi's loss, and knew how heavily Guðrún's murder must be affecting Daníel.

The brook flowing through Hafnarfjörður was calm and the honks of the geese echoed over the water. They were noisy these days, gathering together to prepare for the long trek south for the winter.

Daníel opened the door and seemed genuinely surprised to see her. Áróra pointed to the first-aid box in his hand.

'You're certainly well prepared,' she said and smiled.

Daníel looked slightly abashed and quickly put the box aside as he showed her in.

'Well, yes. I was helping my neighbour,' he muttered, taking her coat and hanging it up.

Áróra took off her shoes and felt a wave of nostalgia. His home had the particular Icelandic smell, the origin of which she had never been able to pin down. Maybe it was these buildings with their thick concrete walls that made the air inside so dry. Daníel slipped past her into the living room and she sensed another aroma that sparked new life in the butterflies that fluttered inside. The smell of him. She would have no objection to burying her face in his neck and breathing in his scent.

'I know you suspect Flosi of abducting and murdering his wife, but I have some information about another aspect that is worth looking into.'

'Really?' Daníel turned, a questioning look on his face.

'Yes,' Áróra said. 'I think Flosi is laundering money for the Russian mafia.'

69

Helena listened as Daníel's phone rang. He didn't answer. She considered knocking at his door on the way to fetch Flosi but decided against it. When he had called to ask her to check with forensics on Flosi's work van, she had the feeling from his voice that he had female company. There was a hurried tone to his words that she hadn't heard before, as if he wanted to get her off the line as soon as possible, and he spoke so quietly it was obvious he was making an effort not to be overheard. She hoped it was the case he was with someone. A shag would do him good. She had long been perplexed at how he seemed completely unaware of his female colleagues' glances and flirting. She envied him this attention; she would have made full use of it to get to know these women better, but in this respect, at least, Daníel seemed to have fallen to earth from some other planet. Such a sweet, handsome guy should have no problem picking up overnight company.

Helena parked by the driveway leading to Flosi's house and waited. She had already called for support and now she just needed Daníel's confirmation to go ahead. She sent him a text message so urgent that he would have no choice but to call as soon as he saw it.

Do you want to arrest Flosi this evening or tomorrow? Call me.

It worked. And he must have heard his phone ringing before, because he called back right away. Again, he spoke hurriedly.

'Hæ, Helena.'

'I hope I'm not interrupting,' she said. 'I need your go-ahead to arrest Flosi. It's up to you whether I pick him up now and let him spend the night in a cell, or we fetch him in the morning and go straight into an interrogation. It's all ready to go, but if you think it's too harsh to have a man who's mourning spend the night

behind bars then we'll wait. Just in case he turns out to be innocent, I mean.'

'Considering you want to arrest him, I assume forensics came
up with something interesting?'

'They did,' Helena said. 'Blood traces in Flosi's van. Splashes
and a small puddle that had been wiped up.'

There was silence for a moment, and Helena could imagine
Daniel's expression; the look of disappointment that so often
made an appearance just as they were about to crack an investigation. It was as if he always hoped that everyone involved with a
case would be innocent. Then Helena heard him draw a deep
breath.

'OK,' Daniel said. 'Call Oddsteinn and let him know that we're
bringing Flosi in now.'

70

It came as no surprise to Flosi when the police came to arrest him. He had already noticed the blue lights before the ring at the doorbell, so he had taken off his gold watch and belt, placing both on the hall sideboard with his phone and keys. Judging by the movies he had seen, he would need none of these things, as anything loose would be taken from him at the station. Then he called out to Sara Sól and told her to call Unnur and ask her to find him a lawyer specialising in defending criminal cases.

Sara Sól was struck dumb. She hurtled down the stairs and threw herself into her father's arms, her eyes awash with tears as she asked again and again what was going on. He held her tight, then at arm's length, his hands on her shoulders as he looked deep into her eyes.

'Don't worry, my love,' he said. 'You know perfectly well that I would never do Guðrún any harm, so we'll let the police do their work and trust them to come to the right conclusions.'

Sara Sól showered him with one question after another, but he was unable to focus on what she was saying. Then the doorbell rang, seeming louder and more piercing than ever before.

'Deep breaths,' he said to Sara Sól, who was more collected now, and she did as he asked. They both took two deep breaths and then he opened the door.

He was relieved that he had given himself enough time to calm Sara Sól down, because if she had lost control then he would also have been overwhelmed. He would not have been able to bear his concern for her wellbeing on top of the fear and humiliation that snatched at him as Helena informed him that he was under arrest on suspicion of involvement in Guðrún's death.

'You do not need to say anything unless you wish to,' Helena said, and moved to one side, as if to ensure that she had eye contact with him, to be certain that he heard what she had to say and understood it. 'You have the right to a defence of your choice. If you have no preference, then a lawyer will be allocated to you.'

'Sara Sól will sort that out for me,' Flosi muttered.

'Fine,' Helena said. 'When we get to the station you will be given a fuller explanation of your rights under the law as a suspect.'

She nodded to one of the uniformed officers who had accompanied her, and he stepped forward holding a set of handcuffs.

'Is this really necessary?' Sara Sól wailed, and Flosi could feel the tears well up inside him at the sound of her anguish.

'It's all right, my love,' he whispered. 'It's all perfectly all right.'

Once he had been handcuffed, he was led out of the house by policemen holding him by each arm, and down the drive to the police car. He was relieved that it was evening, the darkness shielded him to some extent from the gaze of his neighbours, but when he thought it over, he decided that he really didn't care.

His humiliation was total. It would hardly have made any difference if there had been a crowd of a hundred onlookers to witness his martyrdom. There would be whispers of his arrest soon, and the police would hardly be able to keep the news of the body's discovery quiet for long. Before long people would put two and two together – and many of those people would firmly believe that he really had murdered Guðrún.

MONDAY

71

Daníel stood with a cup of coffee in his hands and stared wordlessly out into the garden. The overgrown patch he had fought with for years had been mown smooth, so that his lawn now looked overgrown in comparison. At midnight, when he had gone out to check on Lady Gúgúlú, he hadn't noticed the patch being anything other than its usual unkempt self, and he hadn't been aware of any noise from the garden during the evening or the night either. But then he had been so completely absorbed in Áróra that his senses had been overwhelmed; the scent of her, her softness, the pulsing heartbeat he had felt with his cheek as they climaxed and he sank down onto her breast.

He knocked gently at the garage door before going in with the coffee, imagining that he was waking Lady Gúgúlú up, but she was sitting up in bed, and gave him a knowing glance as she checked her phone with her good eye. Daníel took the pack of painkillers from the table and handed it to her, with the cup.

'Did you, ummm, cut the grass on that untidy patch yesterday or last night?' Daníel asked hesitantly, shaking his head at such a ridiculous question.

Lady Gúgúlú looked at him with her one good eye.

'No. I haven't exactly been in any condition for gardening,' she said, and her tone underscored how outlandish an idea this was.

Daníel laughed apologetically.

'Of course not,' he said. 'It's just that someone has mowed that lousy patch of weeds up by the rock and I just wanted to say thanks. I've been struggling with that part of the garden for years.'

'Ach, darling. You're so blinkered. You always think in two di-

mensions, in terms of what is visible. When all the while the elec-
tromagnetic spectrum of the world is in reality a rainbow.' Lady
Gúgúlú swallowed the painkillers with a gulp of coffee.

Daníel had no idea what that meant. He rarely understood
more than half of what Lady Gúgúlú talked about, but that didn't
matter. He heard in her voice that her comment was well intended, even though it indicated clearly, as so often before, that
his senses were nothing to be proud of.

He tilted her head back and examined her. The bruise had
formed and the whole left side of her face was black, blue and
swollen, and it didn't help matters that grey stubble had begun to
sprout, making her appearance even more gruesome.

'How are you feeling?' Daníel asked.

'The face is the window to the spirit right now, so you can see
for yourself,' she said, taking Daníel by surprise. He had expected
her to tell him that she was fine, to tough it out, pretend nothing
was wrong, shrug it off as she had the night before.

'I have to go to work,' Daníel said. 'You can call me if you need
to.'

'Thank you, darling,' Lady Gúgúlú said.

Daníel paused in the doorway. He wasn't quite sure how to put
his feelings into words.

'Listen, I just wanted to let you know that I'm here for you if
you need anything,' he said.

'Yes, darling. That's what you said.'

'No, I mean, y'know...' he began and hesitated. 'I can listen as
well. I can listen to all sorts of problems if there's anything troubling you. Maybe I've made you listen a few too many times to me
going on about my messed-up love life. In comparison, I know
very little about you.'

'Everyone wants a gay best friend,' Lady Gúgúlú said, and
Daníel felt there was a note of sarcasm in her tone.

'True enough,' he said. 'Take it easy today.'

'I'm just going to watch a series on TV and smoke a little grass,' she said, and then seemed to regret it. 'Oops! I didn't mean to tell you that, darling.'

'I didn't hear it,' Daníel said, relieved that the awkward moment between them had passed. 'I'm far too busy dealing with a murder case.'

72

Áróra looked out of Daníel's kitchen window and saw the geese practising formation take-offs and landings on the brook, with all the honking that went with it. She filled her coffee cup and sat by the round kitchen table, and was suddenly reminded that this was precisely where she had sat the first time they had met since she was a child. When her mother had sent her to Iceland to check up on Ísafold she had recommended that she should speak to Daníel. That had been no more than a few months ago, but it seemed as if years had passed. There had been nothing normal about the passage of time since her arrival in Iceland.

She heard Daníel's voice approach from the garden, and he appeared in the kitchen with his phone to his ear, but his eyes instantly fastened themselves on her and a smile flashed across his face, which she instinctively returned. He ended the call, dropped the phone into his pocket, smiled again as he caught her eye.

She laughed.

'What?' she asked.

'Nothing,' he said. 'It's just so good to look at you.'

Áróra felt her cheeks flush. She didn't understand what was going on inside her. It wasn't as if she was a teenager.

'Stop it,' she said. 'Don't look at me like that.'

He laughed again, and then his expression became serious.

'Flosi has spent the night in a cell and he'll be on his way to be questioned shortly, so I have to be there,' he said apologetically.

She nodded.

'No problem,' she said, getting to her feet. 'I'll see you later.'

But Daníel took her hand.

'Hey, not so fast. I'm going to finish my coffee first.' He pulled her back to the table, and she sat down. 'Could you explain for me properly what you were talking about last night?' he asked, and they both smiled as their eyes met. Their conversation about Flosi's financial affairs hadn't been concluded when the focus of their attention had drifted elsewhere.

'Flosi's offshore account – the one he took the ransom money from – is full of money that comes in from 193 small companies, most of which are probably fronts for some kind for criminal activity. The money goes from the offshore account to other companies, two here in Iceland and one in the States. One of these, Tækjakistan ehf, is certainly a front company and I imagine the other two are as well. From Tækjakistan, and undoubtedly from the other two companies, there's a flow of money to Garðvís ehf, which is Flosi's big, genuine company, and those payments are covered by false invoices.'

'So you reckon that Flosi is directly engaged in laundering the proceeds of crime?'

'Yes,' Áróra said. 'It's a typical scam arrangement. I would bet on Flosi being the bookkeeper. But that's not in the sense that he looks after accounts; it means that he's the individual who allows his company to be used as a conduit for the proceeds of crime. In return, he'll get a slice of the pie, or remuneration of some sort.'

'Wow.'

'Exactly. You can confirm if that's correct by checking whether Garðvís is paying unreasonably large invoices from overseas companies. That would give you evidence of money laundering.'

'This sounds like a job for the district prosecutor or the Financial Supervisory Authority,' Daníel said. 'I have the feeling that this isn't something that CID is equipped to deal with. But didn't you say that there's a Russian connection to all this?'

'Tækjakistan pays rent for its office to Kuzee slf, which seems to be a small company owned by Leonid Kuznetsov. It doesn't seem to have any activity other than to invoice for colossal rents from a few small Icelandic companies, including Tækjakistan. It can't be right to be paying eight hundred thousand krónur a month to rent a tiny space on Smiðjuvegur.'

'Leonid?' Daníel said, his eyes suddenly sharp and engaged. 'You said Leonid?'

'That's right,' Áróra said. 'He's Russian and has Icelandic work and residence permits. If my suspicion is correct, there could well be a connection between this money laundering and Guðrún's abduction.'

'You mean that the Russian mafia might bear a grudge against Flosi?' Daníel asked, now on his feet.

'Yes,' Áróra said. 'That's plausible.'

'Fucking hell,' Daníel said, stooping to kiss her on the mouth with a delightful gentleness.

Áróra laughed, the kiss presenting a bizarre contrast to the curse that had dropped from his lips at the same moment.

73

They'd made little progress questioning Flosi. He sat, hunched and despondent, beside his lawyer, who at intervals whispered to him and reminded him that he was not obliged to answer the questions Helena and Kristján took turns asking. And nothing appeared on the screen of the tablet that Helena held; it was as if nobody was listening in to the interrogation, although she knew that Daníel was watching the feeds from the cameras. She imagined that he was peering at Flosi's face with interest. The reason none of his questions were appearing on her screen must be that Daníel simply had nothing to add to what they were asking.

'I don't know how I can make it plainer than I already have: I didn't abduct and murder Guðrún,' Flosi said, his voice weary and his tone dull, having repeated the same thing over and again.

Many people became angry during such interrogations, losing control of their emotions, yelling and hammering the table in frustration at being repeatedly asked the same question, but Flosi remained calm. He simply seemed tired of replying, but went through the motions for them, with neither conviction nor passion, mouthing the required words.

'I didn't do anything to Guðrún.'

'You had an affair,' Kristján said. 'Some of us would call that doing something.'

Flosi sighed, but he didn't take the bait.

'Certainly,' he said. 'And I can't say I'm proud of it. What I mean is that I did her no harm. I didn't hurt her physically. I would never have done that. As I have already tried to explain, I loved Guðrún and wanted nothing but the best for her, even if the passion had maybe faded from the relationship.'

He remained calm, speaking slowly, and that came as a surprise to Helena. He had been so emotional and had come across as so unstable the first few times they had met. Now it seemed that he had drawn a veil around himself, and there was no way to read his thoughts through it. He could simply be numb with sorrow. Perhaps it was true that he had genuinely loved Guðrún and had been left in shock by her death.

What took Helena most by surprise – and she suspected that Daníel would be wondering the same – was that he had not raised the classic point, demanding why they were not out there searching for the killer, the real murderer, instead of concentrating on him. At some point anyone innocent would ask a question like this. Understandably, as it had to be terrible to be locked up and accused of the murder of a loved one, knowing that the killer was still free.

But Flosi said nothing of the kind. He simply continued to deny everything and looked down at the table, his expression blank.

74

'I don't know what to think,' Daníel said, pacing the floor in front of the whiteboard. His head was buzzing. He had two completely opposing theories he wanted to examine, and both of them looked interesting. One was that Guðrún's death was simply linked to a money-laundering operation, and the other was focused more around Flosi's personal affairs. Daníel had ordered the team to gather all information available concerning Leonid – who worked at Garðvís and was certainly the same Leonid that Áróra had stumbled across in her own investigation. The electronics and cybercrime division had Leonid's computer and had promised to let Daníel know as soon as they had been able to get into it. But now it was Flosi himself who was under scrutiny, and the whole team watched and waited for Daníel, apparently confident that he had a path laid out ahead of him.

'I believe him when he says he didn't abduct or murder her, but the evidence against him is stacking up.' The team hung on his every word, every one of them with the same look of intense concentration. 'You all listened in when he was making his statement. What do you think?'

Palli nodded, as did Kristján and the four officers who had been seconded to the investigation. Helena was the only one who didn't nod in agreement. At the back of the room the commissioner stood leaning against the door frame, her eyes scanning the group.

'This is a man who has definitely hidden information and never offers anything unless it's forced out of him,' Helena said, oddly formal, as she always was in the commissioner's presence. 'So maybe we shouldn't believe what he says.'

'He hasn't lied to me directly,' Daníel said. 'But he certainly keeps things to himself and doesn't share anything unnecessarily.'

'He hides stuff, ducks questions and avoids fuss,' Helena said. 'But I have to admit that when I sat opposite him, I did believe him. At any rate, I believe that he didn't abduct her, and there's no evidence that he did.'

Daníel agreed. If Flosi had been involved with the kidnapping, he would hardly have gone to the accountant to have the cash ready, and he would never have agreed to any police involvement.

'Are we working on the theory that Guðrún staged the abduction to extort money from Flosi, and then he figured out she was hiding in the summer house, went there and killed her?' the commissioner asked.

Daníel nodded, and the whole team followed suit, their eyes flicking between him and the commissioner. He wasn't sure whether or not to expect a rebuke for not locating the summer house earlier. It would come, as it was an unforgivable error on his part, but it wasn't a rebuke that would be administered in front of the team. Once the case had been more or less concluded, she would call him in and between them they would go through everything that had been done, or not done, leaving no stone unturned. But now was not the moment to wonder whether these errors had cost Guðrún her life. Fear and self-reproach could wait until later. There would be a flood of both once it was all over, as there always was. Now they needed to take decisions and follow them through, without allowing the fear of possible consequences to divert them.

'My suggestion is that we continue with the ransom handover and see if someone comes to collect it,' Daníel said.

The commissioner caught his eye and held it.

'You're assuming that the kidnappers aren't aware that the body has been found?' she said.

'Yes,' Daníel said. 'It'll do no harm to go through with it and see what happens. There has been nothing in the news so far about the discovery of the body, and it might remain that way until this evening. That gives us an opportunity. All it costs is a call-out for the Special Unit.'

The commissioner stared thoughtfully into his eyes for a moment, and nodded quickly.

'Agreed,' she said. 'I'll alert them.'

75

Daníel waited for Áróra on the steps of the police station and took a few steps towards her as she appeared from around the corner of the building.

'You missing me already?' she asked with a teasing smile, and Daníel felt himself melt inside at the sight of her and as the memory of the night returned to him.

'Yes,' he said, and resisted the urge to wrap his arms tightly around her. That wouldn't be a smart move, right outside the windows of police headquarters. They went side by side towards the entrance and up the steps, where he opened the door to the station with his pass card.

'There are two things I need to ask you to help us with,' he said as they took the stairs, but he didn't have a chance to tell her more as Rannveig from the electronic and cybercrime division was waiting for them on the landing.

'What news of far beyond?' Daníel asked, and Rannveig laughed. She was a longstanding colleague and they had always got on well. They had joined the force at around the same time. He had been ambitious enough to work his way upward, while she was a systems analyst who had intended to spend just a year there before heading back to university to complete a computer science degree. But she was still here and had become one of the country's leading experts in her field.

'Everything's just fine for those of us who do real investigations while you lot down here enjoy yourselves playing cops and robbers,' she said, extending a hand to Áróra. Daníel introduced them.

'This is my colleague Rannveig, who cracked open Leonid's computer in five minutes flat,' he said. 'And this is Áróra, who is helping us interpret the data.'

The meeting room he had intended to use was occupied, so he decided to take them to the incident room set up to investigate Guðrún's disappearance. By now there were more keys in circulation and a much larger team at work there. Rannveig opened the computer and Áróra took a seat in front of it. She quickly found the accounting software used for Garðvís, and while she went through the figures, Daníel and Rannveig went upstairs for a coffee from the better machine.

When they came back, Áróra had already found what she had been looking for.

'That was quick,' Rannveig said with respect in her voice.

Áróra shook her head.

'When you know what to look for, it's not complicated,' she said. 'Especially when they don't even bother to try and disguise the transactions.' She picked up a pen and sketched a rough diagram. 'Garðvís regularly pays large invoices from three companies in the UK. These are Babylon Gardens Ltd, Geoffrey's Toolbox and GT Box. According to the invoices, these are for distribution services, and as it's not easy to prove that these services have been carried out, this is an ideal route for laundering money.'

'Is there anything to tell us what kind of companies these are? Whether they have legitimate activities, or are fronts for something else?' Daníel asked.

'We can check and see if Interpol has them listed,' Rannveig said, watching Áróra's fingers flicker across the laptop's keyboard while she searched an overseas database.

'According to a simple search, Babylon Gardens invests in property and companies in Moscow,' Áróra said. 'Which means that the money paid into Flosi's offshore account makes its way to the legal economy in Russia, after stopping off at a few places around the world on the way.'

Daníel felt his heart hammering so hard inside him that it was as if it was banging against his ribs. A cold sweat broke out down his back and his throat tightened. Could he have been so completely on the wrong track the whole time?

76

Áróra stood with her arms held high while the female officer clipped a transmitter to her belt and threaded the wire up inside her shirt.

'We'll hear everything you say and you'll hear instructions from us in your ear,' Daníel said as the officer put the earpiece in place. 'Thank you for doing this,' he added. 'Flosi will have to put the ransom money in the right place so everything looks plausible, and you're the only person who can be seen with him. And I know you'll catch up with him easily enough if he tries something stupid.'

The wires all in place and taped in position, Daníel led her over to a large whiteboard that was covered with a huge amount of information. He pointed to a printout of a Google Maps image of Miklatún and explained the little red crosses that had been marked on it.

'You're to drive right around the city. We've already loaded the route into your car's navigation system, so you just need to go where it tells you. When you get to Miklatún, stop in the car park outside Kjarvalsstaðir, and you and Flosi are to walk along this path running along the side of the museum and then turn left. Then you're in the right area. You walk to the middle of the park, Flosi puts down the bag on the grass and you walk back to the car the same way you came.'

'OK,' Áróra said. She was happy at the prospect of being able to help both Flosi and Daníel at the same time, and was both self-confident and aware of the knot of excitement that had formed in her belly, which was linked to what she had confirmed a little earlier from the contents of Leonid's computer. It was as if Daníel sensed her thoughts. He pointed at the map.

'In the bushes all around, by the football ground, by the museum and at the end of the playground, the Special Unit will be hidden and ready. We'll have two drones high up over the park transmitting direct to the control room, so if anyone approaches you and Flosi, we'll see them right away, and the Special Unit will respond. The priority is to protect you both,' he said, and Áróra nodded. 'They are well armed and ready for any eventuality,' Daníel added. 'Because considering the latest information, we don't really know who we can expect to be collecting the money.'

'You're ready to take on the Russian mafia?' Áróra asked.

Daníel smiled.

'I hope so,' he said in a low voice, glanced around and grasped her hand, squeezing it in his. Áróra felt the warmth of his hand for that fleeting moment, and wanted to hold on for longer, to feel the heat of it and the soft palms feeling every inch of her. But she pulled her hand back smartly, as Helena stood up from her desk by the window, came across to them and continued to outline the route planned for her and Flosi.

'When you're back in the car, pull away immediately and drive off slowly, going to the left along Flókagata, take a right along Rauðarárstígur, then left onto Grettisgata, where you turn into the BSRB car park and wait in the car for our guys to fetch you.' Áróra nodded. This was straightforward. Helena pointed to the map. 'I'll be here on Bólstaðarhlíð in an unmarked car and I'll be listening in. I'll have a view over most of the park and can be with you in less than a minute,' she said. Áróra was about to reply, saying that she felt better knowing there was someone she knew close by, but before she could say anything, her eye was caught by a photograph fixed to the white board next to the map of Miklatún.

The picture that had attracted her attention was of a panelled living room, no doubt from the summer house that Flosi had forgotten to tell the police about. The photo was starkly lit, no doubt to show the blue patch on the floor that had to be blood. But it wasn't the blood that attracted Áróra's attention, but the little fire-place at the end of the room.

'The poker's missing,' Áróra said, pointing to it.

'What?' Helena asked, and both she and Daníel leaned close to peer at the picture. 'What's a poker?' Helena added.

'It's a heavy metal tool that you use to shake up the fire,' Áróra said, pleased with herself that she knew such words in Icelandic, recalling her father cursing lousy British heating as he crouched by the fire and poked at the coals.

'But there are just two hooks and two tools,' Daníel said. 'A shovel and a little brush.'

He continued to stare at the picture.

'The poker fits into the middle of the stand,' Áróra said. 'There used to be a set like that in the living room when I was little, and in practically every other house in Britain.'

'Hell,' Daníel said.

'Fuck,' Helena added.

77

Helena used the few spare minutes while she waited in the car to call the Selfoss police and ask them to search carefully around the summer house, the barbecue outside and the garden shed, and anywhere else that the poker could have been left. If it didn't show up anywhere, then there was a good chance that this was the murder weapon. The next step would be to call in divers. It made sense to assume that the murder weapon had been thrown into the sea at the same time as the body. She proudly explained what a poker was used for and sent them pictures of one that Áróra had found online and said had to be similar to the one missing from the hearth in the summer house.

Now there was nothing for it but to wait. They had half an hour until the ransom was supposed to be handed over, and Helena could feel the anxiety building up inside her. Instinct told her that they weren't far from a conclusion, from final explanations, and from tying up the loose ends left by all these events. By tonight the various threads of this case would have been identified. There would be the detailed pathology report, maybe something from the Selfoss police, and Flosi could possibly have more to say later on. Plus, there was a chance, of course, that someone would come and fetch the ransom.

Although Helena knew that it was wrong to hang on to any such expectations in an investigation of this kind, she still hoped that the suggestions Áróra had made about the involvement of the Russian mafia and money laundering had some basis in reality. She hoped that someone would come to fetch the ransom, demonstrating Flosi's innocence. She had believed him when he had sat opposite her that morning and stated that he had neither abducted nor murdered Guðrún. Despite his record of keeping things to himself, looking into his eyes she had been convinced he was telling the truth.

She put a finger to her earpiece to make sure it was in place and a moment later she heard the control room's countdown:

'Ten minutes to handover.'

There was literally nothing to be seen in the park across the street. The Special Unit were good at this. It had to be at least two hours since they had taken their places, lying in the bushes around the park. She couldn't understand how they could lie so completely still for so long, and how they could conceal themselves among shrubs that had mostly lost their leaves, which gave her a clear view but made it difficult to hide.

The control room reported that the drones were in the air, and that Áróra and Flosi were in the car park outside the Kjarvalsstaðir gallery. Helena sat up straighter in her seat, peered out, and within a minute she saw them appear around the corner of the building and head out across the grass. Flosi carried a large sports bag and Áróra walked close to his side, and from a distance Helena could make out that he was shorter by half a head than Áróra. They followed their instructions precisely, walking to the middle of the park by the football ground, where Flosi placed the bag on the grass. For a moment they both glanced around, as if they were expecting someone or something, before turning. She watched their backs as they walked, side by side, back towards Kjarvalsstaðir.

Now they would have to wait again, and Helena wondered why Miklatún had been chosen for the handover. It was a good place, as it was wide open and easy for the criminals to keep watch. But that worked both ways: it was also easy for the police to monitor such an open space. Her thoughts were interrupted as a man passed her car, heading across the street to the park. He was large and beefy, his head shaved but with a showing of dark stubble. He wore baggy, grey tracksuit trousers, trainers and a red windcheater, its sleeves pulled halfway up his forearms, showing clearly his intricate black tattoos.

'A male in his forties heading into the park. Grey trackie bottoms, red jacket,' Helena reported, and the control room replied that the Special Unit had their eyes on him. She watched the man as he went past the bushes and turned into the football ground, and for a moment her heart began to hammer as he seemed to head for the park, for the bag. Then he disappeared from sight and the control room reported that the man was heading for the basketball court, where a group had congregated to play. Helena sighed, but her heart was still beating fast when the control room again crackled in her ear.

'Female heading for the park from the Miklabraut underpass.'

Helena's hand was on the door handle, ready to sprint into action, even though she knew she wasn't supposed to go into the park until the Special Unit had done its work and taken control of the scene. She sat tensed as she listened to the description of the woman.

'Middle-aged. Brown coat. Passed the football pitch. Almost at the crossing. Going into the park.'

Helena left the car and strode across the street. Then she paused, cupping a palm over her ear so she could hear the control room clearly.

'Making for the bag. Maintain positions until she touches it. OK, she has the bag. Go, go, go!'

Helena ran along the pavement until she found a gap between the bushes that allowed her a view of the park. The Special Unit were rushing towards the woman, and it was as if the undergrowth had got to its feet, each of them dressed in camouflaged jumpsuits with little sprigs of foliage on their helmets that trembled as they ran. The woman took to her heels as soon as she saw them, first holding the bag and then throwing it aside. A moment later she had been overpowered. Helena ran into the park as the control room confirmed no further suspicious activity. She felt the ear-piece fall from her ear as she sprinted, dangling over her shoulder on the end of its wire, but she didn't give herself time to replace it. There was something familiar about the figure lying face down in the grass, hands cuffed behind her back. A masked Special Unit officer knelt with a knee between her shoulder blades so that she was unable to move, but the slim, golden legs that emerged from her skirt kicked in the grass in a vain attempt to break free. As Helena arrived, the officer lifted his knee, and turned the woman onto her side so that her face could be seen. It was smeared with mud and grass, but she was still easily recognisable. Helena groaned.

'Fucking hell, Sirra!' she said, short of breath after sprinting across the park. 'Fucking hell.'

78

A compromise acceptable to both Sirra and Daníel had finally been reached. For a long time she had seemed to be in shock, adamant that she would only speak to Helena in private and that she didn't want a lawyer. But eventually Daníel had one called out, who spoke confidentially to Sirra, before she and Helena went to the interview room while Daníel and Oddsteinn the prosecutor watched from behind the one-way window, which was hardly used now that cameras had come into use. Now Sirra was sipping coffee and seemed to have slumped down in her seat, as if the air had been leaking out of her since the dramatic arrest in the park at Miklatún.

Helena sat opposite her, also holding a paper cup, as if to indicate that this was an informal chat over a coffee. She put her folder and pen on the desk in front of her, started the recording and read out the formalities, then paused before leaning forward, seeking to make eye contact, and sighed, heavily and dramatically.

'What the hell, Sirra?'

'Is that how you start a police interrogation? "What the hell"?'

Sirra smiled thinly and sipped her coffee.

'You know I'm not big on formality,' Helena said. 'And in this case, yes. What the hell, Sigurlaug Sigtryggsdóttir? I don't know what the hell else to ask.'

Helena and Daníel had agreed beforehand that she would keep the conversation at a personal level, as that was clearly what Sirra wanted when she had demanded to speak only to Helena.

'No,' Sirra said. 'I don't really know what to say myself. It's all turned so surreal.'

'You could start by telling me how you came to be arrested by the Special Unit on Miklatún, where you were collecting a bag full of ransom money,' Helena said.

Sirra snorted, shaking her head in disgust.

'Ransom money? You mean Flosi's hidden cash.'

'We know that Flosi kept this money in an offshore account, and he'll have to explain a few things to the tax authorities,' Helena said gently. She leaned forward and watched until she had eye contact again. 'The origin of the money doesn't change anything concerning your part in all this, Sirra. This is a serious case, so it'll be better for all concerned if you can speak to me candidly.'

'OK, OK,' Sirra said in resignation, burying her face in her hands. Then she pouted, exhaled a long breath and shifted in her chair. She looked Helena in the eye and nodded, and now she could again see the familiar, determined, glamorous Sirra.

'Good,' Helena said. 'How come you went to Miklatún to collect the bag of money?'

'I was just going along with Guðrún's wishes,' Sirra said. 'It's never been easy for me to say no to her. It's just the way she is. Somehow she manages to be enchanting and pulls you along with her. Even into something as crazy as this.'

Helena remained silent. She decided to use Daníel's approach, waiting for Sirra to continue, and she didn't have to wait long. The silence hadn't reached the point of becoming uncomfortable when Sirra leaned towards her and looked at her with beseeching eyes.

'That's why I wanted to talk to you,' Sirra whispered. 'Because you would understand. I'm so fond of Guðrún. I'm very fond of her.'

There was a strong emphasis on *very*.

'Ah, I get it.' Helena hadn't meant to speak, but the words unexpectedly escaped her. 'Are you saying that you and Guðrún have been in a relationship—?'

Helena didn't finish before Sirra interrupted.

'God, no,' she said. 'Guðrún isn't that way inclined. She loves Flosi. Not that he deserves it. No, this is just me and, ach ... it's awkward. Look, almost two years ago Guðrún and I had a weekend break in Copenhagen just before Christmas, you know, some shopping and a little *hygge*, just for us.'

Sirra fell silent and Helena nodded, as if acknowledging that she understood exactly what Sirra meant by a pre-Christmas *hygge*-break in Copenhagen, even though she had never been on such a trip herself.

'And I'd had too much to drink and tried to kiss her, and that was just ... yeah. Guðrún said thanks, but no thanks, and she was so sweet about it. I wanted the ground to swallow me up, but she seemed to find it so exciting. It was like I had become something for her to work on, *Project Sirra Out of the Closet*. She set me up with a Tinder profile and encouraged me to meet women. Every time we met she'd take the phone off me and swipe a few. You included. Guðrún chose you.'

'Oh.' Helena glanced instinctively at the window and wondered what Sirra's lawyer was thinking. Daníel would hopefully explain the situation without any fuss. 'So Guðrún encouraged you to come to terms with yourself?' she asked.

Sirra nodded.

'Exactly. And you know how much of a step that is, what goes on inside you. How everything looks so different and how you start to understand things differently, from a whole new angle.'

Helena smiled. This was all very familiar. Although she had been young when she had discovered that she was a lesbian, the process was the same as Sirra had been through, the whole metamorphosis, breaking free of the cocoon.

'I'll always be deeply grateful to Guðrún for her support, for the friendship she showed me exactly when I needed it most.' Sirra lifted the paper cup and drank the rest of her coffee. It had to be cold, but her expression didn't show it. 'So it was difficult for me to say no when Guðrún asked me for help,' she added. 'Even though I didn't like the sound of it.'

79

Daníel sat beside Sigurlaug's lawyer and watched as he took constant notes on his pad. He would explain later about the connection between Helena and Sigurlaug, or Sirra, as she called her – and why he had given way, allowing Helena to carry out the questioning despite there being a personal connection.

Helena did it well. She had had to make an effort to break through Sigurlaug's defences, and then she had used his technique, been amiable and her voice warm, maintaining a calm silence and leaving Sigurlaug to fill the gaps.

'I was angry with Flosi on her behalf. He's such a fool not to realise what a diamond Guðrún is,' Sigurlaug said, her voice echoing and sounding slightly nasal through the loudspeaker. 'And I understood very well her fear that Flosi was up to the same tricks again, and that this time the divorce would be tougher as there's no child involved, plus the pre-nup terms and all that stuff. But all the same, I should never have agreed.'

'What was the plan for handing over the money?' Helena asked.

'I was supposed to fetch the money, and at the same time she would turn up back at home,' Sigurlaug said, glancing at the clock on the wall. 'So she should be turning up at their house more or less right now. So you can go there and arrest her as well.'

Daníel felt the hairs rise on the back of his neck. Helena looked up and he felt that they were looking into each other's eyes through the mirrored glass. Sigurlaug didn't know that Guðrún was dead.

'Do you know where Guðrún has been? Where has she been staying over the last few days?' Helena asked, and Daníel admired how she managed to keep her cool.

'She spent the first night at my place, and then I drove her up to her summer house. She was going to stay there until today, and she was going to get a taxi home,' Sigurlaug said.

'Wasn't she concerned that Flosi would go to the summer house looking for her?'

'I don't think they've used the summer house for years. They weren't interested in it. Sara Sól has used it occasionally in the summertime, but that's all. Flosi wasn't supposed to figure out that Guðrún was behind all this. At least, not until the ransom had been paid. I'm not sure if I understand it correctly, but my sense is that Flosi is involved in some dirty business, so this kidnapping was supposed to look like it had something to do with that, and he'd pay up without a word.'

'So Guðrún didn't imagine that Flosi would bring the police into all this?'

'No,' Sigurlaug said. 'She was convinced that he wouldn't contact the police because he had secrets of his own. Looking back, I think she's just been devastated that Flosi found a new woman. She's heartbroken. When she found out that his bit on the side is pregnant, she was convinced that Flosi would abandon her, leaving her with peanuts, and go and marry the one with the bun in the oven. He's old-fashioned like that.'

'How did she find out that Flosi has a mistress and that she's pregnant?' Helena asked.

'She's had the feeling that something has been going on. She said there was the scent of another woman on his clothes, that kind of thing. Then Flosi forgot to shut his computer properly and she opened it to see a pregnancy scan on the screen, from Bergrós.'

Helena nodded, and Daníel approved. The narrative was flowing, and he knew it wouldn't be long before Sigurlaug would continue. He was right. She raised the paper cup to her lips, but didn't drink, and put it aside before continuing.

'He and Guðrún tried for a baby when they first got together and it was constant heartbreak for them both that it didn't work out. Then along comes a pretty little thing and gets knocked up right away. I think Guðrún was right about what would happen, although she obviously shouldn't have tried to extort money from him.'

'Do you know what Guðrún had in mind for that money?' Helena asked.

'She was going to use it to get back on her feet after the divorce. Maybe open a little flower shop. I had offered to help her financially with it, but she felt that Flosi should foot the bill. She felt she had a right to walk away with something after twelve years together. So I agreed to help her with the letters and the practical stuff, to keep the money in my account, drive her to the summer house and all that. And to fetch the ransom, of course.'

Daníel sent Helena a message that this was the moment to tell her about Guðrún. Helena checked the tablet and acknowledged with a quick nod.

'When did you last hear from Guðrún?' she asked.

Sigurlaug paused to think.

'We decided to be in touch as little as possible, but she sent me a message on Thursday evening, using the pay-as-you-go phone she bought at the airport when we went to New York.'

'And what was that message about?'

'Nothing special. Just good night, and some girlfriend stuff. Thanks for all your help, that kind of thing. It seemed a bit weird that she didn't pick up when I tried to call her around midday on Saturday – or maybe not. We had decided to stay safe and talk as little as we could. And then I was busy all weekend, with a course for a big company.'

Sigurlaug suddenly stiffened, looked around the room, her eyes stopping on the glass of the window and resting there for a moment. Her gaze returned to Helena.

'Is Guðrún all right?' she asked hesitantly.

'Sirra,' Helena said, holding her gaze. 'The body of a woman was found in the sea near Thorlákshöfn on Saturday. Not far from the summer house. The body turned out to be Guðrún. She has been murdered. I'm so sorry.'

Sigurlaug stared at Helena in disbelief, shaking her head as if refusing to accept it. She opened her mouth several times, unable to speak. When she finally found her voice, it was hoarse and choked, and Daníel felt a pang of sympathy. This was the part of the job he hated; the sorrow, the defencelessness, the suffering mixed with guilt.

'Dead?' Sigurlaug whispered. 'Guðrún is dead?'

80

It was inconsiderately late in the evening to start the mower, but Daníel didn't expect that either Lady Gúgúlú or his neighbours in the upstairs flat would complain if he were to do it now. He switched on the lights over the decking, which illuminated enough of the lawn for him to mow it. This was the last time the grass would be cut before spring, and he wouldn't have bothered if that wretched patch of weeds hadn't become tidier than the rest of the garden. He laughed to himself as he thought it over: the garden was split into his part and the part that wasn't his, or so it had turned out. Back in the summer he had given up trying to cut that corner by the rocks, both because he simply wasn't able to, for whatever reason, and also because of the entreaties of Lady Gúgúlú, who had a particular love of what she called wild flowers, although chickweed was what most people would have called it.

He hauled the mower out of the garage, filled the tank and started the engine. He started by the garage and took it in strips, back and forth. The smell that rose from the ground wasn't just the usual aroma of freshly mown grass, it was blended with the smell of rotting brown leaves that had collected on the lawn. Autumn was certainly here.

The mower had a built-in drive so it wasn't heavy work and he barely needed to push. The grass collected in the hopper that he had to empty in the middle of each traverse. It was as he was re-placing the freshly emptied hopper that he noticed the supplier's name: Garðvís ehf. He stared at it, taken by surprise by the coinci-dence, and cursing as his thoughts, which needed a little rest, were instantly dragged back to the case. It had been partly solved, as Si-gurlaug had explained how she had helped Guðrún stage her own abduction, but the murder was still unexplained. Guðrún clearly hadn't murdered herself. He was hauled from these reflections by Lady Gúgúlú, who appeared at the door of her garage flat.

'Hæ darling. You're working hard.'

Daníel left the mower where it was and went over to her.

'How are you feeling?' he asked.

She waved a dramatic hand in the air.

'Fine. Just one eye and the ego that are complaining. Everything else works just fine.'

'Pleased to hear it,' Daníel said, and was about to say something about counselling and therapy for victims of violence when the doorbell of his flat chimed.

'Oo-la-la, an evening visitor,' Lady Gúgúlú said. 'Could it be the delightful Áróra?'

Daníel snorted.

'You reckon you can see through the hills like your invisible friends in the rocks?' he said, and heard her laughter follow him as he jumped onto the decking and disappeared through the French doors into his apartment.

'Am I disturbing you?' Áróra asked.

He shook his head.

'No, not at all. Come in,' he said, showing her inside. He half expected her to give him a kiss, or at least touch him, but she went straight into the living room and sat down. 'It's been a hell of a day,' he said, to have something to say, and sat down next to her. 'Thank you for your help.'

'Any news?'

'The poker was found in the heather not far from the summer house. There are blood and fingerprints on it that are being examined.'

'And the other side of it? Flosi's finances?'

'Well, nothing really. The last I heard from the computer-crime division was a confirmation of what you saw right away this morning – a typical money-laundering operation.'

'And are you going to do anything about this?' Áróra asked, and Daníel sat up straighter, suddenly aware that he had a duty as a police officer to uphold. Following the investigation into her sister's disappearance, he suspected that her opinion of the Icelandic police was not high.

'It's a job for the Financial Supervisory Authority, or the Directorate of Tax Investigation. I'll take advice on where it's best to take this, but I know that whichever of them investigates, they would welcome more information, as what we have from Leonid's computer is just a part of the puzzle.'

Áróra nodded knowingly, and Daníel saw immediately that she knew what he meant.

TUESDAY

81

His thoughts on the way to work were all of Áróra, and her powerful body, which accepted him so energetically he could wrap all of himself around her without fear of hurting or crushing her, or unintentionally using a strength greater than hers. Despite his morning shower, he felt that there was still an aroma of her on his skin. A series of daydream vignettes passed through his mind, of the two of them walking together, munching shared popcorn at the cinema, cooking dinner together before curling up in each other's arms in front of the TV. Just for once, as he arrived at the station he needed to put his thoughts in order, to focus his mind on the case he was working on – Flosi's case.

Helena was waiting with everything ready for him. She even had a mug of coffee for him, and he wondered how early she had turned up for work. He took the folder and the coffee from her, and they clinked mugs, as if they were toasting each other, and Helena asked for coffee to be taken to Flosi and his lawyer while they waited in the interview room.

'How are we going to tackle this?' she asked.

Daníel was wondering exactly that. The repeated questioning the day before had yielded nothing. Something more would be needed to force Flosi's hand.

'I'll ratchet up the pressure a little,' Daníel said, and they again clinked mugs before making their way to the interview room.

They took their seats, Helena read out the names and formalities for the recording and then Daníel looked silently at Flosi for a long time.

'Well, Flosi,' he said gently. 'Is there anything you'd like to tell us before we start?'

A quick smile flashed across Flosi's downcast face, and he glanced at the lawyer, who shook his head.

'Let's leave out the fishing,' the lawyer said. Daníel knew him. This was an older man with a glistening bald head. Daniel had encountered him under similar circumstances before, but couldn't put his finger on exactly when. 'Let's see what you have.'

'Fine,' Daníel said, opening the folder and taking out the photograph of the Luminol patch in the back of the van.

'This is what's left of a pool of blood that was found in the back of the new Garðvís van that you were using for most of Saturday.' Flosi shrugged, so Daníel continued. 'We have a witness who confirms that you took this vehicle from Garðvís on Saturday morning, leaving your own car there, returning the van late in the afternoon and then going home in your own car.' Daníel fell silent and watched Flosi, who also said nothing. 'What did you need the company van for?'

'I don't remember. Maybe I needed to go to the tip or something, and needed a bigger car.'

Daníel saw the lawyer jab Flosi smartly with his elbow. That was quite right of him. There was nothing to be gained by lying. That would lead to a trap it could be difficult to escape later.

'Our forensics team has identified the same tyre pattern as the van at both the summer house and in the mud at Laxaslóð, where we believe Guðrún was thrown into the sea,' Helena said and slid a photograph of the tyre pattern across to the lawyer.

Daníel saw that her words hit Flosi hard. He closed his eyes for a moment, quickly shaking his head as if he were trying to erase an image from his mind.

'I did Guðrún no harm,' he whispered.

'Well, considering you're an innocent man and did Guðrún no harm, we can turn to other possibilities,' Daníel said, and took out a statement detailing Garðvís's overseas transactions, placing it in front of Flosi. 'We took a look at the international business your employee, Leonid Kuznetsov, has been conducting.'

Flosi stiffened in his seat, cleared his throat, and for a second his eyes flashed this way and that, as if he was seeking inspiration from every corner of the room.

'Why on earth are you looking into the company's finances? How does this have any bearing at all on Guðrún's death?' the lawyer asked, reaching to pull the statement closer so he could examine it. But Flosi clapped a hand firmly on the sheet of paper, snatched it away and pushed it back across the table to Daníel.

'We believe there could be a link,' Daníel said. 'If you're laundering money for the Russian mafia, then there could certainly be a connection.'

The lawyer scowled and began to mutter something, but Daníel didn't hear what he said, because Flosi hammered the table with his fist.

'Enough,' he snapped. 'No more bullshit. I give up. I confess. I murdered Guðrún.'

82

Áróra didn't need to introduce herself as she arrived for a meeting with the heads of the Financial Supervisory Authority and the Directorate of Tax Investigation at its stylish offices on Borgartún. If they hadn't known who she was before, it was clear that they had now done their homework well and knew what she wanted before the meeting began.

'Of course we need to seek special authorisation to purchase information from you,' the head of the Directorate of Tax Investigation said.

Áróra nodded in agreement.

'Of course. Twenty million krónur is a lot of money. But you would undoubtedly be able to secure significantly higher amounts, plus there would be tax revenue that could be levied on undeclared earnings.'

She knew that she would have to add a little conviction to bring this off, as authorities were often reluctant to embark on investigations that crossed many borders. This was work that demanded an understanding of numerous rules and regulations, as well as co-operation with institutions in other countries, all of which could become long, complex processes. It was in the shadow of all this that international criminal organisations were able to operate.

Áróra stood up, walked around the table with her laptop in her hands, placed it between the two directors and pulled up a chair so that they had to move apart to make space for her. Then she began opening files. First was the pdf document concerning her overview of Flosi's account. Michael would be angry that she had leaked this, but on the other hand, the last thing he wanted was to be caught up in the Russian mafia's business dealings.

'This is Flosi's offshore account,' she said. 'He's used it to collect commissions on sales that are part of his legitimate business over the last thirty years. There was a healthy amount of money on there, over two million euros. But around three years ago small amounts began to collect in this account, payments from small companies in the UK and around the Nordic region. I counted 193 companies that pay into Flosi's account several times a month.'

The head of the Directorate of Tax Investigation leaned closer and peered at the screen, while the head of the Financial Supervisory Authority leaned back in his chair and nodded. Áróra scrolled further down the document and pointed to a couple of lines that she had highlighted in yellow.

'Then there are the withdrawals. Each month there are large payments that go to three accounts. There's INExport inc. in the States, and there are Tækjakistan ehf and Garðvís ehf, which are registered Icelandic companies. I have examined one of these three, Tækjakistan; it's a front company that does nothing but maintain a pretend office. Money flows through this from the off-shore account and to the legitimate activities of Flosi's family company, Garðvís.'

Áróra opened the data on Tækjakistan's accounts that she had obtained using her Trojan horse, and explained what she had discovered.

'The company's only revenue is payments from Flosi's offshore account and its outgoings, apart from the salary paid to the thug who spends all day playing computer games, are sky-high rental payments to the building's owner, which is Leonid Kuznetsov, a Russian national with an Icelandic residence permit, and...' Áróra scrolled further down through the document '...paying the sub-stantial invoices it receives from Garðvís, which is also where this Leonid Kuznetsov works.'

'Interesting,' said the head of the Financial Supervisory Authority, and the head of the Directorate of Tax Investigation nodded his agreement.

'These are significant amounts,' Áróra said, and she could almost sense them mentally calculating how much would accrue to Revenue and Customs if they were to investigate and work their way through the case. Áróra closed the document and opened another in which she had collected the screenshots that she had sneaked from Leonid's computer at the police station.

'These pictures show payments from Garðvís to Babylon Gardens in the UK. According to a web search, this company is a major investor in property and companies in Moscow,' Áróra said. 'So all this money that's most likely generated by illegal activities in the UK and the Nordic countries, is paid into an offshore account, goes from there to Iceland and Britain, and ends up in the legitimate Russian economy.'

'These are just screenshots,' the head of the Directorate of Tax Investigation said, pointing at the screen.

'That's right,' Áróra said. 'But that's all I have from this end of the scam. But Leonid Kuznetsov's computer is currently being held by CID, so if you can get access to it using a court order, then you have the whole process in your hands – an unbroken chain forming a massive money laundering operation. And the data I've shown you is yours for twenty million krónur.'

Áróra closed her laptop and stood up.

'But you need to make a quick decision, as my other option is to take this to the TV, as Kveikur would snap this up for a documentary. But I would prefer you to take this on and investigate with the police, as my concern is that this Leonid and the Russian mafia have their hooks into Flosi, and that he's their bookkeeper, possibly under duress.'

83

'It doesn't add up,' Daníel said, leaning against the wall in the corridor outside the interview room.

Helena agreed with him, but knew she was expected to put forward suggestions for alternative scenarios.

'Could he have suffered some sort of blackout?' she said. 'So that he could have killed her but has no memory of how?'

Daníel mulled it over for a moment. He was the unlikeliest person to fall victim to tunnel vision, but sometimes it was as if he went to the opposite extreme and was unable to accept the most plausible option.

'We know he used the van on Saturday,' Helena continued. 'That's confirmed by witnesses. There are matching tyre tracks both by the summer house where Guðrún was murdered and by the rocks where she was dropped in the sea. Then there's everything that supports motive – the lover, the baby on the way and all that.'

'There's something about how he immediately changed tack when I mentioned the Russian mafia that's suspicious,' Daníel said. 'That angle clearly hurts.'

'If he's genuinely laundering money, then that would be uncomfortable, quite apart from Guðrún's death,' Helena said.

She could see that he was deep in thought. Then he looked into her eyes.

'I find it very difficult to accept that he murdered her, although I admit that I'm maybe a little too close to him after spending a week in his company to be able to see things with the right clarity.'

'OK,' Helena said. 'Let's suppose he's shielding someone. Is that someone he fears, such as the Russian mafia, or someone he's fond of?'

Daníel nodded and his lower lip protruded as he thought.

'Fine,' he said. 'Let's take things down that route.'

He opened the interview room door and Helena followed him inside. The air-conditioning was working at full blast and the room wasn't hot, but she could sense the tension in the air. When they had started that morning, Flosi had come across as tired and downtrodden, but now he seemed agitated. She could feel that they were getting close to something.

'Guðrún's death is in no way connected to my business,' Flosi said as soon as they entered the room. 'I don't care to have my entirely blameless staff mixed up in all this. I am responsible for her death.'

'What puzzles us is that you can't give us satisfactory answers to various aspects of all this,' Daníel said. 'We know about the journey that took you east of the mountain, and that you wrapped her up in the carpet, put the body in the van and dropped her in the water not far from Laxaslóð, to the west of Thorlákshöfn.'

'When exactly did you deposit her body in the sea?' Helena asked.

'During the day sometime. I had other things on my mind than checking the time.'

'Around midday, afternoon, or when?' Helena asked, in no mood to let him get away with such an easy answer.

'Before midday. Probably not long before midday.'

'The evidence supports all this,' Daníel said. 'You took an unmarked company van from Garðvís and drove eastwards out of town on Saturday morning. We have witnesses and CCTV data, and tracking your phone also confirms this.'

'How exactly did her death occur?' Helena asked. 'What led up to it and what circumstances led to you become responsible for her death?'

'It's all very hazy,' Flosi said quickly. 'We argued and it got very heated. I pushed her without meaning to, and she fell and cracked her head on something.'

'On what?'

'I don't recall. The corner of the table, or something. There was blood everywhere.'

'Try to remember, Flosi,' Daníel said gently. 'This is a very important aspect.'

Flosi sat in silence, and then shrugged.

'Like I said, it's all hazy.'

Helena cleared her throat so that both Flosi and the lawyer looked at her expectantly, but she didn't speak right away, pausing before opening her mouth.

'According to the pathology report, she didn't fall against something,' she said.

This seemed to grab Flosi's attention.

'Really?'

'The pathologist's opinion is that she was repeatedly clubbed around the head with a heavy implement.'

Flosi looked down and said nothing, and Helena glanced quickly at Daníel. They had both seen it. Flosi was devastated and at a loss.

'This could not have been accidental. She received numerous blows to the head so that her skull was fractured, with the result that there was damage to the brain, according to the pathologist's initial examination.' Daníel closed the folder he was holding. 'The Selfoss police found the murder weapon in the heather some distance from the summer house. It is bloodstained, but the handle had been wiped so there are no usable fingerprints on it.'

'I could well have hit her on the head,' Flosi muttered, his eyes on the table in front of him.

'With what, Flosi?' Helena asked. 'What did you hit her with?'

'I don't remember. Something I picked up. The thing you found in the heather. A hammer?'

'Or a jemmy?'

'Yes, could be.'

'Which was it,' Helena asked. 'Jemmy or hammer?'

'It was a jemmy,' Flosi said. 'The jemmy from the toolbox. I remember now.'

Daníel looked disbelievingly at Flosi, and stood up.

'It's sad that you're such a lousy liar, Flosi,' he said, and left the room.

'We'll break for lunch,' Helena said. She switched off the recording and followed Daníel out of the room.

84

Flosi sat at the table in the deserted interview room and tried to collect his thoughts. They seemed to flutter around him, and try as he might to chase them, the result was always the same anguish. The lawyer had gone to fetch them some lunch and had asked Flosi what he wanted, but he hadn't been able to reply.

He didn't care what he had to eat, or if there was anything at all. Right now all he wanted was relief from the pain. He who had always been so fortunate, sailing through life with a breeze of good luck behind him – now he had crashed into a disaster that was easily as bad as life had been good before.

He closed his eyes and lay forward across the table. He rested his cheek on the cold surface and allowed his thoughts to drift back to Friday, the last day he had lived without pain. As things looked right now, it might turn out to be the last pain-free day of his life. Guðrún had been no trouble. She had just opened the door and asked him to come inside the summer house, where she had clearly been for a while, more than likely since her disappearance.

'You figured me out,' she said, wearing the expression that he had always found so disarming. It was the look that told him she knew she had overstepped a limit.

He hadn't been able to be angry. He hadn't exploded with fury and yelled at her as he had been preparing to do the whole time he had been driving into the countryside east of Reykjavík, and for a while before that – ever since Daníel and Áróra had told him the likelihood was that Guðrún had staged her own abduction. The night before had been a sleepless one; he had shivered with fury, waiting for the morning so he could pretend to go to work, when in fact he had driven eastwards along the south coast road to check his hunch that Guðrún had hidden away in the summer house.

She had stood there with that naughty-girl expression on her face, and he had melted on the spot. The anxiety of the last few days had been building up into a knot deep in his belly, and he had broken down and told her how much he loved her, that he regretted not having appreciated her and the life they had built together. She had shed tears too and said that she had no longer been able to trust him once she knew another woman was expecting his child, that she had stumbled across the scan image in his email. That was her reason for a measure as desperate as staging her own kidnapping. She knew that deep inside he loved her and would do anything to protect her from harm. On the other hand, divorces tended to be bitter, hate-filled affairs, and she was concerned that she would come out of it badly.

There and then he forgave her and she forgave him, and they made love right there on the carpet with a passion that they both thought had been forgotten long ago, and afterwards she heated soup for them both. It was one of those wonderfully thick vegetable soups that she made with such skill. After lunch she had filled the hot tub and they had sat in it, surrounded by autumn colours, and she had told him that she would remain at his side whatever happened with the child. He could be a weekend dad and she would be a good step-mother, and together they could make a success of its upbringing.

They had decided that Guðrún would call Sigurlaug and tell her not to collect the ransom, while Guðrún would take a taxi to town and appear at home on Monday, where she would give the police some vague answers. The idea was that she would be adamant that she had been abducted, but without giving any clear descriptions of the kidnappers. She would say that she had been drugged the whole time. Her story would be that they had approached and bundled her into a car as she had walked to

Fjarðarkaup. After that they must have gone to the house to leave the ransom demand and make something of a mess. Maybe it wasn't entirely convincing, but if she stuck to her guns there would be no way for the police to prosecute her for staging her own abduction. As long as she kept to her story, there was no evidence that she had kidnapped herself.

Driving back to town, Flosi had been happier than he remembered ever having been. The heavy grey clouds overhead did nothing to dampen the beauty of the autumn colours of the heaths that were so unbelievably bright, in spite of the gloom.

The door of the interview room opened, and Helena put her head inside.

'Would you like coffee or a soft drink while you wait for lunch, Flosi?' she asked, and he was about to reply when he caught sight of his daughter standing behind her.

'Sara,' he called out, and Sara Sól turned and saw him, her jaw dropping in surprise, and her lips said a silent *Dad*.

But then Helena quickly stepped inside and shut the door.

'I'm sorry,' she said. 'You're in custody and aren't to see anyone.'

'What's my daughter doing here?' Flosi asked, feeling the desperation swell inside him.

'There's a lawyer with her,' Helena said. 'Nothing to worry about.'

'Lawyer?' Flosi felt a heavy cloud of darkness settle over him. 'Why would she need a lawyer?'

Helena sighed and perched on the chair opposite him, looking at him as if he were an obtuse child.

'Daníel doesn't believe your confession,' she said. 'He thinks you could be shielding your daughter so he's going to question her. He thinks that you could be shouldering the guilt for her.'

A blackness closed in on Flosi and he felt himself struggling for breath. He had reached his limit and had sunk as deep as was possible in misfortune. He couldn't continue.

'Let Sara Sól go,' he gasped, aware of the choking sob in his own voice. 'It was Bergrós. It was Bergrós who murdered Guðrún.'

85

Daníel hadn't felt comfortable playing on Flosi's paternal instincts, but all the same, it had worked. His suspicion had been that Flosi was shielding Leonid or some other shady figures, but it had turned out he was playing the knight in shining armour to protect his mistress. He had needed some prompting to abandon such a ridiculous idea. Nobody should take the blame for someone else in such a case.

The guilty party, Bergrós, sat hunched at the interview room table. She had confessed as soon as she had been arrested, and had continued to confess her crime to everyone she encountered at the station, including the officer who brought her a soft drink, Helena, who sat with her and waited, and the lawyer Flosi arranged to represent her. There was no doubt that there was a brooding guilt that she needed to relieve herself of, maybe in some kind of resignation at what she had done. Now that Daníel entered the room, she trembled and wept tears that fell to the table and nodded her head constantly, muttering to herself.

'It was me. I did it. I'm a murderer.'

Daníel had seldom seen guilt make such a clear appearance. Every cell in Bergrós' body seemed to be anguished.

Helena read out the time and date, confirmed the names and ID numbers of those present, went over the reason for her statement being taken, and stressed that Bergrós should ensure that her account was truthful and accurate.

'Well, Bergrós,' Daníel said, once the formalities had been concluded, 'Flosi did everything he could to shoulder your guilt. He confessed to murder to protect you.'

Bergrós sniffed.

'I didn't ask him to,' she said. 'He did that of his own accord because he loves me.'

Daníel nodded and tried to catch her eye, but she looked down, avoiding his gaze.

'Flosi is quite a gentleman and does his best to protect the women in his life,' he agreed, glancing at Helena to let her know it was time she spoke. She could be the bad cop.

'Flosi was prepared to shoulder the guilt for murdering the wife he loved, to protect you, and you—'

Helena got no further as Bergrós broke in.

'He'd long ago fallen out of love with Guðrún,' she hissed, and her green eyes flashed. She glared at Helena, shifting to sit upright in her chair, so Daníel could finally take a proper look at her face. Her upper lip trembled slightly, tiny quivers that seemed to be involuntary.

'How did you know that Guðrún was at the summer house?' Daníel asked in his gentle tone so that Bergrós turned to him in surprise, the wind taken out of her sails – exactly his intention.

'I ... I just knew,' she said, and Daníel could have sworn he saw her cheeks flush a little red behind the dark freckles.

'You were going to let him take the blame,' Helena said. 'That tells us that maybe you don't love him as much as he loves you.'

Bergrós stared at Helena as if wishing that looks could cut through skin and bone.

'I had no idea that he was going to confess to the whole thing. He must have been thinking of our child!' she snapped. 'He doesn't want his baby to be born in prison.'

'How did you know that Guðrún was at the summer house?' Daníel repeated. Flosi had already denied that he had ever told Bergrós about it.

Bergrós looked sideways at Daníel, as if he were interrupting a serious conversation between herself and Helena.

'I just guessed,' she said, almost absently, eyes still fixed on Helena.

'Flosi was prepared to take the blame because you told him it had been an accident,' Helena said, unblinking as she held Bergrós' eye. 'You told him that you had pushed her and that she had fallen and knocked her head against something.'

Helena opened a picture on her tablet and turned it towards Bergrós. The image was of Guðrún's body lying on a steel table, her head turned to one side to show the gaping wound above her ear. Bergrós turned away, looking down at the table, and Helena slid the tablet across to her, forcing her to face up to what she had done.

'She didn't fall, did she?' Helena continued. 'You beat her around the head, again and again and again, until she was dead.'

Bergrós shut her eyes, as if trying to avoid the picture on the tablet screen.

'What made you go to the summer house?' Daníel asked yet again in his measured tone.

Bergrós' lawyer sighed.

'Can't we move on from this line of questioning?' he said. 'My client has confessed and is prepared to co-operate.'

Daníel ignored him.

'Why go to the summer house, Bergrós? What prompted you to do that? How did you know about the summer house?'

Bergrós opened her eyes and glanced from Helena and back to Daníel in confused anger.

'I followed Flosi, OK? What was I supposed to do? He didn't answer messages or emails and sent someone who works for him to tell me to keep away, that he couldn't talk to me because of something to do with Guðrún. What was I meant to think? Was I supposed to let him just ghost me and our baby?'

'So you followed him. Where from? His house in Hafnarfjör-ður?'

'Yes.'

Bergrós' anger seemed to have ebbed away and Daníel leaned forward to establish eye contact again.

'Talk to us, Bergrós. Tell us how all this worked out. You followed Flosi on Friday? He went out early that day and was going to go to work.'

'He didn't go to work,' Bergrós said. 'I was outside early and I was going to be ready to speak to him face to face, because he wasn't answering the phone or my messages, and I couldn't go to his house because of his wife. Guðrún.'

'So at that point you believed that Guðrún was at home at their house in Hafnarfjörður?'

'Yes. I was going to tail Flosi and talk to him if he stopped somewhere to buy pastries for the staff – he does that sometimes. Or I was going to catch him outside his work. I wanted a proper explanation for why he was ghosting me, and to find out if we were still OK together.'

'So it was a surprise when he didn't drive to work?'

'Yes,' Bergrós said. 'When I saw he was heading eastwards out of the city I considered turning around, thought this might be some business trip to a builder's merchant somewhere. But I decided to keep going and followed him, expecting that he'd stop at a kiosk sooner or later and I'd be able to talk to him. Maybe we could sit down and talk over a coffee.'

Bergrós fell silent and looked down at her hands, and Daníel was relieved that he and Helena had worked together for long enough that she knew as well as he did that once a suspect had begun a narrative, silence could serve better than a question.

'When we drove down from the Threnglsin Pass, quite a way outside Thorlákshöfn he turned off onto some track, up to a summer house, got out of the car and went inside.'

'He wasn't aware of being followed?' Daníel asked cautiously.

Bergrós shook her head.

'No. I stopped by the road a good way away and waited. I thought he might be meeting someone for work, so after a couple of hours, the usual time for a meeting, I turned around and parked by the main road, where there are road works, and walked up to the summer house. I went behind it and saw Flosi around the back, in the hot tub. With his wife.'

Her final few words were just a whisper, but in a voice so high and thin that it could have been a child's. Daníel waited, and so did Helena, and the tension in the air was almost palpable. They really were about to conclude this one.

'Something happened inside me,' Bergrós said. 'Seeing him there with her in the tub. They were naked, kissing, stroking each other,' she said, her voice cracking and tears running down her cheeks. The lawyer reached for a tissue, took one from the box and handed it to Bergrós. 'So when Flosi left...' she sniffed, and got no further, burying her face in her hands.

'You decided to go inside and kill Guðrún?' Helena said bluntly.

'No. It wasn't like that!' Bergrós looked up and put a hand on her belly. 'When Flosi left, I was going to follow him and speak to him, but somehow I couldn't. I went home. I was just in complete shock. I couldn't sleep that night and didn't know what to do. So in the morning I went back that way to the summer house to talk to Guðrún. I wanted to show her the bump, show her that Flosi would be happier with me. He's always longed for another child.'

'And what?' Daníel asked quietly.

'She knew about the pregnancy. She knew about me. She said that she and Flosi had made a plan. They would be weekend parents. She even offered for them to have custody of the baby and I could be a weekend mummy. The fucking spoilt bitch thinking she could take my baby away! So I hit her. With some metal thing that was next to the fireplace.'

'The poker,' Helena murmured.

'Yes. Whatever it's called,' Bergrós said.

86

'Your lawyer's obviously on the ball,' Helena said as Sirra got into her car outside the police station.' If they consider there's no reason to keep you in custody.'

'He said that my part in all this was actually resolved,' Sirra said. 'It's just as well. Another night in that cell would have killed me. I can hardly believe you think it's acceptable for people to be locked away in there for days on end.'

'People are rarely there for more than one night. Any longer than that and you would have been transferred to the lovely Hótel Hólmsheiði.'

Helena smiled, and Sirra extended a hand, placed it on Helena's forearm and squeezed.

'Thank you for everything,' she said.

'You mean for having you arrested?'

'No. For talking to me. For listening. And for giving me a lift home.'

Helena turned out onto Sæbraut, put her foot down, and heard Sirra sigh in the seat next to her.

'It's so good to see the sea,' she said. 'It's as if your thoughts become smaller when you're locked in such a tiny cell.'

She gazed out of the window and said no more until they were at Laugarnes.

'Was it Flosi?' she asked hesitatingly, as if she didn't want to hear the reply.

'No,' Helena said. 'It was Bergrós, the mother of Flosi's unborn child.'

'His piece on the side?'

'Yes. She killed Guðrún at the summer house, then called Flosi, and he came and helped her clean up and dispose of the body.' Helena bit her tongue as she heard Sirra wince. It was as if she had done her physical harm. 'I'm so sorry, Sirra,' she said. 'You have all my sympathy.'

Sirra nodded and stared numbly straight ahead until they were outside her place in Laugardalur.

'But why?' she asked as the car rolled to a halt. 'It seems so pointless to ... kill Guðrún. Flosi was going to leave her anyway and get together with the mistress. Why murder Guðrún, who hadn't done her any harm?'

'It seems to have been envy,' Helena said. 'Flosi and Guðrún were reconciled. Bergrós saw them together and freaked out.'

'Reconciled? But...' Sirra had been taken by surprise. 'Had Flosi figured out the plot and the staged kidnapping?'

'That's it,' Helena said. 'They were going to have Guðrún make an appearance, and hoped that it would all fizzle out. Guðrún was going to phone you and let you know not to fetch the cash. But she died before she could make the call.'

Sirra wiped tears from her eyes with the back of her hand.

'I know I'm not exactly at my best right now,' she said. 'But would you like to come in for a drink?'

Helena smiled and shook her head, and Sirra opened the door and got out of the car.

'Thanks for the lift,' she said. 'And for telling me about how Guðrún died. The last twenty-four hours have been pure hell.'

Helena looked at her and felt a pang of sympathy at the sight of her tousled hair and creased clothes. Sirra, usually such a glamorous figure, went up to her own front door with her handbag in her arms, holding it like a baby and taking slow, cautious steps, as if she didn't trust the ground beneath her feet.

'Sirra,' Helena called, and Sirra turned. 'When your case is closed and out of police hands, then I'd be up for a drink.'

Sirra stared back in surprise, and finally Helena saw a smile cross her face and she nodded. Helena started the car and headed back to the station. There was much still to be done.

87

Daníel was in the unsettled mood that always descended on him at the conclusion of a murder investigation. He was indescribably relieved, so much so that he longed to crack open the bottle of champagne he had bought on the way home and revel in his own delight for a few hours. At the same time, his heart was heavy with a disgust sprinkled with sorrow. The last thing Flosi had said to him stuck in his mind, as if the words had been carved indelibly into his memory.

'The hardest thing I've ever done was to throw Guðrún off that cliff,' he had said.

The image of Guðrún's body floating like a bloodstained angel in the sea was fixed in Daníel's mind, while Flosi's words echoed repeatedly in his memory.

He spent a long time under the shower, shaved and scrubbed his face with a flannel, allowing the hot water to overwhelm his senses, as if it could wash away those memories: the vision of the dead woman in the sea, her husband's regret, the gleam of fury in the eyes of the mistress, concern for the future of the child she carried. He knew from experience that it would fade. He would concentrate on going over the case records, writing reports, following the case as it was handed to the prosecutor, and then his heart would be lighter. But now he could concentrate on Áróra, who was coming to dinner.

He put on clean jeans and took a white shirt from the dry cleaner's plastic wrapping, and when he had applied some of the post-shave moisturiser his daughter had given him, he followed it with a generous splash of aftershave on his throat. Áróra had told him that she liked the smell of it. She had whispered to him in bed, breathing deep, as if she had wanted to inhale him whole, inside her, deep inside. He shivered with pleasure at the thought.

He took two woollen blankets out onto the decking and placed them on the garden chairs, switched on the gas heater and placed it where it would do its best to keep them warm while they sat outside in the still evening air. He had lit a couple of candles and placed them in glass jars on the windbreak when he heard the doorbell.

A little later Áróra sat with a glass of champagne in her hand, watching him at work at the barbecue. They had kissed and laughed, and the echo of Flosi's miserable voice had begun to fade. He had seared the fatty edge of the fillet of lamb and turned it over, away from the direct heat, and closed the barbecue. It would need a few more minutes.

'There's something I need to tell you, Áróra,' he said, and sat in the chair next to her. 'As the investigation into your sister's disappearance is still open, I've had to take myself off it now that we have a relationship.'

Áróra put the champagne glass down, hard.

'What do you mean by that?'

'We are forbidden involvement in cases in which there's a personal connection,' he said. 'So I took myself off the investigation and the head of CID will allocate it to someone else.'

'But I want you to continue to investigate this,' she said. 'You're the best detective in Iceland. Everyone says that. You're the guy who never gives up. If anyone can find out what happened to my sister, it's going to be you.'

'There are plenty of excellent police...' he began as she got to her feet.

'We may have slept together, but that doesn't mean we're in a relationship,' she said. 'I want you to investigate Ísafold's disappearance. You have to stay with the search!'

She went to the edge of the decking and stepped down onto

the grass. There was desperation in her eyes, and he was about to go over to her and take her in his arms, but she strode away, the hurt clear on her face as she vanished around the corner of the building.

He had known well enough that she wouldn't be happy with him signing off the investigation, considering she seemed to be settling in Iceland with the aim of being able to search for her sister. And she seemed to have such an unshakeable belief that he was the man who could resolve this mystery. All the same, he hadn't expected such a powerful reaction. It had become clear that this was a more painful and sensitive matter than he had realised.

Daníel stood by the barbecue and thought that his legs were about to give way beneath him. The smell of food cooking on the coals suddenly became unbearable along with the insistent echo of Flosi's voice and the vision of Guðrún's body floating in the sea, arms undulating like wings in the swell.

'You make a tragic hero, darling,' said Lady Gúgúlú as she appeared from the darkness, wrapped in a dressing gown and with a large turban around her head. 'The tragedy is that your greatest talent is the obstacle to your happiness. Why do you have to be such a good cop?'

Daníel was so relieved at the interruption that he forgot to scold Lady Gúgúlú for having listened in. He opened the barbecue and the fillet of lamb looked ready.

'Would you like champagne with your dinner?' he asked, and there was no need to ask Lady Gúgúlú twice as she planted herself on the garden chair.

88

The door to her flat stood ajar when Áróra came home. If she hadn't just told Daníel that they didn't have a happy future together ahead of them, she would have called him right now. She would have gone out to the car and waited for him to arrive and go into the flat with her. But this notion, that she had almost allowed herself to rely on a man, irritated her so much that she pushed the thought aside and marched straight in.

The hoodie-clad thug from Tækjakistan who was waiting behind the door for her used the same tactic as before. He shoved her so that she lost her balance and pressed his forearm against her throat as he forced her up against the wall in the hall. She could hardly believe that she had fallen for the same trick twice in a row. She knew how to get out of it, as she had done it before, as the blue bruises around both the man's eyes showed. But this time it was hopeless as he hadn't come alone. He had brought two guys dressed in shell suits and with gold chains around their necks, one of them standing and waiting, ready to take over if she managed to free herself from the reception thug's grasp, while the other one dragged out all the drawers from the IKEA chest and emptied them onto the floor, disappointed at how little there was to be found there.

Áróra wondered what they were looking for and tried to figure out a plan of how she could break free and get out of the door, or just loosen the chokehold so that she could scream and attract the attention of the neighbours upstairs. If they were at home. She hadn't noticed if the lights were on when she approached the house. She had been too occupied thinking of Daníel, and that she had hurt him. Again. And if by that she had hurt herself. The expression on his face when she had snapped at him that she wanted him to continue investigating her sister's disappearance flashed through her thoughts and triggered the tears.

'The fucking bitch is crying,' the hoodie guy called, laughing, clearly imagining that this was his doing.

Áróra felt an urge to wrench herself free and beat him to a pulp, but she allowed wisdom to prevail. She knew from past experience that she could handle him, but was in no doubt that three of them would be too much for her.

'Good. Very good. This is how we want her,' said a fourth man, who now appeared from the living room, a Slavic lilt in his English. He was different, dressed in a shirt and a high-quality woollen coat over it, and his hair was barbered in a way that wasn't simply an all-over crop. His steps clicked on the tiles as he walked; he wore smart shoes, not trainers like the others. If her guess was correct, this had to be Leonid Kuznetsov.

'We just wanted to let you know, Áróra, that we know who you are and what you do, and we also know where your mother lives,' he said, holding up her laptop. 'We'll take this with us. And I'd like your phone as well.'

The one who had searched the chest of drawers reacted as if he had been given an order, rounded on Áróra and went through her pockets. He took her phone and handed it to the man in the coat.

'Very good,' he said as he made for the door. 'I don't suppose you want any more visits from us,' he added, and then smiled. 'And your mother definitely wouldn't want another visit.'

Áróra would have shaken her head if she had been able to move, but instead she blinked rapidly to indicate her agreement.

'Very good,' he said. 'Very, very good.'

He dropped her phone into his pocket and turned in the doorway, smiling amiably, as if he were leaving after a pleasant chat over coffee.

'Just to be sure we're in agreement, nobody is selling anything to anyone, are they?'

Áróra blinked rapidly. The man in the coat jerked his head quickly to one side, and the hoodie guy released his grip. She sank to her knees and gasped for air, grimaced and felt the relief at being able to breathe, filling her body with oxygen and feeling it flow to the starved cells.

When she looked up, they had gone. She sat still for a moment and stared at the new chest of drawers, wondering if the drawers had been damaged when the man had hauled them out and hurled them to the floor. At the same time, she wondered how these men could know that she had offered to sell the authorities information about them. They clearly had a long reach.

She got to her feet and went to the bedroom, pulling out the bedside table to get the spare phone that was taped to the back of it. As soon as it was working, she punched in Michael's number and paced the floor while she waited for it to make the connection. She almost wept tears of relief when he answered.

'I take it you've had a visit from some Russian gentlemen?' he said, and she closed her eyes and sighed.

'Was yours bad?'

'No. But I don't want another one,' he said.

'No,' Áróra said. 'Neither do I.'

'You're not thinking of selling information to the Icelandic tax authorities, are you?' he asked.

'No,' Áróra said. 'It was a possibility, but these Russians have taken my computer and all my files.'

This wasn't completely true, as she naturally had copies of everything. She always had a backup. But she wouldn't use it. She knew checkmate when she saw it. This was one of the most valuable lessons that martial arts had taught her, knowing when it was time to submit. *A competition isn't worth broken bones,* her father had always said, and this was a piece of wisdom she was coming to appreciate more and more as the years went on.

'I'm sorry,' Michael said. 'Sorry I got you caught up in this dirty business.'

Áróra laughed, wincing at the pain in her throat.

'And I'm sorry I tried to sell information that you let me see in confidence,' she said.

Now it was Michael's turn to laugh.

'I know you were doing it for the right reasons,' he said. 'But these guys are no shrinking violets. I'll find a way to get out of this and Flosi can find some other accountant to manage his fishy business.'

Áróra said goodbye to Michael, and had to smother a stab of fear as she punched in her mother's number. Hopefully she hadn't had a visit as well.

'Thanks for the flowers, darling,' her mother said in a cheerful voice as she answered the phone.

'Flowers?'

'The ones your friend delivered,' her mother replied. 'He said he was from Iceland, but I couldn't place his accent. But he brought me the flowers you sent. Thank you, sweetheart.'

'You're welcome, Mum,' Áróra said, shivering at the thought that these men really had found her mother, and from the relief that their visit to her had been no worse than that. They did not make empty threats.

The phone to her ear, Áróra went through the flat and looked at the damage while she chatted about this and that with her mother. The contents of the kitchen cupboards had been smashed on the floor, but otherwise little harm had been done. She felt a strange wish that there had been more to wreck, almost a regret that there had not been more to her life here, more substance.

'Mum,' she said, stopping by the map of the Suðurnes region that lay on the living-room floor. This was the map marked with the roads she had searched. 'I bought a flat in Reykjavík.'

There was silence on the line for moment, as if her mother

needed to digest this information. Then she spoke more gently than Áróra could have expected.

'You know that she might never be found, my love.'

Áróra felt a sob rise in her throat and coughed to conceal it.

'I know she'll be found, Mum.'

Áróra picked up the map and smoothed it out on the coffee table, and her finger traced a track near Sandgerði that she hadn't yet checked. If tomorrow turned out to be a windless day, she could fly the drone.

'Sooner or later she'll be found, and we can lay her to rest properly. Next to Dad.'

Acknowledgements

Red as Blood was inspired by a mysterious case in Norway, in which Anne-Elisabeth Hagen disappeared on the 31st of October from her home in an Oslo suburb. A ransom note was left in the house but despite the efforts of the Norwegian police, Anne-Elisabeth has never been seen again and her disappearance remains a mystery.

Any similarity to the Hagen case ends, however, after the opening pages of *Red as Blood*, and I want to emphasise that the book is not based on it. The book is a product of my imagination and is the second instalment in my An Áróra Investigation series.

Being a writer is a privilege. Doing what you most enjoy in life as a job is the best situation one can possibly think of. I am eternally grateful to my readers for their enthusiasm and loyalty, and hope I can continue entertaining you all for years to come.

But to get a book out in the world takes more than a writer. It needs a team of dedicated and creative professionals, to whom I am indebted for doing such an amazing job in getting my work ready for publication.

Iceland's number-one crime editor, Sigríður Rögnvaldsdóttir, is always the first person to read my books and is my guiding hand when the original Icelandic version is published by Forlagið.

Translator extraordinaire Quentin Bates then does his magic to get the story into English. He is what we call in Iceland a *snillingur*. English-language editor West Camel then polishes the manuscript to perfection so that Karen Sullivan publisher of Orenda Books will approve. Thank you both for your professionalism, guidance and friendship.

But the text of the book is not the only thing that matters. A book needs a cover, and I have been so lucky to have Mark Swan design mine. I could not be happier with how *Red as Blood* looks.